LATECOMERS

LATECOMERS

Anita Brookner

PANTHEON BOOKS ▪ NEW YORK

First American Edition

Copyright © 1988 by Anita Brookner

All rights reserved under International and Pan-
American Copyright Conventions. Published in the
United States by Pantheon Books, a division of Ran-
dom House, Inc., New York. Originally published in
Great Britain by Jonathan Cape Ltd.

Library of Congress Cataloging-in-Publication Data

Brookner, Anita.
Latecomers.

I. Title.
PR6052.R5816L38   1988   823'.914   88-43100
ISBN 0-394-57172-X

Manufactured in the United States of America

LATECOMERS

Hartmann, a voluptuary, lowered a spoonful of brown sugar crystals into his coffee cup, then placed a square of bitter chocolate on his tongue, and, while it was dissolving, lit his first cigarette. The ensuing mélange of tastes and aromas pleased him profoundly, as did the blue tracery of smoke above the white linen tablecloth, the spray of yellow carnations in the silver vase, and his manicured hand on which the wedding ring fitted loosely, without those deep indentations that afflict the man who has gained weight or age, a man to whom in any case his wedding might be presumed to be an affair of the irrelevant past. Hartmann gazed around the hotel dining-room, coming to rest benevolently on the youngish men with briefcases at the adjoining tables – middle management, he believed they were called – for whom lunch was inextricably bound up with discussions of a business nature. My dears, you do not look well, thought Hartmann: your complexions are not clear, your haircuts unbecoming. You give your time and attention to business and save too little for yourselves. There is not a lot of point in talking about a zero-growth scenario, as you are apparently prepared to do, if you are going to dispatch a lobster cocktail followed by steak and kidney pie: mineral water will not save you. He himself ate sparingly, grilled fish with a vegetable, followed by coffee. He had long ago learned the pleasures of sobriety, of extracting the essence from the example, of attaining and completing rather than striving and collapsing. He would not even allow himself a second cigarette. That would come much later, after his frugal dinner. Since his wife had started going to evening classes, he preferred to prepare something for himself. Before going back to the office he would select and buy cheese: another treat, another exercise in worth.

Hartmann aspired to the sublime. If, as Hegel says, in the true sublime a sharp consciousness of inadequacy is required, Hartmann resided somewhere in the more comfortable territory of the false sublime, for inadequacy rarely troubled him. He considered his life's work to lie in the perfecting of simple pleasures, mainly of a physical or domestic nature, far from the strife and pain of more ambitious purposes. The idea of God, for example, he rejected as derogating from his own serene existence. To the proposition, 'I am that I am', Hartmann, if he ever thought about it, would have replied, '*Et moi?*', not meaning any disrespect, but rather acknowledging a simple division of activities in which paths would never cross. On the other hand, a mundane task supremely devised and carried out, however small – the buying of cheese, for example – filled him with a sense of completion for which many more metaphysically inclined men might envy him. Hartmann's joy was apparent in his beautifully cut hair, his expensive suit, his manicured hands, the faint aura of cologne that heralded his approach; in his mild and habitually smiling face, too, his expressive walk, in which the body, leaning slightly forward, seemed to indicate amiability, a desire to please. He was now middle-aged, in the closing stages of middle age, even *old*, he daringly thought. He had an impressionistic attitude towards his age, as he did towards his daughter's marriage, sometimes resigned to it, sometimes deciding to ignore it entirely. Thus it occasionally pleased him to take up the benign posture of an elderly man while safe in the secret knowledge that he had plenty of time in hand. Now in his sixties, he felt himself to be unchanged from his earlier self, but noticeably improved on the miserable boy whom he tried not to remember. There were in fact certain memories that Hartmann had consigned to the dust, or to that repository that can only be approached in dreams. For this reason Hartmann took a sedative every night and ensured untroubled sleep. He defended this practice, as he defended all his habits, as sensible: his own glossy head was his best justification. 'I eat well. I sleep well', he was in the habit of saying, when asked how he did. 'What else is there?' He knew there was more, but thought that wisdom consisted in reducing the purchase of such nebulous matters or indeed of any imponderables that might darken his own impeccable consciousness.

However, no man is free of his own history. Hartmann was no exception. But in the interests of damage limitation he had struck a bargain with the fates: he would, in so far as he could, employ the maximum good will at his disposal in an effort to screen out the undesirable, the inadvertent, those shocks against which the mere mortal is powerless. He would, he had long ago decided, be deliberately euphoric. It was a technique which he could practise and perfect, although sometimes it nearly eluded him. Thus, from his earliest days, he remembered scenes that might have been devised by Proust. He remembered his father, in a magnificently

3

odorous and gleaming emporium, pointing with his cane to a pineapple, a box of peaches, and asking for them to be taken out to the car. Or himself, when tiny, walking with his nurse in the Englische Garten. Or first love, at the age of ten, and a game of hide-and-seek with the beloved at Nymphenburg, beside the long paths rustling with fallen leaves and the commotion of birds. He did not remember, because he had never witnessed the event, his elegant parents, dressed for some *fête-champêtre*, being hoisted, slightly puzzled, on to farm carts, but behaving with good grace, thinking this part of the entertainment. They were driven off, never to be seen again, but how could he know that? How could one remember absence? Was it not one's duty to fill the void, when there were so many agreeable ways of doing so? He had a sense of his own life progressing to its conclusion and was therefore ruthless in dispensing with the past, since every minute of the present must be valued. And, after all, he had survived: that was all that mattered in any life. And he was here, in this hotel dining-room, waiting for his bill, replete, contented, even lively. What mattered was to intensify the pleasure, to ensure that it might be repeated. On such satisfactions Hartmann constructed his happiness.

He cast a long lingering glance at the middle management, now flushed and talkative, and reflected how even his business life managed to avoid such infelicities. It may have pleased his gloomy partner, Fibich, to behave like a harassed salesman, to eat a sandwich at his desk or to stir his tea furiously with an HB pencil, but that was not his way. Fibich felt guilty about having made so much money so easily: that was *his* way. Hartmann mentally shrugged his shoulders at the folly of such a reaction. He had never been ambitious, driven, ruthless, as so many men seemed to be. Even Fibich

4

thought such behaviour ridiculous. There was even, to Hartmann, something reassuring about the absurdity of their trade: greetings cards, of a cruel and tasteless nature, which had paid their way very nicely for about twenty years, until Hartmann, who did little work but was valued for his *Fingerspitzengefühl*, his flair, his sixth sense, suggested that the market in this commodity was self-limiting, and that there were fortunes to be made in photocopying machines. They had both been printers by trade in the years that Hartmann had forgotten about, and it was easy for them to diversify from their original specialization. Of course the work was anathema to them both, but the money was charming, delightful. Fibich, clutching his neuralgic head, might groan at every suggestion that Hartmann put to him, but it was understood between them that they would agree on everything, as they did, and always had done, the ebullient Hartmann literally dragging Fibich along with him, into sheds, warehouses, shops, wherever their greetings cards had led them. And now they sat in splendour in Spanish Place, in an office got up to look like a flat, for domesticity was important to them both. Each had a room or salon, in which decisions were taken; coffee was served morning and afternoon. Their accountant, Roger Myers, and their company secretary, John Goodman, shared the apartment, though slightly less expansively; their typists were encouraged to take time off for shopping. Thus a family atmosphere was maintained, for which neither Hartmann nor Fibich thought to take any particular credit. It was simply that they preferred to feel themselves at home, for the idea of home was central to their lives.

In that unexamined area that informed their first beginnings Hartmann was aware of much that he had decided to forget or to overlook: those years at the print works which had been the final discomfort of their anxiety-ridden adolescence. Indeed, with his customary fleetness, Hartmann was able to turn even this memory to good account. I have come through, he said to himself. What he meant by this was that he was no longer an apprentice, nor would he ever be one again. And even the print shop had been a welcome release after the horrors of school: if Hartmann ever thought to congratulate himself, and he did frequently, it was because he was no longer at school. Sent to London as a frightened boy to live with his father's sister, Marie, who had providently married an Englishman named Jessop, and staring from the window of the taxi at the huge red-brick cottage in Compayne Gardens which he did not recognize as an apartment house, he struggled with his tears and the incomprehensible language until the ultimate betrayal took place, and he was sent away to school. Here, unfortunately, the memories were vivid and would not always go away. Doubly, even trebly an outsider, he knew, even on his first day, that he was doomed. Had it not been for the accident of being paired with Fibich – but both were forbidden to speak German – he would have died or killed himself. Only the knowledge that someone else's experience reflected his own reality saved him, although Fibich was arguably worse off even than Hartmann, for he knew no one. Aunt Marie, visiting one weekend and arousing much ribald attention from the other boys with her tweed cape and the pheasant feathers in the band of her brown felt hat, immediately said that Hartmann must bring Fibich home with him, meaning to her gloomy flat in Compayne Gardens, and the winding hilly streets so unlike home. And so they had been together since childhood and could no more think of living apart than they could of divorcing their wives, although their temperaments were diametrically opposed and they rarely thought alike on any matter. It was even natural to them to live separated by no more than a single storey: two apartments in Ashley Gardens, near Victoria, had attracted them, not because they particularly liked the district, but because each would feel the other near at hand. They had retained the habit of closeness, of being allies: everything was called in to reinforce their bond. They were both called Thomas, and turned as one whenever the name was spoken. For this reason their wives addressed them as Hartmann and Fibich, as they addressed each other, and always had.

Hartmann, waiting for the bill, frowned. He felt discomfort at the insistence of such memories, which were no longer relevant to anything that crossed his amiable mind in the sunshine of his deliverance. This ritual of lunch, which he enacted so often and so regularly, bore somewhere in its train the memory of meals unspeakable, eaten in fear, never properly digested. Those school meals were, in effect, the source of all the loving little luxuries with which he surrounded his present life, just as the aromatic dormitories proclaimed his future need for sybaritic comfort. The bleak wet Surrey countryside in winter, and the incomprehensible hours spent running up and down a muddy field, ensured his devotion to London, its soft mornings, its stony heart, the inexorable streets in which the doctors and the dentists plied their trades, and the suburbs with their flowering trees and the motor bicycles on the pavements. Everything amused him now, all prospects were viewed with indulgence. He was a sophisticated man, sophisticated enough to know that fond recollection of the past was mere sentimentality; this, as it were, intellectual attitude reinforced his active physical discomfort whenever schooldays were discussed. He was apt to turn away questions about his early life, which, now that he was middle-aged, or old, depending how he felt, and successful, were often forthcoming. It was Fibich, who, with a groan, alluded to past ordeals, until silenced by a nod from Hartmann. The past still worked actively in Fibich, seemed from time to time almost to take him over. Hartmann acted as his censor, bringing him forcibly back to the present. 'It is over', he would say, simply. On his face, when he spoke these words, there would pass, unknown to himself, an air of great weariness that was at odds with his dismissal of times long gone. Of course, he remembered them perfectly, or would have done had he allowed himself to dwell on them. He even remembered them better than Fibich, whose obsessional examination of these memories had led him for a short time to a psychoanalyst. When he read *Oliver Twist* Hartmann marvelled that Dickens had had such an acute understanding of the misery of boys. Girls, he thought, did not, could not, suffer so much. He thanked Heaven that his only child was a daughter.

He sat back with a sigh. Since, in this context, reminiscence was safe, permitted, he cast a selective look back to his beginnings. Schooldays still loomed large: he took this to be a sign of his assimilation, since schooldays figured so impressively in the accounts that Englishmen gave of themselves. His school, their school, in fact, had been one of those decrepit but expensive establishments created and run by an ex-army officer and his harassed wife that proliferated in England in the years before the Second World War. The masters were incompetent, irascible, lacking all faith in what they were doing, lurching from one expedient to another, aware that what little luck they possessed was running out. Hartmann and Fibich, metaphorically and

8

almost physically twin souls, marvelled at the bad but fattening food, the indifferent hygiene, the rudeness of the servants, all of whom were emboldened by the increasing haplessness of the headmaster and his wife to indulge in forms of self-expression that both Hartmann and Fibich found to be unacceptable. The Matron, in particular, caused them acute discomfort. She was a youngish woman called Joy, thick-legged, red-cheeked, apparently quite at home in this community of half-grown men. Hartmann, even at the age of fifteen, found something retarded in her make-up. Fibich, the younger and more agonized of the two, winced at her jovial enquiries into the state of his bowels, information that he could not bear to disclose to another living soul, particularly when it was required of him in a loud and cheerful voice which, he felt, demanded his collusion in urgent and unwelcome terms. His frightened modesty often spurred her to excessive attention. She had a way of cross-questioning him while rolling up pairs of socks with swift thick fingers, pretending to be not very interested in his answers but studying his long lowered eyelashes in repeated sidelong glances. There was some-thing menacing as well as flirtatious about these inter-views. Fibich heroically fought back the symptoms of genuine maladies in order not to be ministered to by her, and carried on with a fearful toothache, which he hoped to have the courage to endure until he could take it back with him to Compayne Gardens and there ask for help.

The man who looked after the boiler and was supposed to be responsible for maintenance – the luke-warm water, the damp slimy towels in the downstairs cloakrooms, the windows that were never quite open enough to dispel the smell of boys – lived in the basement surrounded by tins of dried-up paint, his radio permanently tuned to a foreign station playing nostalgic tea-time music. Although it was said of this man, Henderson by name, that he had a taste for small boys, inducing them into his malodorous quarters with offers of tea and biscuits, Hartmann and Fibich found themselves lingering in the passage outside his rooms just in order to listen to the music. The announcer's voice, which they strained to hear, would be abruptly eclipsed, as if Henderson were angry at such alien intrusion into his domain. Seconds later the music would be resurrected, all too faint echo of the life they had left behind, too careless of its existence to have studied it more closely. Some genetic trace kept them yearning for its sweetness, its suavity, even its falseness, while their stomachs suffered from the weight of potatoes, sausages and custard they were forced to ingest.

Since he had come to this country at the age of twelve, this ordeal had lasted a long time. Then came apprenticeship to the printer, until the order of release came in the form of a letter from Switzerland informing them of the deaths of both their parents. Certain monies had been put aside for them, and these, together with reparations after the war, had enabled them to set up on their own. The day they had both installed themselves in their first little office in the Farringdon Road had been one of deep emotion for them both. Nothing, perhaps, would ever affect them so again, apart from the birth, health, and destiny of their children.

Since that time Hartmann had been blithe. He was modest about his good spirits, was not foolish enough to think that he had earned them. Luck, quite simply, had come his way, that was all. Throughout his adolescence he had been frightened. The first step towards emancipation had been his ability to master the language. This had come with a rush, as he was about to leave school; it was as if the prospect of freedom had released something in him, had suddenly induced ability where there was none before. The second step, oddly enough, had been his National Service, which had been an unexpected introduction to conviviality. Sent to mind stores in Wiltshire, there was little for him to do except check deliveries, and he was much in demand as a source of supplies. Fibich, whose stoicism in the face of toothache had left him with a legacy of migraines, was not accepted for the army. He remained in London, at the printing works, lodging with Aunt Marie, whom he now considered to be an authentic relation. It was the first time the two had been separated. Fibich sent his cigarette ration to Hartmann, who was gradually discovering the delights of generosity. Open-handed among the boxes of dried bananas and the sacks of dried egg, Hartmann marvelled at the ease of friendships based on mutual interest. He found his fellow conscripts charming (his favourite adjective), and, as he listened to their plans for the future, he began to dwell on the possibility of making plans of his own. Fibich had been keen on the idea of publishing – he was the more learned, the more serious of the two of them – but Hartmann saw that they must attack from the flank. They would never know enough to be insiders, that was clear. The trick, therefore, was to find a trade which was in a sense superfluous but also gratifying. That was how the greetings cards had been conceived. In the beginning the cards had been sentimental. A Happy Birthday to my dear Wife, they proclaimed. Or, Baby is One Today! Gradually they allowed realism to creep in, and found that the more outrageous the message the more eagerly it was bought. Get Well cards soon topped their sales, particularly lugubrious or insensitively cheerful greetings for the post-operative patient. They

11

had never looked back.

The odious feel of rough khaki on the backs of his knees and of his neck also inspired in Hartmann at this time his love of luxury. In this he was aided by the sight of his fellow conscripts sprucing themselves up for a night out. Such applications of grease and water, such furious polishing of boots! Hartmann had tried to emulate this activity when they kindly included him in their invitations to spend the evening in a pub, but such exercises were not for him, any more than the flat beer and the dark and aromatic room in which it was consumed were for him. Instead he took advantage of their absence to strip wash himself, writing to Fibich to send him bars of scented soap. And ever since those days he had been a devotee of his morning toilet, and his bathroom was filled with scented essences, with rose-flavoured mouth-wash, and with colognes which he would pat into the skin of his face, so that his wife, on kissing him goodbye, would say to him, 'You smell better than I do.'

Now he had reached the age when the odours of the body are more insistent and more difficult to dispel, when the day's work, minimal though it was, felt like a more serious operation than in the early days when there had been so much more to do, when waking from sleep was a more lengthy process. These days his wife enlivened her hitherto flawless complexion with a geranium flush. He had no feelings of resentment against the passing years, counting each day a triumph, particularly when the winter sun shone strongly, as it did today. Rather he welcomed old age, or what he supposed was old age, having done too well, spent his time too fruitfully, to wish it all back again. Certain attitudes of mind and body were no longer available to him, or if available no longer becoming. The young men at the adjoining tables (and he was forced to revise their status upwards, hearing one of them remark that he had passed the previous evening at Annabel's) aroused no feelings of envy, that mean-minded desire that he occasionally noted among his contemporaries to deplore young people's lack of style, or what was considered their lack of style. Silver-haired now, and with a slightly more prominent stomach, Hartmann was still recognizable to himself, as was Fibich, as gaunt as ever, but with expensively rearranged teeth. The skin of Hartmann's face was still dry and glossy, although the body was more capacious: dressed, he managed to mask from himself the sight of the unwieldy forked animal that had earlier emerged from the bed. Upright, bathed, burnished, he still evoked a smile from the face in the mirror; his wedding ring was still loose on his finger. And after his lunch, which he preferred to take alone, he could now afford to wander a little in the sun, a pleasure denied to him in those days when the sun had never seemed to shine at all, when the only refuge from the hard-packed dirty snow was the single bar of Aunt Marie's electric fire. Stoical, she had refused to 'give in', as she put it, to the cold, although her own early years had been warmed by district central heating. Now both Fibich and Hartmann insisted on almost tropical heat, and the air inside their homes was soothed by scents of cigars, lavender polish, and rich cooking that never entirely dispersed. He vaguely remembered such scents from the parental home, which he otherwise did not remember at all, or did not try to. It was Fibich, at the suggestion of his analyst, who longed to return, but was fearful of doing so, and thus existed on the horns of a dilemma that would never be resolved. Hartmann's solution to this problem had been breathtaking in its simplicity: get rid of the analyst. 'A meddler,'

13

Hartmann had said. And, 'Psychiatrists! What do they know?' Hartmann understood that Fibich was still unhappy, and occasionally, but only occasionally, acknowledged the reason. But why dwell on the past, particularly when the past was so uncongenial? Better to eat a good lunch, rejoicing in prosperity, and then to select a piece of Brie, a piece of Cantal, perhaps to point to a fine pineapple, in preparation for his evening meal. Television was marvellous at keeping one in the present. He loved the American soap operas, rejoicing in the extravagance.

The head waiter came up to bid him good-day: Hartmann was a customer of long standing.

'The family well?' Hartmann asked, genuine in his enquiry.

'Very well, sir, thank you. We saw Mr Fibich the other day.'

'And the account for Mr Goodman and Mr Myers is up-to-date?'

'Yes, sir, all taken care of.'

'Good-day then, Monsieur Pierre. Thank you.'

'Thank you, sir.'

They appreciated each other wonderfully.

Out in the street the winter sun was at its zenith, soon to retire its light and its shadows. Hartmann waved his hand to the woman arranging a jacket in the window of the dress-shop – he had known her for thirty years – and strolled in the direction of Selfridges. A little shopping, the purchase of the evening paper, and he would be back at the office in time for a second cup of coffee. Very civilized, he thought. Well, he had earned it. And this evening his daughter was coming round, an occasion for great rejoicing. He would ask Fibich and his wife to join them, since they both loved her. And their boy doing so well: a miracle. It was an uncertain profession, of course, and nothing was guaranteed, but it seemed that he had the gift. This, he was aware, was an attitude of indulgence in him for this particular young man, for the idleness of which he approved in women was, generally speaking, anathema to him in men. (He ignored his own, which was in any case ornamented with much ceremony of a business-like nature.) But enough of that. Today was another blessed day, like so many. Had he been a praying man, but of course he wasn't, he would have given thanks. Instead he settled the collar of his coat more closely round his neck, and stepped devoutly towards Selfridges.

2

Hartmann's wife, Yvette, had been attractive as a girl and had managed to preserve her appeal into middle age. Although younger than Hartmann she had always had a grown-up air, based largely on a set of mannerisms which belonged, or seemed to belong, to the generation that had gone before her. Apart from fleeting expressions of blankness or loss, she breezily broadcast an air of established and traditional womanhood, which nevertheless managed to sidestep the essential business of being female. Her peculiar attraction was based not on looks so much as on various forms of self-advertisement. She still entered a room with a sort of pre-emptive bustle, as if drawing on herself the attention of a crowd: she always assumed an audience, and frequently got one. She liked to imagine people saying 'Who is she? Who is that beautifully groomed woman with the blonde hair?' When she had first started work, in the far-off days when she was in her early twenties, she had always managed to give the impression that she was chairing the committee of a charity ball. She bestowed her activity, rather than letting it be harnessed to anyone else's needs, or even to the needs of the occasion. She was a typist in the company run by

Hartmann and Fibich, and not a particularly good one, but although they were irritated by her lack of attention and her dubious punctuality, her altogether sunny indifference to the demands of the work they politely asked her to do, they both found themselves hypnotized by her self-importance and waited with genuine interest for her appearance at the office. However late she happened to be, Yvette regarded her arrival at work, or what she thought of as her entrance, as the high point of the day. After that had been registered (and she knew the importance of first impressions) she tended to let her attention lapse from what followed. She shed about her an aura of femininity which made men thoughtful because it did not seem aimed in their direction: on the contrary, it seemed to exclude them, as if she herself belonged to a sect which considered them to be of little importance. She was faultlessly put together, wore her carefully varied blouses and skirts as if they came from couture houses, and gave off waves of a scent which, though inexpensive, nevertheless created trails which insinuated themselves into the hallway and the corridors.

Her strongest card, and she used it quite unconsciously, was her refusal to take work – any work – seriously. She implied, without words, that work was not her sphere, that she was, in fact, destined for another life, that she was an object of luxury rather than of labour. If Fibich went into the room shared by the two typists to ask for a file or to wonder why his letters had not been done, he would find her brewing up tea, with many a dainty shake of a braceleted wrist. 'I've told Jill to lie down,' she would say. 'She's not herself today. I've given her a couple of aspirin. I think she should go home when she's had a bit of a rest.' For gradually she had seduced the other typist, a younger girl, into a

17

protective observance of her own interests, so that both of them would spend the day discussing new ways of doing their hair or answering questionnaires in magazines. A low burden of continuous conversation issued from behind the door of their room. At the threat of the onset of work one or other of them would consider herself a trifle unwell. Neither Hartmann nor Fibich was brave enough to ask what the matter was, since a look of reproach usually preceded the announcement, as if all women's ills could rightly be laid at the door of men. As Yvette was the stronger personality of the two she usually ensured that Jill would declare herself incapacitated and in need of her ministrations. Fibich, kept waiting while the tea was dispensed, and even cajoled into drinking a cup himself, could not help admiring Yvette's white hands with their rosy nails, her thin gold bracelet on her spotless cuff. 'Now then,' she would eventually and tolerantly ask. 'What can I do for you? Of course, this has put me out. You've got to take into account that I'm virtually single-handed here. I can't be expected to do the work of two people. I really need a junior.' Fibich would end up taking the letters home with him. Fortunately he had a friend with her own typewriter and she would rattle them off in the course of an evening. Work often got done this way.

In those days women did not labour out of any sense that the work itself imposed rules and laws superior to their own personal inclinations. Those who did were thought unlikely to get a man. It was Yvette's very frivolousness – expressed in her blithe indifference to the demands of a growing business – that seduced Hartmann, that and her excellent presentation. The trail of scent, the spotless cuffs, the white hands, and of course the enhanced awareness of herself that promised an exalted deployment of her attributes, all amused him, beguiled him, and though he privately thought her rather absurd, not altogether serious, and perhaps even a little pathetic, there came a point beyond which he could no longer deny himself the pleasure of her company, or rather, the spectacle of her personality. The working day was too short, it seemed to him, to contain the enigma and the fascination of Yvette. After remarkably little hesitation, and with a shrug at his own weakness, he married her.

As it turned out, Yvette's genius was equal to Hartmann's own. Never, in the course of their lives together, had he seen her in a state of dereliction. From dawn to dusk, and, more important, from dusk to dawn, she remained a pleasure for the eye, and for the senses, or for most of the senses. The promise of the rosy nails and the spotless cuffs had been kept, had increased, gaining, with each new access of prosperity, orders of magnitude which had in themselves something hieratic, celebratory. Nor was her care confined to her own person, although that continued to come first. She was a competent, even a creative housewife, who could be trusted with Hartmann's tastes and pleasures. Her interior was lavish and yet comfortable; her cooking elaborate, rich, and reassuring. She remained convinced of herself as an outstandingly worthy cause. She frequently expressed surprise at women who claimed equal rights with men, for she considered that women had everything to gain and men everything to lose where their interests were concerned. She tended to pity men for their natural and inevitable inadequacies.

All this was an entertainment to Hartmann, who, contemplating the high standard of comfort to which Yvette had brought him, considered the promise magnificently kept. On her more intimate incapacities he kept silent, for she was unaware of them herself and would not in any case have believed him had he informed her on this point. Indeed, part of her happiness, her unaltered sense of her own superiority, was due to a sense of virginity preserved, or at least prolonged, and anything more robust, more Dionysiac, than her usual reluctant performance she would have dubbed an unimportant concession that some women, not necessarily those of whom she approved, were forced to make to men in order to gain their consent on a matter of detail. She herself, she thought, evolved in a higher sphere. She despised profoundly women who betrayed the slightest flaw in their appearance, as if this advertised a sluttishness in their dispositions at which she would instinctively and fastidiously shudder.

This curious position, not uncommon before the great awakening that was to overtake women in the years of liberation, had its causal derivation in a circumstance which Yvette could scarcely remember, for, like Hartmann, she had no interest in the past, and whereas he had made a knowing selection of his reminiscences, subjecting his early life to an extreme form of censorship, Yvette behaved as if the history of Yvette ('Who is she? Who is that marvellously groomed woman with the blonde hair?') had not existed before the time when she herself had assumed control of it. There was, however, a picture in her mind – she could not call it a memory for she could not understand it: it was more like a dream, in that she could contemplate it from outside, almost from another's point of view – that she had been forced to verify, incurious though she was, by means of information gleaned with difficulty from her mother, Martine. In this picture she was a tiny child in a train which she somehow knew to be speeding south. When she asked her mother about this she saw, from the expression on her mother's face, that the older woman had been woken into grievous life by the reminiscence. And as she heard the story she realized why she could not remember it, for it belonged not to herself but to her mother and to her mother's life. As Yvette understood the story, her mother, Martine Besnard, had been travelling from Paris to Bordeaux to visit her sister, Alice. The picture that Yvette had in her mind was of herself, tiny, in a pleated skirt, docile, *tartine* in hand. She heard her mother say, '*Mange, mange, ma fille*': she felt the shadow of her mother bending over her to smooth back her flyaway hair. She later learned that her mother, a young widow, had been forced through lack of money to take refuge with her sister, who had married well, and to throw herself on the generosity of her brother-in-law. Yvette was charmed by this fairy-tale beginning and listened to the story as if it were indeed a romance, with herself at the centre of it, although from the high colour that invaded the older woman's cheeks as she told it the adventure had been unwelcome, distasteful, hazardous, and indeed so grave a risk that Martine's face flushed as she recounted it.

To Yvette the story had no resonance except as a novelette, the kind in which she believed implicitly, despite her relative sophistication, and this too was a common position among women in the days that preceded enlightenment. And yet something remained of it, enough to give her a heightened sense of the necessity of material comfort, of the security she was now able to extend to the mother whose early words, '*Mange, mange, ma fille*', had been accompanied by the cast shadow of her protective body.

The truth was slightly different, as Hartmann was to learn. On that occasion, the occasion that Yvette remembered as essentially picturesque, Martine Besnard had been fuelled by a desperate and unyielding purpose. She had fought hard to contain two overriding impulses: to feed the child and to go to a place where she might be guaranteed sustenance. Her sister, Alice, had married a substantial man in the wine trade. When the exigencies of keeping the child in Paris, in an apartment designed only for her icy mother-in-law, became too exhausting, she took off for Bordeaux, desirous of luxury, yet deeply reluctant to play the poor relation. The child's pointed face reminded her of her late husband, whose activities, from the outset of the Occupation, had caused her such grief. He had been killed while she was still wondering how to divorce him. On that point she was uncharacteristically vague. The relief of his death had been considerable, although with him disappeared all her subsistence. Had it not been for the little stock of money she had seen him hide under a floorboard both she and the child would have starved. It was with the last of that money that she had bought the train tickets to Bordeaux.

Only one hope sustained her: that she would meet someone, as her sister had done, who would give her a better life. The flush of effort in her cheeks could, she knew, so easily deepen into an ailment, an affliction, and who then would look after the child? So that when Edward Cazenove, the representative of an English wine shipper, came to Bordeaux after the war, and returned there on several occasions, she decided to marry him, although she did not particularly like him. To begin with he was unattractive, with a reddish face, flat hair, and uneasy eyes. That the uneasiness came from timidity rather than dishonesty did not, in Martine's view, excuse it: a man had no business to be timid. But he was lonely, polite, and he appeared to be fond of the little girl, and Martine, thinking of the room she had vacated in the rue Washington, took courage and ended her connection with France. They married from Alice's house and went back to his bachelor apartment in Manchester Square. The child cried a little, but not much. The high flush in Martine's cheeks subsided, although privately she considered her new life inferior. One day, after putting a casserole of rabbit into the oven, she looked out of the window on to the silent square and admitted to herself that she would have done better to have waited a little. But waiting demanded so much courage, and she was not a brave woman. She had done what she could. Even now she wondered if she would ever be warm again: London was as bitter as Paris had been. It was at this point that she gave up hopes for her own life and transferred all her yearning to her child. If it lay within her power, Yvette would never have to make the same disappointing decision that she herself had made. Yvette would be happy, and, better still, protected. Yvette would have expectations like any other girl and would be in a position to fulfil them. From that moment Martine abandoned herself to the pleasures of food, such as there was, and good wine, of which there was more than enough. Yvette remembered her parents, or rather her mother and stepfather, of whom she became rather fond, as a passive, rather silent couple, with a high and steady colour, drinking down the good wine at every meal, and flushing further in grateful response to its unfailing benefits.

With that recital out of the way, relations between mother and daughter became amiable but distant. Yvette saw nothing of the frightened young widow in her mother, a substantial and normally uncommunicative woman with a thin mouth, her colour still high, who preferred these days to keep her own counsel, quite willing to off-load the daughter she had brought into

23

safe harbour, as if the effort were self-limiting and had now served its purpose. She and Cazenove, to whom she had finally become rather attached, preferred to spend their winters in Nice, where they reverted to being French. Seated at a table outside a café on the Promenade des Anglais, they would watch disapprovingly as the first tourists arrived. '*Nice n'est plus Nice,*' they would say to their favourite waiter, shaking their heads. These days the high colour spread down their necks to disappear beneath their collars. When they window-shopped in the rue de France, Cazenove carried his wife's handbag. They managed, modestly, but quite comfortably. Hartmann helped.

Yvette regarded her mother's story with complaisance. She did not see it as tragic or even fatal, one of those throws of the dice that change lives; she did not consider that she might have evolved differently had that accident of going to Bordeaux not taken place. She continued to regard it as something of a fairy tale, part of the myth, the charm that she had always claimed for herself and that had landed her safely in the serene waters of her own marriage. What she remembered, typically, was her own contribution to this happy state. Childhood was an irrelevance: what was of passionate interest to her was the way she had designed her life as a woman. Self-love had saved her, when she was the poorest girl at her Swiss school, Les Colombes. Too much to drink had by that stage had its effect on Cazenove's career, an occupational hazard which was nevertheless unsympathetically dealt with. In the years that coincided with Yvette's adolescence he sat at home in Manchester Square, and the money came from his rapidly diminishing savings and regular donations from Martine's sister, Alice. The finishing school had been Martine's last effort to secure her daughter a future, made in the teeth of opposition both from Cazenove and from Alice. With resources so slender and so hazardous, Martine had indoctrinated her daughter with a need to succeed, a purpose which a young girl like Yvette could hardly take as seriously as her mother appeared to do. But, luckily or unluckily, Yvette thought of herself as desirable and possessed to a high degree that amorous disposition that young girls usually turn towards a favoured adult. But there was no favoured adult in Yvette's cosmology; she no longer felt ineluctably attached to her mother and her stepfather, to whom she had never seriously considered herself related. Her amorousness was therefore devoted entirely to herself. Scanning her face in the glass, she saw not the fine skin, the strong but widely spaced teeth, the fair hair already rising high on the forehead and giving a hint of future recession, but her secret possession, her perfect body. It was the knowledge of its perfection that sustained her, that enabled her to look in the glass and think, 'I am the best'. It was a body that might have been designed by a Salon painter of the Second Empire, by Baudry or Bouguereau, one of those legendary hourglass shapes that bloom extravagantly but harmoniously above and below a narrow waist. When other girls went out to drink chocolate in the nearby town, she stayed quite contentedly in the school dormitory, buffing her nails or washing one of her two cashmere sweaters, themselves passed on to her by an unknown French cousin. Few clothes meant strenuous and vigilant upkeep, and sometimes she was bored. But when her spirits momentarily fell, she knew that she could always raise them by walking lightly in her nightgown between the rows of beds, as if she had forgotten something in the bathroom, and see the faces grow discontented as her splendid breasts passed by. Further display she planned only for the delectation of a husband, that same husband to have received discreet advertisements in order to help him make up his mind. It was only when he was safely in the net that he would discover that its promise was not kept to any recognizable extent by its performance. Yvette herself was never to perceive this, for the evidence of her splendour was always there for her to admire. Nor did she wonder that her so splendid body gave her such scant information. She was, to a surprising extent in one so endowed, ignorant of sensual impulses, chaste. It was monogamy she craved, as the one adventure of her life that would enable and entitle her to live as she pleased for ever after. It was in this fashion that her mother lived on inside her. And the smile stayed on her face, for she never doubted her victory.

It was this assurance, together with her bustling fastidiousness, that had brought Hartmann to her side, and on the whole he was not disappointed. He appreciated her more as the years took their toll than he had when they were first married. She still amused him, and she was still unaware that she did so. She had seemed a little frightened as a bride, and indeed she had been woefully inexperienced, for her mother's efforts had been all in the direction of preparedness and not at all towards that of pleasure. The finishing school had been followed by a few weeks taking lessons in typing and shorthand from a retired secretary who lived on the top floor, under the roof, of the next-door building. Yvette had hated these lessons so much, had hated in fact the greasy hair and the muddy complexion of the retired secretary, that she had taken in little of what the woman was trying to teach her. Hence her unwillingness to work when her mother had found her the job with Hartmann and Fibich, had found it by dint of going to an expensive employment agency and doing all the interviewing herself, while Yvette, appalled, had listened to the clattering typewriters and wondered if she could ever pass the test that they were going to inflict on her. She passed it, but only just, and then took the only job that called for general office duties rather than typing and shorthand. Nevertheless, Yvette described herself to her friends as a secretary. Fibich shook his head, but Hartmann found himself quite touched by her pretensions, by her appearance, and by the occasional blank look of absence on her face, in her eyes, as if she were waiting for someone to rescue her from a dilemma which she did not fully understand. Ariadne on Naxos, he had thought. So he had been Bacchus.

In the early days, when he discovered that the splendour of that body was in fact limited to what could be displayed rather than enjoyed, Hartmann took a mistress. His attitude towards this woman was ambiguous. On the one hand he found in her all the passion that was lacking in his marriage, but on the other hand he disliked her. He disliked her for reasons which had to do entirely with himself. She was a quiet woman, not bad looking, but certainly not remarkable, shrewd, cool, and tactful. He could be sure of her discretion, and yet he felt uneasy with her. He felt that he could only have relaxed with a woman of a coarser disposition, a dangerous, frankly down-market sort of woman, the sort of woman with whom he need not mind his manners. Whereas Elizabeth – a cool discreet sort of name – treated him with an amiable respect that forced his respect in return. Her deportment, in fact, was entirely appropriate in a wife but not in a mistress. Since Yvette remained disconcertingly innocent of her physical shortcomings, and found it impossible, and uninteresting, to speculate about the capacities of other women, there was certainly nothing in Hartmann's conduct that robbed her of her status.

And yet it was precisely a matter of status that created such discomfort between Hartmann and his mistress. If anything, Elizabeth was slightly superior in breeding to Yvette, whose touching childhood, the half-remembered episode of her mother urging her to eat in the train to Bordeaux – an episode which so moved him when he first heard it – seemed to clothe her in a vulnerability of which she remained unaccountably unaware. In short, when he was in bed with Elizabeth, he felt guilty; she had the effect of reinforcing his fidelity to his wife. She continued to receive him with the same thoughtful deference, pretending not to notice the studious lack of love, the absence of endearments, his very reluctance to call her by her name, as if literally distancing her from his real, his authentic life. It was as if he sent his *doppelgänger* to make love to her. And the love-making itself, the necessary quantity of their association, had a brutality, a facelessness, that excited them both but did not compensate for all that was missing on both sides. She could have loved him, but would not allow herself to do so, for she understood him rather well. Thus, through each other they came into contact with their lesser selves. When he left her Hartmann was astonished to feel such melancholy.

On the evenings of the days on which he visited his mistress he was more than ever affectionate towards his wife. He appreciated anew his handsome drawing-room, on which Yvette had lavished such care; he even appreciated his wife's little fussy self-regarding ceremonies. Safely back in the land of husbands and wives, on whom society smiles, he would vow to put an end to it. And one day he had. Elizabeth had behaved perfectly, and there were no harsh words. What she had felt he never knew. These days he greeted her through the window of the dress shop she owned, and she would always smile back.

It amazed Yvette that married women could have flirtations. Why did they need to, when the business of flirting had already been brought to an honourable conclusion? In that sense she was virtuous. Her days passed in relative but nonetheless real innocence, shopping, rearranging her linen cupboard or her wardrobe, lunching with friends, strolling down Bond Street. Recently she had begun to imagine herself a little too hard-worked, a little too tied to the house (for the women's movement had caught up with her): she had declared that she would not cook dinner, would in fact go to evening classes. She was aware of the impact that this declaration made. In reality nothing much interested her, but she found a group that discussed great works of French literature, and she decided that, with her fine accent, she would make a good impression there. Rather touchingly, to Hartmann, she was set to reading *La Princesse de Clèves*, the first book on the list, which she found puzzling but to which she was attracted. She would come home momentarily thoughtful, as if pondering matters which had not previously engaged her attention. But once in the flat, where Hartmann would be sitting in front of the television, she would find the ideas that had suggested themselves, had indeed been eagerly discussed by the group, ridiculous, and would retire to pamper herself with a leisurely bath and a flattering nightgown. Every night she virtually dressed up to go to bed, comfortable in the knowledge that she could at last sleep undisturbed.

These days the splendid body was more voluminous, the hair dyed to an uncompromising shade of gold. With her new amplitude her bustling demeanour made a more genuine impression. Although still inclined not to take her seriously, Hartmann trusted her absolutely. He realized that she too would soon be old, that they would be old together. A vein in her left leg occasioned her some discomfort, and once, when he went into the bedroom before she had finished undressing, he saw that between the black satin straps of her ambitious underwear the flesh of her back had become turgid, the back itself slightly but noticeably rounded. She had never complained, but remained happy with the original bargain. She was still, despite *La Princesse de Clèves*, an old-fashioned woman. She still kissed him goodnight before turning over resolutely on her side. And she was there every morning to ask him how he had slept (for sleep was becoming important to them both), to serve him his coffee in his special cup, and to reassure him that, in spite of age, nothing had really changed.

Fibich remembered. Fibich remembered Aunt Marie, whom he called 'Aunt', and the flat filled with implacable Gothic furniture where he had spent so many years wondering if his bewilderment would ever end. He remembered blundering through his life, never knowing or indeed discovering whether his actions were acceptable or whether they were as futile as he believed them to be. The years before his arrival were lost, and it was their loss that had sent him to the analyst. And no momentous retrieval had taken place, nothing that he thought might at last supply him with an identity. All that remained of that enterprise, apart from the agonizing possibility of a deliberate return to his birthplace, in itself an exercise in human archaeology and therefore in a sense hedged about with superstition, was the odd fragment, the odd image, extracted under kindly coercion from a mass of fear which was very slow to abate. He had, for example, an image of himself as a very small, very plump boy, engulfed in a large wing chair which he knew to be called the Voltaire, feeling lazy, replete, and secure in the dying light of a winter afternoon. He deduced that he must have been put there to rest after a family meal, perhaps a Sunday lunch, but he could not reach back and discover who had been present, nor could he remember the room or rooms in which these activities had taken place.

But he knew that he could not have invented this image, which returned to him quite clearly from time to time. The fact that he saw himself as fat was crucial, since for all of his adult life he had been laughably, cadaverously thin. For as long as he could remember his mind had been occupied with thoughts of food, of which there never seemed to be enough; at the school he did not even mind that the food had been disgusting, for all that mattered was that the food should be there. He was never to be fully secure in the knowledge that there would be another meal, not even as a married man, with a wife who knew all his needs. Much as he had loved his infant son, he had felt an involuntary pang when his wife had first turned to the child and occupied herself with cutting up the food in his little dish. He had felt a sadness then, and a terrible shame, that his wants were to be subordinated to those of the child, and that he still minded. The analyst had been very keen on that episode.

He feared the future. For as long as he could remember he had feared the future. He was plagued by dreams that had no connecting thread apart from the incongruousness of their settings, and the fact that a great deal of cleaning, of housework, seemed to be involved. He dreamed of being approached, amiably, by notable men, men in public life – a government minister, a newspaper tycoon – all of whom seemed to be well disposed towards him. In these dreams some sort of rendezvous was proposed, one which he knew would be to his advantage, but before this could take place he would have to scrub out a derelict kitchen or an obscure bathroom, while outside the sun shone and crowds strolled by on ample pavements. He was troubled, too, by tiny jealousies, envying Hartmann's easy acceptance of the world as it was, not reaching back towards a past which he had never properly possessed. He was five years younger than Hartmann, had left home at the age of seven, and therefore could hardly hope to recapture his lost life, particularly as advancing age was affecting him more quickly, so that these days he hardly knew himself, with his distinguished grey hair, his hesitant walk, and his habitually anxious face, from which his renewed teeth beamed forth a message of sturdiness which he himself could not believe. Often his tongue would creep cautiously round his mouth to make sure that his teeth were still there.

He would retire, he sometimes thought, and devote his time to sorting out these matters before it was too late, and he would do this without the benefit of outside interference, by which he meant the analyst, Mrs Gebhardt, with her transfixing but fallacious maternal aura and the kindly smile built on a foundation of indifference. In the meantime, part of the past, the most expendable part, was still with him, so that he seemed still to be possessed by the tedium and the incomprehensibility of that segment of his life which was of no value to him, while the essential part, the part that would have explained his character and would have furnished him with a lineage was irrevocably missing. Quite simply, there had been no one to tell him about it. He felt, alarmingly, that he was only alive by the skin of his teeth.

Of his curious life since his arrival at the school, and then at Aunt Marie's flat in Compayne Gardens, he remembered a great deal, but the memory was uninteresting, tedious, and he was even a little annoyed at its tenacity. Aunt had been kind, but being childless herself was devoid of that instinctive warmth that Fibich craved. She had been kind through inadvertence, through absent-mindedness, never quite realizing that children need to know that they are the object of constant attention rather than of haphazard and lightning sallies into their conversation or their activities. The flat in Compayne Gardens had been filled with black furniture of a convoluted nature, so that every bureau and credenza, of which there had been several, looked as if they had been designed by the Brothers Grimm. Paintings, in an amateurish and discordant style, hung on every wall, for Aunt's late husband, Mr Jessop, had been an artist, of a kind that had congregated in Hampstead in the years before the war, blessed with an income that had allowed him to go on turning out his orange and green abstracts without much care that nobody ever bought them. They were frequently given away to friends as wedding or anniversary presents: the friends would nod thoughtfully and remark that he was 'evolving'. Nevertheless many remained, stacked two or three deep in the small room that was destined to receive Fibich, so that to the nightmare of the furniture was added the constant awareness of cruel landscapes in the style of the early Derain, Provence under a Hampstead sky, or alternately, Hampstead as it might be on the outskirts of Avignon. 'My husband was a Fauve,' Aunt had said, showing him to his room, by which Fibich had slowly come to understand that the late Jessop had had carnivorous instincts. He had shuddered and turned the pictures to the wall. Aunt's kindness showed through in the fact that she had not noticed this, or had not objected to it if she had noticed it. Or perhaps she was as tired of the pictures as he would have been had he had to live with them all his married life.

Aunt had come to England as a girl, to marry Mr Jessop, and in deference to his calling had dressed artistically, with amber beads and flying hair and the tweed cape that had caused so much mirth when she visited the boys at their school. The tweed cape had been purchased before she left home, and was of so excellent a quality that it never wore out, and was quite in fashion when the style came round again in the fifties. *La vie de bohème* had left Aunt with a more secure knowledge of how to provide mulled wine for fifteen or twenty friends who might drop in of an evening to discuss the Marxist interpretation of history than an understanding of how to feed starving boys on inadequate rations every day during their holidays from school. She tended to cook everything at once, usually on a Friday evening, so that they could count on one meal of a certain splendour, while the rest of the week was given over to unappetizing expedients. It was to Aunt's credit that she invested this one meal with considerable ceremony, lighting candles, spreading a damask cloth. A shadowy girl, a niece of her late husband, was invited, and came early on Friday afternoons to help with the preparations. The meal was invariable: braised tongue *à l'orientale*, followed by baked apples. Sometimes there were Kentish cobnuts to follow, and Fibich was given the task of cracking them. He remembered passing the shelled nuts to the shadowy girl, whose name was Christine Hardy. Later in the evening she would disappear silently to do the washing-up.

An ache, which he was not old enough or bold enough to recognize as boredom, would seize him as soon as the cloth was once more gathered into its folds, and the rest of the weekend had to be endured. Walks were encouraged, for Aunt had not felt the cold, and the single bar of the electric fire was not switched on until evening, and then only reluctantly. Traversing the Heath with Hartmann, who was the only other person he knew, Fibich would wonder if this life would ever end, since he knew he could not go home again. His terror and despair were without measure. Sometimes, in the evenings, he would forfeit his place in front of the electric fire and disappear to be sick. Aunt knew this, although it was never mentioned. It was Hartmann who took care of him, although Fibich was adept at being sick without anyone noticing. 'Sit here, Thomas,' Aunt would say, as he came back, white-faced, into the drawing-room. 'Sit down and get warm. You are quite safe here, you know.' She was good in that way, never got alarmed or hysterical, so that the symptom passed as he grew older, although he always had a sensitive stomach and loathed unusual food, regarding it with suspicion and the fatal knowledge that it was sure to upset him. With that, a tremendous appetite for farinaceous material, as much bread and starch as could be obtained. He grew rapidly, but it was hard for him to believe that he had ever been that fat child who sat so replete, his digestive system becalmed, in the chair called the Voltaire. 'Not *the* Voltaire, *a* Voltaire,' Aunt had explained to him much later. 'It is a chair with a high back and wings. Very comfortable. We had them at home.' In her drawing-room one sat on springy sofas with bulging arms that were too low, relics of the days when she had set up house. The more substantial objects she had somehow brought with her, as she had the green and white plates, elaborately scrolled, from which they had eaten their baked apples. In the bathroom a rust stain crept down the inside of the old-fashioned claw-footed tub, under the taps. The water was hot, but they were enjoined not to waste it. 'The King of England uses only five inches of bath water,' Aunt would tell them. 'See that you do the same.'

Through the tears occasioned by his recent bouts of vomiting Fibich saw the haze of girandoles twinkling sadly against the beige walls. With the blackout curtains drawn the room was dim, but no dimmer than it was during the daytime, when the intrusive furniture loomed. The washing-up done, the shadowy girl would come in with a tray of tea. 'Thank you, dear,' Aunt would say, and would put extra sugar from her ration into Fibich's cup. Such kindnesses he remembered.

Occasionally friends from the old days would drop in, fat men in stained tweed suits, women with unadorned faces. Aunt herself was handsome, ramrodbacked, even elegant. The flyaway hair of her early days had long been disciplined into a kind of scroll that was cleverly tucked round her head. Her eyes were not good, and sometimes she would don a pair of tinted glasses. She looked curiously out of place as she sat among her husband's erstwhile companions, and, had she known it, remarks were occasionally passed in the neighbourhood. But she did not know it, or if she did she ignored it: she was not without a certain grandeur. And her efforts were commendable. She spent her days collecting unglamorous material for salvage, or knitting (badly) for men in the services. The Vicar called, largely to show his broadmindedness, for she told him with a ringing laugh that she was a free-thinker. She was particularly good with bombed-out families, whom she tirelessly strove to see rehoused. She was never ill, or lazy, or negligent. On the whole, she was a distinguished woman, although her presence remained uncomfortable. She was their only relative, so that in later life Hartmann and Fibich and the girl, Christine, had communal memories of her. Once she had taken all three of them to hear Myra Hess play Bach at the National Gallery.

When Hartmann went into the army Fibich stayed with Aunt, paying her a small sum out of his wages at the print works. She aged quickly after the war, seemed to lose her iron nerve and her equable spirits. Perhaps the strain of having the boys in her flat had at last begun to tell. She had never wanted children, and would have been quite happy on her own, with her numerous activities to fill up her spare time. But now she began to rely on Fibich to keep her company in the evenings, to mend things about the flat, to carry the shopping. Her eyesight had deteriorated quite rapidly, and she no longer read. Together they would listen to the wireless, silently united for the Brains Trust or the play on Saturday evening, the highlight of the week. Aunt particularly liked plays with detectives in them or criminals pretending to be decent members of society. 'Ha, I see your game,' she would cry. With hair still dark, back still straight, but colour haphazardly applied to her cheeks, she suddenly looked bizarrely foreign. Yet she still never left her bedroom without being fully dressed and groomed, accountable to the world.

With his first meagre stipend Fibich bought her a bunch of violets, which she held to her cheek for a moment before laying them aside. Fibich put them in a fish-paste jar, thinking them too humble for a vase. With his second stipend he bought a reproduction of Dürer's *Praying Hands*, out of some obscure religious and national impulse. 'What a horror,' said Aunt, gazing at it severely through narrowed eyes. 'I hate that finicky style.' 'But he is a great Renaissance master,' objected Fibich, who was rapidly losing faith in his purchase. 'Hardly,' said Aunt. 'A most unhealthy mind. No trace of your Latin exuberance there. A crabbed

soul. Still, if you like it, I can hardly discourage you.'
Fibich had, in buying it, aspired to nobility. Now he
was disappointed. It stayed on the wall of his room until
its piety began to irritate him, after which he took it down.

He grew immensely tall and very handsome, a condition of which he was unaware. He remained miserable
and ashamed, largely on account of his appetite which
continued to torment him. He saw himself marooned
forever in Aunt's spare room, to which he would
smuggle jars of peanut butter or packets of Lyons cup
cakes. Aunt took less and less interest in maintaining the
household, and in desperation Fibich learned to cook.
The girl, Christine Hardy, still visited occasionally, and
she taught him the rudiments: soon he was able to make
a good clear soup and a dish of savoury rice and a
compote of dried fruits, all of which Aunt greeted with
enthusiasm. His cuisine was tailored to her taste. He
saw that he was to be responsible for her for the rest of
her life, or possibly his, and indeed he knew that
Hartmann, still absent, relied on him to keep some sort
of a home for them both. Fibich, with his anxious
mournful temperament, had nurturing instincts,
although what he longed for was to be in receipt of
those instincts from someone else. Yet it seemed that
this could never be. As he loped home from the printing
works in his dirty shirt, a precious shin bone and a
pound of carrots in his shopping bag, he had nothing to
which he could look forward except Hartmann's return.
When the letter came from the Red Cross, informing
him of his parents' death (but he had always known that
they were dead) and of the instructions they had given
and of the money waiting for him in Switzerland, he did
not immediately register that he need no longer lead
such a menial existence. He continued to go to the
printing works, postponing all decisions until Hart-

mann came home. As far as he was concerned, nothing had changed. He did not see the admiring glances that some girls directed at him, or if he did he was too shy to acknowledge them let alone interpret them. He rarely greeted people, for he was afraid of revealing his bad teeth. He was tolerated at the works, but had few friends. He asked nobody home: it was not the sort of home to which one asked friends. He and Aunt drifted on together, in the dim rooms, listening to the wireless, talking only very occasionally, retiring early. Sleep, which in early life never failed Fibich, was his enduring treat, and was to remain so until its dramatic interruption by dreams, just when he thought he was old enough to relax.

When Fibich was nineteen, Aunt entered on to her last illness. A feebleness overtook her, and she frequently leaned her head back in her chair and closed her eyes: Fibich did not know whether she slept or fainted. He consulted the girl, Christine, and they both agreed that one of them would always stay with her, so that when Fibich went to work Christine would move in. He would find her there in the evenings, and had the rare experience of coming home to a cooked meal. Aunt was silent but seemed serene: she smiled at them in her intervals of lucidity, bore no grudges, was visited by no urgencies or recriminations, put her entire trust in her unlikely helpers. The doctor left pills, which Fibich threw away. He knew quite well what was happening, and hoped he would be equal to the task. He was grateful to Aunt for the good manners with which she had conducted her life and was now conducting her last days. In all the years he had lived with her he had learned nothing about her, and now it was too late to ask the questions which he should have asked before. Perhaps, he thought, she might have liked to talk about her life before they met, about Jessop, and the friends, and the adventure that had brought her to this part of the world. He was grateful to her for not ever having burdened him with her own feelings, for now he realized how importunate the presence of two frightened boys must have been. Every evening he supported, half-carried, her to her room, and helped to settle her in her high walnut bed. He left both their doors open, so that he could hear her if she called in the night.

When he came home one late November evening he heard a low unconscious moaning sound and saw that Christine's face was white and frightened. The sound swelled and faded, sometimes developing into a hoarse one-sided conversation. 'She has been like this all the afternoon,' said Christine. 'It is the end,' replied Fibich. Together they dragged Aunt into her room, for she was now a dead weight, and too absorbed in her internal monologue to pay them any attention. Her feet trailed on the floor, and Christine had to go back and pick up her discarded slippers. Once she was installed in her bed her talking stopped; soon the moans began again, and in the short intervals between them her face would be contorted by frowns, as if someone or something were giving her intense displeasure. Fibich urged Christine to go home, for he knew that the task belonged to him. She was reluctant to leave; however he impressed upon her that he would need her the following day, and finally she left. Fibich knew that Aunt would not last the night. He sat by her bed, scrutinizing the animated face with its closed eyes, occasionally holding the hand that twitched rhythmically on the coverlet. Time swept by, not with agonizing slowness, as he had half feared, but with a species of exultation; every time he looked at the clock it was to notice, amazed, that another hour had passed. In the street outside the sound of the final car died away, and then everything was silent. At two in the morning Aunt opened her eyes, seemed on the verge of saying something, struggled with what seemed increasing excitement, looked him full in the face, then fell back, dead. Fibich pulled the sheet over her face, and sat with her until it was light.

Christine, when she came, shed a few tears; then she calmed herself and went into the kitchen to put on a kettle for tea. That seemed to be the appropriate thing to do. Fibich telephoned the doctor, and was told what arrangements would have to be made. He felt a distaste, a weariness, as if he had encountered death many times before. Midway through the morning hunger possessed him, and with this sign of normality he knew that he would survive the ordeal, as he had survived everything else. The presence of Christine, a silent girl at the best of times, and these were not the best, helped him to play his part. When the doorbell rang he got up to let the doctor in, but there stood Hartmann, jovial, in his khaki, at last released from the army. It was then that Fibich wept.

Since then he had let himself be guided by Hartmann. It was Hartmann who set up the idea of the business, with a gambler's confidence that had won over Fibich. In time the idea that their monies might have been used separately disappeared, and they genuinely had all things in common. Their early experiences had given them the identity they needed, and as long as they stayed together this identity became more reassuring, so that in middle age they seemed to have as substantial a life as anyone else of their acquaintance. And it had to be said that Hartmann's sunny and insouciant attitude was marvellously attractive to have around, and that it preserved Fibich from his worst excesses of melancholy. The melancholy was still there, of course; it was never to disappear. But for the years of their young manhood, with their ridiculous business established and even prospering, he knew some lightness of heart. With their wives, the two men would go on holiday together, hiring villas in Normandy, buying cars, briefly acting as *bons viveurs*. Hartmann acted this way as if he had been born to it: Fibich did it as an act of daring, to see if he would be either stopped or arrested. The habit of caution, of self-effacement, was too deeply engrained in him to be entirely vanquished. But no one seemed to think he should not be enjoying himself; he was never summoned to the headmaster's study. Briefly, he put on weight, and his appetite settled down to near normal. When he saw the sun at his window he was nearly a happy man.

Yet in his mind he never entirely left the flat in Compayne Gardens, where he had stayed for five years after Aunt Marie's death, until Hartmann, who was the first to marry, found the two homes where they could be as nearly together as was compatible with their married state. Hartmann, who could not wait to leave lugubrious Compayne Gardens, the red-brick houses, the untidily winding streets, moved out as soon as he seriously contemplated marriage to Yvette. He had brought her home to Compayne Gardens, where Fibich had behaved impeccably: he treated her with respect, as Hartmann did not, and would listen to her for hours. However, Hartmann had a more active courtship in mind, and secured the flat in Ashley Gardens after no more than a brief search: his pleasures had always inspired his most effective actions. He then set about enquiring of his neighbours whether they had plans to move on, and asked them to warn him if and when they found somewhere else to their liking. Fibich lived on soberly in Compayne Gardens, still carrying his shopping bag, with its shin bone and its pound of carrots. He was still strikingly handsome, and still unaware of it. He was beginning, slowly, to come alive, but it was taking a very long time. As if he dared not trust the sun which reappeared at his window, as if he dared not believe that he was now free to invent his own life, he regularly dusted the Gothic furniture, kept Aunt Marie's bedroom aired, and sat quietly in the evenings, listening to the wireless. He threw out the Dürer reproduction, though, and managed to offload many of Jessop's paintings at one of the new junk shops that were springing up in the district. He was happy to visit Hartmann and Yvette, and not made envious by their comfort. He was an abstracted and uncommunicative man, active only when he was at work, more often than not sunk into what passed in him for reverie when at home. He turned out to be trustworthy, simple, honourable, the serious element in an enterprise that Hartmann continued to consider something of a joke. Only the neighbours found him slightly odd, curiously unwilling to join them. For Fibich needed all his spare time to himself, as if the task of discovering himself required all his best energies. But now sleep, in which he placed his faith as the element that would restore him to himself, and which for so long had been his infinite resource, began to fail him. The night that sleep failed him for the first time, and the following nights when the same thing happened again, alerted him to the fact that his troubles were not yet over. He had been lucky for a while, that was all. It could not last. He had always known that it could not and would not last. So that, ironically, when the spectre of childhood might at last seem to have been laid to rest, he began to be the old Fibich again. With his connections in Hampstead, he had no difficulty in finding an analyst.

44

4

Christine Fibich, who had been born Christine Hardy, had always known that she would marry Fibich, although he had not always known it himself. From her first sight of him, pale, teary, but oddly glamorous with his long elegant legs and dark hair, she had thought, 'I can make you better.' But for a very long time he had not seemed to notice her. It was only when Aunt Marie became ill that he began to take her presence for granted, even to rely on it. She was aware that her connection with this strange household was tenuous, but she felt at home there, much more so than in the tragic flat in West End Lane, where her father and her stepmother always seemed to be returning to darkened rooms after another pointless quarrel. Her mother had been sister to Mr Jessop and had thus been a Jessop herself before marrying Mr Hardy, a morose widower, and dying shortly after Christine's birth, presumably of disappointment. Mr Hardy, a widower once more, had been much in demand among the ladies of the Bridge Club, despite his lack of obvious attractions: he was unmarried, that was enough, and to women of a certain age he possessed advantages. He seemed to be independently wealthy, for he did no work and was to be seen reading the financial pages of the worthier newspapers. He was in fact a retired businessman: in his heyday he had owned a chain of florists' shops, had sold out when they were doing well, and had subsequently invested his money wisely. His days passed in calculations of a financial nature, although his wealth, which was modest but real enough, did not seem to benefit him. No flower graced the interior of his gloomy apartment, which was decorated in shades of brown and illuminated by the weakest of lights. Government restrictions were seized on by him as an excuse not to replace the heavy walnut furniture, which seemed to be covered by a fine spray of dust and cigarette ash. The fringes of the Turkey carpets were swollen with dirt, and stood up like the epaulettes on the uniform of a Napoleonic soldier. Brown velvet curtains hung lifelessly at every window and when pulled for the blackout released more dust into the stagnant air. Windows were never, or rarely, opened. He insisted on an even temperature, not noticing the smell, which was compounded of ancient cooking and unwashed ashtrays.

Rita Gifford was the divorcée who won his hand. Initially energetic, a characteristic which was held over from her original employment as a hospital sister, she too was living on a small capital and was determined never to work again. She was a highly-coloured woman with a heavy body which tapered down to elegant legs and feet; after a few games of bridge she inveigled Mr Hardy to a tea dance, at which she knew she could be seen to her best advantage. She was a woman who liked being married, or rather who liked the status of marriage, for she did not much care for men. What was initially perceived as vivacity was in reality an argumentative disposition, which she managed to keep in check until after the wedding. She had, in fact, overestimated Mr Hardy's assets, and although she did not care for children any more than she cared for men, she thought that the girl, Christine, could just be tolerated as part of the bargain. There was no love lost between herself and Mr Hardy: there was no love at all, not even affection, but Mr Hardy, who was too out of sympathy with women in general to understand his daughter, thought that he was making a move in the right direction by getting a woman into the house to look after her. Having done this he could legitimately take no further interest. If he thought of his third marriage at all in philosophical terms, which he did not, it would have been seen as a benevolent provision for his only child. Further than this he did not seem to want to look. Nor was he much interested in how he and Mrs Gifford would spend their time together. He probably calculated on a number of bridge evenings, which would be convenient, as he hated going out. He thought that that should be enough. The rest of the time she could devote to his comfort, or rather to the preservation of those maniacal habits which were the rule by which he lived.

But once installed, Rita Gifford, or Rita Hardy, as she now was, discovered that she rather disliked him. The necessities of her life once guaranteed, she began to crave the superfluous, and when that was not forthcoming to decline into headaches, moods, petty clashes of opinion which charged the atmosphere and were resolved by a banging of doors when she retired into the bedroom for one of those mysterious siestas which kept the flat under permanent curfew. Mr Hardy preferred to take his rest in the drawing-room, which was soon filled with loud snoring noises. When Christine came home from school she would find them both asleep, discordantly, and she soon learned to make herself a sandwich and to take it to her room, which she would not leave

47

until much later in the evening, when people arrived to play cards. Her after-image of her father was of a stout figure, head thrown back, legs thrust out, fast asleep and snoring loudly. She soon learned to read with her fingers in her ears to drown out the noise.

She was a modest girl, who did not even presume to be unhappy, although she was often accused of upsetting her stepmother. Indeed she came to be used as a bone of contention for the obscure resentments which now bound Mr and Mrs Hardy together. However self-effacing she tried, and managed, to be she was blamed for everything, for coming in, for going out, for having a long face, for not playing bridge (she was fourteen at the time), for reading too much, for not having any friends. For she had the wit to know that she could never bring anyone home. Children know that their peers are both cruel and honest and will judge each other's parents without mercy: it is their first experience of adult anxiety. She also had the wit to know that she would learn nothing at home that could prepare her for another life. She therefore got into the habit of visiting her aunt, Mrs Jessop, her dead mother's sister-in-law, who was conveniently situated a few minutes away. Marie, absent-minded but well-meaning, took her presence for granted, and when Christine timidly asked if she might learn to cook, responded gallantly and with some relief, glad of the help and of the opportunity to teach, in equal measure. Thus Christine learned the rudiments of home-making. It was her only act of independence. Trained to keep silent, she saw her only chance as being allowed to remain silent in a more harmonious environment. She wondered if anyone would have her as a nun, but as she did not believe in God was forced to dismiss this idea as unrealistic.

Gradually she allowed herself to think of Aunt

Marie's household as her real home. Nobody noticed her absence at West End Lane, and she knew instinctively that she was wise to keep out of her stepmother's way. 'Always under my feet,' she had overheard that lady say to her father, and, more meanly, to her face, 'A girl your age could be earning her living. It's not as if you had looks on your side.' Yet she was not the original wicked stepmother for she seemed too often to be incapacitated, moaning with 'one of my heads', and spending little time in the kitchen except to make numerous cups of tea which she would carry off to her room. Soon Christine was putting her new-found expertise to work at home. Thus she cooked in both houses, thinking and hoping that she was practising for the life ahead, but not knowing what that would be. In the evenings Mrs Hardy would step forth momentarily refreshed, her face newly made-up, to prepare for the card-playing guests. Having slept all the afternoon, both Mr and Mrs Hardy liked to retire late. Often Christine would return from Compayne Gardens to a flat full of biscuit crumbs and cigarette smoke. She soon learned to clear up the next morning before going to school.

She was timidly aware of being an anachronism. She tried to love her father but was baulked in the attempt, for he was not at home with children and thought that his obligation to her ended when he had introduced the new Mrs Hardy into her life. Mrs Hardy, for her part, though generally antagonistic to Mr Hardy, was possessive. 'Your father and I would like to be alone, Christine', was one of her commonest remarks, as a door was once more closed in Christine's face. Murmurings behind these closed doors gave some hint of an amorous exchange, although it was hard and even disgusting to imagine this. Christine preferred to leave for the aseptic atmosphere of the Jessop household, where she was learning to master Aunt Marie's braised tongue *à l'orientale*. She liked the boys too. She liked Hartmann, who was good-natured and who never teased her. She particularly liked Fibich, whom she saw as one of her own kind. He was her reassurance that she was not entirely alone.

When Mr Hardy fell ill, after a lifetime of inertia, cogitation, and smoking, Christine was devotedly at his bedside, thinking that at last, now that they were allowed to be together without much interference from Mrs Hardy (who, for all her hospital training, preferred to make herself scarce) they might be close, might discover the bonds of affection that had been so mysteriously absent for as long as she cared to remember. She had no idea that he might die. When it became apparent that he would, she slept in a chair at his bedside. One night she was alerted to the fact of a final alteration by the noise of his breathing. 'Father,' she said, leaning forward in a thrill of dedication. 'Father. Tell me what to do.' There was an interval of noise and silence, alternately mingled. 'Father,' she said. 'Tell me.' After an immense effort Mr Hardy turned his head in her direction. 'Don't sell Glaxo,' he said, and fell back, dead.

Upon receipt of the news Mrs Hardy retired to bed for a week, during which time Christine, by now extremely frightened, was obliged to wait on her. Grim-faced, a fact which she ascribed to one of her heads, Mrs Hardy was not communicative, although when the bridge cronies came to pay visits of condolence she would reveal herself as a woman of sorrows, and murmur, 'Don't ask me what I've been through.' 'I can imagine,' one or other of the visitors would respond sympathetically. 'No,' she would reply. 'No words can express . . .', and would let her hand fall in a noble gesture of despair. Christine had an inkling that she was referring to the marriage rather than the bereavement, but of course did not allow the thought to take root. She herself was in a state of loneliness compounded by a terrible fear, fear that she might have to spend the rest of her life ministering to Mrs Hardy who would never get up again. Mrs Hardy did in fact remain in a reclining position until the will was proved: the money, of which there was a surprising amount, was left equally to them both. After that Mrs Hardy seemed to recover her energies. One day Christine came home to find four suitcases in the hall, and beside them Mrs Hardy, in a fur coat that had belonged to Christine's mother, waiting for her.

'Well, Christine, I'm off,' she said. 'You can stay here. He left you the flat. You'll have enough to manage on for life if you're careful.'

'But where will you be?' asked Christine.

'I'm off to Bournemouth. I'll leave you my address, although I can't promise to be in touch. I'm going into the hotel business with my brother-in-law. My first husband's brother, that is. He's on his own, like me.' The light of remarriage was already kindling in her eye. 'Look after everything and don't forget to lock the doors.' There was a ring at the bell. 'My taxi,' she said. 'Well, that's about everything, isn't it?' She put out her hand, which Christine, after a moment, realized she was supposed to shake.

'Buy yourself some new clothes or something,' said Mrs Hardy. 'You look awful. And take that expression off your face. Men hate a misery. As far as that goes,' she added, 'the best of luck. You'll need it.'

Then she was gone.

Mrs Hardy's departure, rather than the death of Mr

51

Hardy, affected Christine in an odd way: she became nervous in the silent flat and frequently had to slow down her rapid breathing in order to strain her ears for untoward noises. She continued to make herself a sandwich in the cavernous kitchen and to scuttle back with it to her bedroom. Dust thickened in the drawing-room and in Mrs Hardy's bedroom, for she no longer dared to go into these shadowy apartments which were still redolent of the scents of their previous inhabitants. All day she would try to read, and in the evenings, for which she longed, she would go to Compayne Gardens. By this time Aunt Marie was failing and did not question her presence. Thus Christine was not able to confide her troubles, and she laid them to rest regretfully, as if realizing that nothing in her early life was a matter of record. The task of explaining Mr Hardy would in any case have been a difficult one, although she had practised saying to herself, 'My father is dead', to see if any tears came. But she did not weep, and she finally realized that what she felt was relief, or would have been, could she get rid of the fear that dogged her. When Fibich walked her home in the evenings she would dread the moment when he would turn and leave her. This was additional proof to her that they were meant for each other.

When Hartmann came back from the army, he sized her up. 'Buy yourself something new, Christine,' he said. 'They are wearing longer skirts now. The New Look.' He hated to see a woman in a state of self-neglect: he experienced it as an insult to himself. Christine looked at him in amazement. 'Perhaps you'd like to go to a concert one evening?' he said boldly, ignoring Fibich. He felt that he must limber up in order to practise his re-entry into society. He meant no harm: anyone would do, for he had nothing nefarious in mind.

Christine declined his invitation as if he had been suggesting adultery. Her place was with Fibich, listening to the wireless in Compayne Gardens. It was like being married already.

But how to alert Fibich to this idea? For she was not beautiful, not stimulating, had no experience, and little acquaintance with the ways in which these matters were arranged. Hartmann had cast a seasoned eye over her slender figure, which, once she had bought herself a couple of the long full skirts which had already been in fashion for some time, was seen to advantage. But his seasoned eye also told him that she was all virtue, that her heavy hair would be loosened for no other purpose than to brush it for the night, and the large blue eyes that looked at him so trustingly were in fact only hiding calculations of what to prepare for their dinner. Mentally he consigned her to Fibich, if only to put his mind at rest, for as the prospect of his own life grew brighter in his imagination he felt that he must make arrangements for Fibich's care. He knew that Fibich would not survive for long alone, although he now seemed relatively happy with Hartmann returned and Christine in the background. Fibich was living, in fact, a sort of protracted adolescence, with Hartmann as his brother and Christine as his sister.

It was natural to Christine to help Fibich with his work, to type those letters which Yvette had not managed to finish or even to start, owing to the pressure of other commitments. She liked to think of them both as united in as many ways as possible. She was intrigued by the idea of Yvette, but once she heard that Hartmann wanted to become engaged to her lost no more sleep on her account: in fact relief that it was not Fibich who was so affected made her put her best efforts into cooking a good meal when Hartmann brought Yvette home to

Compayne Gardens for the first time. The evening was unexpectedly convivial. Christine saw in Yvette a woman of style and confidence who might hand down vital information: her admiration was entirely genuine. Yvette saw a decent little soul whom she could bend to her will, and one, moreover, with no figure to speak of. Cautiously, they agreed to go shopping together, to find items for Yvette's trousseau. The idea delighted Hartmann who was already euphoric and paternalistic. But it was Christine who came back from their first expedition with short hair that revealed an elegant jawline. The hair was already beginning to go grey. A wing of the lighter colour swept across the brown like a blush.

Christine felt the full weight of Fibich's existential anxiety. Nevertheless she forced herself to remain calm. Her new hair and her longer skirts gave her a little confidence, but with Hartmann's marriage in the air she grew wistful. Uneducated in the ways of love, she matched Fibich in innocence, except for this odd drive she had always felt towards partnership. Anxiously she wondered what she lacked and thought perhaps she had been too presumptuous in her hopes. She tried to turn for guidance to the God in whom she did not believe, read her Bible, willed herself into imagining a state in which justice would roll down like many waters. This beautiful dream, common to the entire human race, gave her strength when she thought about it, although she did not see how she personally could make it come to pass. She continued to sit with Fibich in the evenings, and when Hartmann moved out to Ashley Gardens and Yvette was busy decorating the new flat, a process which was described to Christine in many telephone calls, she moved her typewriter into Aunt Marie's, now Fibich's, sitting-room, and consigned her life to hope, good deeds, and blind faith.

It was hardly love, although there was no other beloved object in Christine's life. Perhaps there never had been. It was yearning, longing, a desire to compensate for all the loveless years. She hardly thought of herself at all, certainly not as one possessing certain attractions – for she now looked unusual and even distinguished – but rather as an attendant, an acolyte who might, if circumstances were favourable, turn into a permanent employee, her status at last assured. She did not know that Hartmann had calculated on her remaining in Fibich's life, or even that Fibich himself did. She did not see why anything should ever change, and neither did Fibich.

As Hartmann's wedding approached she bestirred herself to go out and buy a new dress. 'Blue,' she said uninterestedly to the salesgirl, for weddings made her increasingly sad. 'Blue is my colour.' So she had once been told and she never questioned the fact, indeed scarcely considered herself worthy of having a colour at all. As a matronly blue garment was being laid to rest in tissue paper, she caught sight of a dress on a model which she instinctively allocated to a more promising sort of woman than she knew herself to be. As her bill was being made out, something drove her to ask, 'Could I try that?' When she caught sight of herself in the grey-green silk dress, with its narrow bodice and full skirts, she blushed with excitement. Her two wings of grey hair framed a face with unusually pink cheeks and brilliant eyes. Something about the colour of the dress had turned her eyes to an almost transparent grey. She felt nervous but determined. 'I'll take this one,' she said. If she had made a mistake it hardly mattered. After all, she thought, no one will be looking at me. So she had been frequently admonished as a small child. 'No one will be looking at you, Christine,' she had heard ancestral voices say. Or command.

She enjoyed the wedding. Yvette's mother had provided as much food as she could lay her hands on, and Cazenove had laid on many bottles of champagne. After the second glass Christine's flush deepened, and her eyes became more brilliant. When Fibich took her home, she said, 'It seems so silly each to go back to an empty flat.' Fibich, also enlivened by the festivity, looked at her. The flush was fading now, but the eyes were enormous. 'I'm not ready to make any changes,' he said awkwardly. 'Until Hartmann gets back from his honeymoon I shall have a great deal of work to do.' The eyes became beseeching. 'We could become engaged, if you like,' he added. 'It's just that I don't want to get married yet.' That night, after he had left her at her door, Christine wept for joy.

But that was not the end of the matter. The engagement lasted for two years, for Fibich was never ready. Finally Hartmann took him on one side and told him what to do: Hartmann prevailed, while Christine still piously waited. After a register office marriage, Christine and Thomas Fibich went back to Compayne Gardens as man and wife.

The happiness that Christine felt was tinged with wonder. 'I am married,' she said to herself. 'I have got married.' Love-making, to which she took with unexpected ease and delight, did not surprise her, and if it turned Fibich and herself into more ruthless versions of the persons they knew each other to be, she was not to know that this process, which amused her, fuelled Fibich's already extreme anxiety. His silences she put down to tiredness, for he was working hard. Indeed, he seemed to want to go to the office at times when they might have been alone together; however, she knew that she must not try to change him. When Hartmann announced that he had found them a flat just below the one occupied by himself and Yvette, she hesitated. As she surveyed the empty rooms that were hers to furnish as she pleased, she felt a thrill of the old fear. 'How will I manage?' she thought. Had it not been for Fibich's blind trust in Hartmann, she would have suggested remaining at Compayne Gardens. But Yvette was pregnant and not feeling well: Christine knew that she would be needed. Slowly, and with many mistakes, using and wasting the money that had never been of any use to her, she prepared their new home. On their first night there, both she and Fibich slept badly, waking many times to search instinctively for a window, a door. Everything was in the wrong place. They never entirely got used to this.

But as the years passed her contentment became thin, brittle, and then began to vanish altogether. Fibich remained distant, self-absorbed, and his self-absorption took him away from her. She put this down to pressures at work until she could no longer make this excuse to herself. The holidays in Normandy, the parties that Hartmann and Yvette gave so successfully, dwindled. Enraptured by their small daughter, Hartmann and Yvette kept more to themselves, leaving Fibich with too much time and with too little conversation with which to beguile his wife. Now that his problems were confided to the analyst, there was little left to be discussed between them. This act of his signified to Christine the end of their intimate life. Although they could not envisage any other kind of existence, for each knew that they had been fated for the other, it was not quite clear how they were to continue. Slowly, as if by osmosis, Fibich passed his fears over to Christine, who began to feel, as she had once felt in her father's gloomy house, an outsider.

And as the years went on, an inner melancholy turned her to silence. The poor remnants of her early life gathered around her in those hours of winter afternoons when the light fades and the night begins too early. Sitting on her sofa in the somehow unresolved furnishings of her drawing-room she would wonder, for the thousandth time, why her surroundings did not please her. Thinking out of the way her cold blue velvet curtains and her pinkish carpet, reflecting yet again that the pink cushions did not really enliven the inert blue velvet chairs, she would wonder uninterestedly if she should change everything. If she changed the chairs she would have to change the curtains, for everything dishearteningly matched everything else. Her taste, if she were asked (but she never was) was indeterminate and therefore of no use to her. Instinct told her that rooms should be dark, featureless, rich with ennui, and this she recognized as a memory from her earliest childhood. Her drawing-room exasperated her by being too insistently blue, an antagonistic colour without a hint of warmth. For this reason she kept the heating on at full strength, so that the room smelled permanently dry. This she attempted to palliate with bowls of pot-pourri, which added their own faded aroma to the iron stillness. In the distance a radio burbled. Overhead, Marianne Hartmann fell down, cried, and was comforted.

On rainy days, when Christine awoke in the warm wet dark, a sense of hopelessness would descend on her: she felt as if her physical disintegration were taking place minute by minute. Her thick hair seemed clouded with moisture, her hands felt damp, her feet enlarged. Instinctively she would put a hand to her eyes as if to brush away cobwebs. Waterlogged, she would resign

58

herself to staying indoors, turning on the lights in the hot flat, nowadays habitually indecisive. The afternoons, especially, were endless. Outside the window a drowned world, leaves sticking to pavements, trees stripped bare, cars refusing to start. It was no comfort to her to reflect on her good fortune in not having to turn out and queue for buses, spend the day in wet shoes, and lumber home, devitalized, after hours of prolonged discomfort. What she longed for, in the sultry stifling air, was a cleansing wind, both physical and metaphorical; she wanted the sinews of her body to tighten, as they had briefly tightened when she was an all too hapless girl; she wanted the chambers of her mind to be scoured by bracing certainties. In these moods she would think briefly of her unhappy early years, doomed to silence in her father's house, ordered not to upset her stepmother, she who was upset by everything. She would think of the kind of marriage for which this sort of youth prepared one, and the gratitude that was still her strongest emotion. She knew now that this was wrong, and a worm of subversion began to turn in her mind. She sometimes surprised herself into thinking that she no longer wanted to be respectable, that she would have felt more in character as a woman who had finally let go and lived with some irony, but a great deal of acceptance, on expedients: any old food, anyone's money. Lovers undoubtedly, for she would allow her own needs to surface from the deep underground chamber to which she had prematurely consigned them. Looking out on the wet street, hearing only the hiss of tyres and the indistinguishable burden of the radio, she could see herself in many slovenly attitudes, fat perhaps, smelling of cigarettes, coarse and wily. When Fibich came home on the evenings of such days he would find her as immaculate as ever. But the vacancy that had

59

lately established itself around her would communicate itself to him, and to his own habitual anguish would be added the consciousness of hers.

5

The children of Hartmann and Fibich were beautiful. Their beauty seemed to Hartmann ratification of the fact that the good times were come ('Look! We have come through!'), while to Fibich it meant that their very beauty might put them in jeopardy. Marianne Hartmann and Toto Fibich were born six years apart, and, like everything else between the two families, were held in common. It was even Hartmann's wish that they might eventually marry, despite the difference in their ages, but this idea was quashed by Yvette. 'A girl needs an older man,' she said firmly. 'A younger man means trouble.' In any event she intended to choose Marianne's husband herself, for she knew that her instincts had guided her wisely in this matter. Where would she, Yvette, be if she had not chosen an older husband (by several years, as it happened) and had had to spend her life worrying about a man who might at that very moment be making a fool of himself with young girls? One heard about such things all the time. That Hartmann might have had a speculative eye never crossed her mind. In any event, she had made him too comfortable to doubt him, had studied his culinary needs, his love of luxury, his disposition towards geniality. She had held parties in her apricot, green, and white drawing-room that were exemplary in their lavishness, had exhausted herself unstintingly in their preparation, had left nothing to chance, had retired late, had risen early to inspect the results of last night's cooking, had frequently had to disappear when the room was full of enthusiastic guests, to reappear in a more elaborate guise, having been momentarily overcome by the heat or the excitement. Hartmann was used to her re-entrance, heralded by a fresh blast of scent, a high flush on her cheeks, and a new toilette to fuel the anticipation. Such evenings – and the old-fashioned feminine codes by which she lived – appeased him at a profound level. It was as if she had experienced his early life for him and was now compensating on his behalf for all that had gone before.

Her pregnancy was to him the final proof that she was in fact the ideal wife for him, despite the fact that in youth he had not exactly loved her. It was when he came home and saw her lying on a couch, her fine ankles a little swollen, her face worried and distant, that he opened his heart to her. He knew that she was frightened. She expressed a longing for his company, hated to see him leave in the mornings, looked wistfully after him when he left the room. The practical and unawakened girl who had first intrigued him now moved him, although his own spirits were so high at the prospect of a child that he could not see how she might have grounds for fear. For what could go wrong? She was a healthy woman. Her mother was there, with sage dry advice. Christine came over daily with covered dishes for Hartmann's supper, when Yvette was too queasy to cook; Hartmann himself was bidden to dine with Christine and Fibich, and sometimes did, although his wife's woeful face made him disconsolate. Her pregnancy was awkward but not difficult; nevertheless, she repudiated every manifestation of it with cries of alarm. She derived no excitement from the baby's first movement, ran to the telephone to summon Christine, accused her mother of being heartless for not weeping with her. Finally her bulk depressed her so much that she took to her bed, despite their concerted encouragements. Her worries were not so much for her condition as for her silhouette. She felt a profound terror that her splendid body might never be hers to call her own again.

The anxieties of her pregnancy resolved themselves into massive relief once the child was born, and made her into an able and even unsentimental mother. In this way she proved once more to be excellent. She seemed to set her sights on getting the baby to move on as quickly as possible, not to linger in infancy, to enjoy dependence or incapacity, but rather to grow up into a semblance of Yvette herself, a good and successful wife. Whereas Hartmann could not bear to let a day of the child's life pass, wanting to keep her small and helpless for as long as possible. Looking at her velvet hands, the beautiful soles of her unmarked feet, he marvelled, ecstatic. When she uttered her first word, which was, rewardingly, 'Dada', he felt a darkness, an inner trembling: his breaking heart, perhaps. Finally enslaved, brought into submission, subjection even, he would dart up in the night, thinking he heard a cry, in reality in order to inspect her anew. 'Go to sleep, Hartmann,' Yvette would say. 'You will spoil her.' It was, of course, what he longed to do, to keep her for himself, to imprint himself on her life and to be imprinted on by hers: she was the favourite and he meant to be the same, to be singled out, for ever, to outlast the others, whenever they might come. He put down money in her name. That way, he thought, she need not marry if she did not want to.

He grew used to her, gradually, reverted to his old hedonistic ways. The child was well-behaved, a little solemn. Sometimes he caught sight in her face of something of her mother's expression when he had first known her: a serious absent look, waiting, waiting. Always immaculate, she had her mother's fastidiousness, could not bear a crumpled dress, held out hands to be washed. Her grandmother examined her, pronounced herself satisfied, and went off to the south of France. This decree of viability reassured Hartmann, as did Yvette's quite surprising expertise. Order and docility reigned. Food was not spat out, mugs were not overturned, nights were peaceful. The child's very obedience rewarded them both. She is happy here, thought Hartmann. Maybe she will never leave us. But Yvette poured scorn on his sentimentality. Grooming her for her future fate, Yvette dressed her stylishly, in salopettes which her mother sent from France, in a smart blue jacket. When Hartmann came home in the evenings (earlier and earlier) he would sink to his heels, his arms open, for Marianne to run to him. The day when Yvette said, 'She is too old for that now,' was, briefly, the saddest day of his life.

Marianne was the only one who could dispel Fibich's melancholy. He adored her, looked on her as their ruined inheritance made good. He and Christine went to shameless lengths to be allowed to spend the evening looking after her, presenting Hartmann with theatre tickets, or capturing the child for the afternoon when Yvette once more felt the need to go shopping. Sometimes on Sundays they lunched together, Hartmann's and Fibich's eyes on the child as she strove with the big knife and fork on which Yvette insisted.

64

'Uncle Fibich,' she said to him one day. 'I am half French.'

'Are you?' he answered gravely. 'Which half? This half or this half?' He lightly pinched first one cheek and then the other.

She giggled and ran to her mother. Later she came back, slipped her hand into his, and said, 'This half.'

Their farewells, once Marianne had gone to bed, were wistful, abstracted, as if the important business of the day were done, as if conviviality could not profitably be resurrected until another Sunday, when the enchantment would be repeated. Fibich felt that Marianne existed by virtue of a special dispensation of fortune. When her starry blue eyes grew solemn as she sat still, gazing at something they could not see, he grew anxious. He was never entirely able to take her for granted, another bond he shared with Hartmann. But Yvette was entirely matter of fact, thereby sealing her dominance. And having no fears for her, nor wishing her to be too protected, shared her generously with the others. A good mother, all told. Unknown to them, she already had her daughter's engagement party in mind.

When Fibich and Christine went home on these Sunday evenings they were thoughtful. Each had a separate sadness to contemplate which crystallized around the sight of the child being carried away to bed by Hartmann. Neither of them dared to think that they might be in a similiar position. They both considered themselves to be disqualified from such felicity, not by fortune but by disposition. Such energy as was necessary to create such a situation for themselves had been denied them. They blamed no one, not each other, not themselves; they were too modest for that. Each knew, instinctively, that they had been barren from birth, blighted like the fig tree in the Bible, on which no fruit could grow. With a peculiar passivity which they had in common, they saw no remedy, not even the obvious one of intention. The shadows of their early lives gathered around them like heavy clouds. Christine moved wordlessly about the kitchen, brought out sandwiches and a bottle of wine on a tray. Neither spoke of their common sorrow. Such evenings were inevitably silent.

So that when Christine, after eight years of marriage, and sitting listlessly in her blue drawing-room, was told disapprovingly by Yvette, who had recovered her legendary figure, that she was putting on weight, she did not make the obvious connection. She was a strong woman – she had had to be – had never paid any attention to variations within her body, had thought that same body to be of little importance. It was Yvette who interrogated her, brought her triumphantly the unhoped-for message. A visit to the doctor confirmed that she was three months pregnant. When she told Fibich he was incredulous. 'Are you sure?' he stammered. 'Are you sure?' And, later, 'That it should happen to me!'

'It is happening to *me*,' she told him with a smile, no longer impatient with his ingrowing preoccupations.

Her pregnancy was uneventful; she stayed calm throughout. An inner strength, sign of the divine afflatus, possessed her. In the afternoons she walked conscientiously, dropping in occasionally to nearby Westminster Abbey to give thanks to the God in whom she had never believed. Credit where credit was due, she thought, for there was no doubt in her mind that it was a miracle. Fibich she somewhat discounted, losing some of the desire to please him that had always informed her actions; for the first time in her life she considered herself to be of some consequence. She had

66

moved on from the importunate girl that she had known so well. Her eye was no longer drawn to children, to babies in prams; she knew that her own child would be superior. A spirit of vainglory touched her, and she was to remember this in later life, when a reckoning was in order. She was never to forgive herself for this confidence, so out of character, so positively dangerous in its implications. She tried to fashion herself on the model of Yvette, to whom no form of confidence was alien. Hartmann noticed the change in her and was approving. In fact all four of them glowed with approval. Christine allowed herself the luxury of criticizing Fibich, sent him to an expensive barber to have his once romantic hair disciplined. He, a happy man, accepted this as a sign of normality, part of his transformation. He told his analyst, a woman barely older than he was, that he needed a break from her ministrations. Looking him over with a practised eye, she opened her diary to the empty months ahead, and said, 'Shall we make another appointment? To see how we are getting on?'

The child, a boy, was born without fuss in five hours. They called him Thomas, which soon became short-ened to Toto. He too was beautiful, but what was immediately noticeable about him was his strength. 'The infant Hercules,' marvelled Hartmann. From the first he strained away from his mother, his cheeks flushed with effort. When he was five months old, and two teeth like tiny white seeds had emerged in his lower jaw, he banged restlessly with his spoon, squirming in his mother's lap, perpetually in ardent motion. He responded to every form of excitement, above all to Yvette's. She, entranced by the sight of the handsome and extravagant child, would swoop on him with high-pitched cries, which he would imitate. 'And how

is he? And how is he? And how's our baby today, then?'
And he would reach ecstatically towards her, pushing
Christine's face aside. A grave seven-year-old Marianne
would watch from the doorway, frightened by so
disruptive a presence. When ordered by her mother to
admire him she would resist, until Christine took her
hand. When he laughed at her she would dart back. He
had a way of laughing that was hurtful, obscurely
insulting. His mother felt this keenly, sensing once
again her own inadequacy. Only Yvette was untouched
by this quality.

From the first the roles appeared to be reversed. It
would have seemed, to a stranger coming into the room
for the first time, as if Marianne, the docile, the silent,
were Christine's child and Toto Yvette's. It was in fact
Christine who first noticed this. She would lift the
heavy bulk of her son into Yvette's arms with a feeling
of relief and take Marianne into the kitchen to ask her
help in preparing the tea. Hartmann admired the child
unreservedly. Fibich was not so sure. Fibich felt him to
be rough, rougher than he could ever be. Toto was
occasionally raucous, testing his strength. He spurned
help, seemed to have within him a fund of expletives,
although he could not yet talk. Watching him strug-
gling with sounds they felt one day a heightened
anticipation of his first words. Silently, with held
breath, they waited, urging him on. His cheeks flushed
an ominous red. 'Dada', they said. 'Mama. Baba.'

'Toto,' he burst out. They collapsed with joy and
laughter.

Every day brought him a new toy which, with a
wide-armed gesture, he flung across the room. Fibich
felt these rejections keenly. Told to quieten the child
down for the night (for Toto hated to sleep) Fibich
would pick up the toys with an air of apology for the

68

way in which they had been treated, and try to rehabilitate them into his son's life.

'Here's a nice bear,' he might say awkwardly. 'What is his name, I wonder?'

No answer would come. He thought he could see contempt in Toto's eye.

'I think his name is Teddy,' he ploughed gamely on.

When still no answer was forthcoming he would sigh and make as if to retreat.

'Teddy will keep you company,' he would say, placing the bear in the cot.

When he reached the door and looked back, to blow his son a kiss, he would see that he had set up a furious rocking.

'Neddy,' Toto would shout. 'Neddy, Neddy, Neddy.'

Fibich would sigh again and tell him to go to sleep. Secretly he began to envisage the time when his son was old enough to learn feelings as well as words, hoping against hope that those feelings would incline him favourably towards his mother and his father.

Fibich was wise enough to know that desire is infinite and attainment finite, that any home, any marriage, and even any child, might fail to correspond with his initial image of such situations or events, and that even in the most auspicious circumstances a curious sense of bewilderment, even disappointment, might come to him unbidden. He therefore responded to the phenomenon of his son with a certain melancholy, as if, once again, life had baffled or deceived him. Whereas Hartmann was all joy, having left the mirage of another life far behind, or being blessed with no such mirage, Fibich felt, when he contemplated the life to which he was now committed, a resignation from which fear was not entirely absent. Is that all? This was the thought that

69

occurred to him, and at the same time he would wordlessly confess, This is too much for me. I did not bargain for such disruption, such alienation. Just when he thought he had internalized one change, accommodated himself to a home that he could make for himself, a home that did not pre-exist him, and in addition to this had married a wife whom he had apparently chosen for himself, he was faced with a son whom he could not understand, whose very being was foreign to him. And this was even more disconcerting than the first two changes, which had, after all, been partially brought about, or at least assisted, by the will of others. Toto seemed to present him with a task for which he had no preparation and for which he found himself permanently at a loss. He himself, innocent, submissive, felt so much more of a child than Toto, in whom he discerned the rudiments of an enormous will, as yet unspecific, but striking in its authority. It was not merely that Toto possessed the rude health, the untrammelled energy that he himself had been denied: that, surely, was a matter for congratulation. What he sensed, and what perturbed him, was inaccessibility. They would never, he felt, understand one another. And without understanding, could each properly love the other?

It was almost a relief to him to go up to Hartmann's flat and watch Hartmann with his daughter. For here was fatherhood as he would have wished to enjoy it. As Marianne played quietly – and she was always quiet – or pretended to help her mother, Hartmann would overflow with praises and caresses. When he read to her she would listen in complete silence, even when, as Fibich could see, her attention was elsewhere. And when Hartmann pressed her cheek to his, her arm would go obediently round his neck. She went to school without protest: there were no tears, no bouts of sickness, no night terrors. Bringing a little friend home with her she would submit politely to the other child's wishes. She was, if anything, too passive, and her mother tried in vain to galvanize her into more volatile activities. But for Hartmann she was so like his idea of a daughter that he was entirely fulfilled in contemplation of her existence. A Victorian child, thought Fibich, her eyes perpetually turned upward, desirous of the light, serious in expression, devoted to her father. Daddy's girl, destined to be a helpmate, an honourable wife. Not made for the rough and tumble of this world: unquestioning, unprotesting, preserved from danger, or so they dared to think.

In comparison with Marianne, Toto represented something cruder, crueller: the life force, perhaps. Even in his embryonic infant form Toto seemed to reach out, beyond the confines of his existence. To Fibich's worried eyes he had immortal longings in him. He saw that he would be unequal to the task of being Toto's father, and through the child longed to experience his own childhood, to retreat into certainties of which he had no conscious knowledge but for which he felt a renewed longing. As he watched the child crash destructively through his early years, he winced at the implied brutality: when his protecting hands were roughly struck away he felt sadness, and a kind of perplexity. Was it for this that he had been preserved, had served his apprenticeship, so that an existence entirely unrelated to his own could come into being? He despaired of ever making sense of all or any of it. And yet he knew that his task as a man was to do just that, to bring into completion the ragged fragments of a destiny of which he felt himself to be the most lamentable, the most fallible of elements. The connections he tried to make between what had gone before and this indomitable stranger caused him pain, literally resulted in headaches. He took to watching the child sleep, feeling closer to him then than when he filled the flat with his energy, his presence. Even the sleeping face seemed replete with intention. Fibich entirely failed to see what would become of him. The child took from his parents only those commodities that ensured his continuity: food, clothing, warmth. These he took roughly, purposefully, as essential ingredients for his future. The task of outgrowing his infancy seemed to preoccupy him, as if it were a task for which he was overqualified, as if he were already exasperated by the smallness of his size, his uncertain grasp.

It was his lack of inhibition that most intimidated Fibich. Ready to shout, to scream, to impose himself, Toto lived every moment of his early years in the accepted, but least acceptable, sense. He wearied them excessively. Often Fibich would return home in the evening to find Christine looking pale with exhaustion and would attempt to relieve her by putting Toto to bed, giving him his bath, reading him his story, trying, timidly, to interest him, to win his attention. It was only when he himself tired of the childish literature that was thought suitable to Toto's age group and read him poetry that Toto would grow momentarily silent, hypnotized by the rhythm of the verses, to which he would submit with a solemn gaze, although he could not have understood a word of what was being said. 'More,' he would cry, 'more', as *Childe Harold's Pilgrimage* was unfolded before him, and Fibich, proud at last to have found a device of his own choosing with which to bring his son into submission, would read on until he was hoarse. Still the boy showed no sign of sleepiness, but went on fixing him with his brilliant eyes, in which, now, could be discerned no light of mockery. Rather the eyes seemed fixed on some inner vision, induced by the scansion of the verses, as if, finally, he had found something worthy of his immense attention. When Christine called to him that dinner was ready, Fibich would call back, 'Soon. In a minute', unwilling to relinquish that moment in which, however briefly, he might think he had gained the upper hand. His attempts to leave the room were met with a storm of tears, a writhing in the bed that seemed to bespeak despair, deprivation, as if the source of future growth had been denied. Frequently Toto would wake in the night and could only be silenced by a further reading. But now, tired out, he would listen with glazed eyes, his thumb in his mouth. They were all very soon exhausted. Fibich began to envisage a thought that he would previously never have entertained: Toto might have to be sent away to school.

When Toto was five he would get out of his bed and enter the drawing-room when Fibich and Christine had friends to dinner. Excited by the company, he would run round, humming to himself, cannoning into the guests, drinking from their glasses. If his parents were watching television he would stand in front of it, wagging his head from side to side. Remonstrances, reprobations would be greeted with a storm of tears. Hartmann, softened by the sight of Toto's rough little hand, with its rim of black under one of the nails, would try to comfort him. Only Yvette could succeed. From the safe haven of Yvette's arms Toto would stare resentfully at his mother.

Where had they found the strength to produce such an unnatural child? For they felt him to be a foundling, a visitant who showed them nothing of their own true natures. It was almost as if their weaknesses were being punished rather than rewarded. Obscurely they felt

73

themselves to be in the wrong. Christine in particular was alarmed at the antipathy she aroused in the boy and recognized reluctantly that she was beginning to feel something of the same emotion: distaste. Fibich was more divided. He adored the child, adored in particular that brutal strength, an instinct that he had been denied. But he thought the boy might turn into a bully if not curbed and, reluctantly, despite his own experience, decided to contact a famous school on his son's behalf. This decision caused a great crisis in his soul, a feeling of betrayal. Yet at ten Toto was almost beyond them both. Christine in particular had many occasions on which to remember her earlier glow of confidence, of carelessness, of *belle indifférence*. Though they were united in their uneasiness, both continued to glory in the boy's robust health and strength, his ability to eat anything, his tirelessness. Seeing his son finally collapse into sleep after a day of superhuman activity, Fibich would think, 'That is how bodies are supposed to behave!' He knew that after his brief and intense periods of rest – of total unconsciousness for five or at the most six hours – Toto would be up, instantly restless, roaming the kitchen in search of his breakfast, shaming his parents who liked to emerge cautiously from the world of the night, weakened by the information they had brought back with them from the kingdom of the shades. His activities on the bicycle he had forced them to buy him terrified them. Fibich, seeing him ride down Victoria Street with his arms folded, nearly had a heart attack. The boy was fearless, superb. But they failed to solve the enigma of his personality.

'He will be a lady-killer,' said Yvette, admiring his fine brown skin, his dark brown, almost black, hair, the easy lines of his rapidly growing frame. He had inherited Fibich's build, or rather his outline, and seemed to have improved on the original model, rather as if Fibich, to whom his height and thinness were problematic, had been the unsuccessful prototype for the final production. 'We are thinking of sending him away to school,' said Christine awkwardly, expecting censure. But, 'Of course, you must. There is nothing for him to do around here', and the matter was dismissed. Fibich, as was his habit, consulted Hartmann, who, with a shrug, agreed. 'He is not like we were,' he assured Fibich. 'He is naturally tough. And, anyway, the circumstances are different.' For a moment ghosts walked on their graves. 'It is important that he makes friends,' said Fibich, by way of excuse. For the only other child they knew well was Marianne, and she did not seem to like Toto very much, fearing his rough hands on her hair. Once, unknown to both sets of parents, he had tried to push her against a window. She had easily recovered herself – it was no more than a kind of insistent nudge, after all – but she avoided him. Although she paid him little attention she sensed in him something threatening in a way she could not identify. He would do things, she seemed to feel, or thought she felt, out of boredom, without motive, just to pass the time, fill up the emptiness. His perpetual preparedness for deeds as yet unperformed made her wary. She blamed herself as much as she did Toto. She knew herself to be something of a coward, self-effacing, too quiet and passive to win her mother's wholehearted approval. Sometimes she felt more at home with Christine, who did not urge her to be other than she was. Nevertheless she took the opportunity of visiting Christine when she knew Toto to be out of the house.

On the day they took him to boarding school they were both nervous, but, it seemed, without reason. Toto darted away from them as soon as he decently

75

could. Had they but known it, he was ashamed of them, ashamed in particular of their grey hair, as if they showed by this very fact that they were not normal parents, had in secret been indecently engaged in activities reserved for the young and beautiful. He had become sexually aware at a very young age: they sensed this and understood that their modesty, or, more properly, their shame, would do him no favours. They hoped to have him returned to them tamed and civilized, what Fibich secretly thought of as 'a little gentleman'. This was his favourite term of approbation: he would not employ anyone whom he did not think of as a little gentleman. They handed him over to stronger spirits than themselves with a feeling of relief.

Nevertheless the day of his departure affected Fibich badly. He went straight back to the office, where Goodman and Myers, both little gentlemen, greeted him with their usual deference. Everything unsettled him, including their good manners. Goodman, in particular, moist-eyed with the effort to express his assiduity, got on his nerves.

'That fellow embarrasses me,' he said to Hartmann. 'He is too eager.'

Hartmann waved a dismissive hand. 'So let him be eager. Embarrassment will not kill you.'

Fibich left the office late and returned to a strangely empty flat, ignoring or trying to ignore the fact that Christine had been crying. He tried to adopt a robust attitude, pretending to himself that all was in order. But that night he had a worrying dream. He dreamed that he was looking out of his window, across their strip of garden, and saw to his horror that a huge tower was being erected about three feet from his gaze. This tower, a rough Brueghel-ish creation which he recognized as Broadcasting House, completely blocked his

76

view. With the speed and ingenuity which he could command in dreams, he immediately negotiated to buy another flat, one with a different aspect, in which the tower could not possibly annoy him, could not even be glimpsed on the horizon. But when he leaned proprietorially on his window-sill and looked out on his new landscape he saw to his horror that the view was precisely the view from the flat in Compayne Gardens, and that he himself, shrunken in size to that of a ten-year-old boy, was returned to the self he thought he had outgrown.

He took this dream as an omen, although he did not immediately understand what it was an omen of. He began to watch himself again, to take note of his progress, even to keep a journal of his dreams. It was as if, by sending the boy away to school, he had re-entered the time machine. Christine noted this, but in her sadness said nothing.

6

The gift of beauty may not necessarily be fatal; on the other hand it may distort the prospects of those who possess it. Women who have been beautiful in their heyday have been accustomed to a position of dominance which may be unearned in any other respect. Early in life they have been entranced by their own euphoric ability to wield influence, first in small matters, then, when they are at the height of their powers, in matters not so small. They become disconcerted and then inconsolable when the beauty fades, and with it the power and the influence. Never reconciled to the stoicism that may be the lot of those less headily endowed, such women may become bad companions in later years, aggrieved at the sudden restrictions imposed by age and with no resource but reminiscence. In the fire of youth, with the beauty still intact and seemingly acquired for ever, the confidence is unimpaired, for the gift appears to others like a sign of superiority, in comparison with which all other accomplishments are counted as negligible. There are many children who have been told, 'Never mind. You are the clever one', and who have never got over it. In men the gift is even more alarming, for it lasts appreciably longer, thus prompting wistfulness and envy rather than true friendship. In the wrong hands a possession such as this can ruin several lives. Only a capacity for hard work can outlast its many temptations.

Toto Fibich was so astonishingly handsome that his parents often wished for a more ordinary-looking son, one who would talk to them more easily, be less in demand, be more familiar, more humble, less of a star. He had Fibich's height and leanness, his mother's formerly brown hair and still startling eyes, and, from nowhere they could think of, a fine burnished skin which gave him an air of perpetual summer. He looked extremely English, but it was the kind of Englishness that has something legendary about it, that cannot be matched up with known prototype, which flatters fantasies with an aura of ancestral perfection. This entirely factitious image had nothing to do with the realities of Toto's ancestry, a disjunction which caused Fibich to marvel, half in pleasure, half in regret. Perhaps he would have liked to see more reminiscence of his past in his son's attitudes, some ghost of what had been lost in an expression, a gesture, even a turn of the head. He was, on the other hand, overjoyed to find in Toto no echo of his own former self, whom he remembered as a miserable shambling figure, perpetually bent under a weight of anxiety, perpetually carrying a shopping bag up the steep streets of West Hampstead. That he no longer looked like or in fact was this figure was a piece of information which he would have dismissed as irrelevant, for although these days he was expensively barbered and tailored, and looked every inch the successful business man, he still tended to behave with caution, even with fear, and thus lacked the ability to bring his new persona to life. The confidence that such a transformation should have conferred on him eluded

79

him perpetually. He suspected that his son despised him, hated in particular his countless nervous turns of the head, his pursed lips, his hesitations. To his son, he knew, he would never be a hero. The best gift that he could have conferred on Toto would have been, oddly enough, an equal form of contempt, masking as amusement or superior experience. In that way respect could have grown. It would not have been an ideal form of respect, but they would have recognized and used it for what it could have been: a *modus vivendi* adopted in default of anything better. Fibich was yearning, brooding, fearful of having such a treasure in his charge, unequal to the task of guiding him, and experiencing at every turn the feeling that in the important matters of life – always excepting the matter of survival – his son had already outstripped him.

Christine too entertained confused feelings towards her son. She felt, in particular, a premonitory sense of loss, for it became quite evident, when Toto went up to Oxford, that he would only ever return home as a visitor or on a temporary basis. In addition to this physical loss of the boy's presence, she remembered how he had repudiated her as a baby, and she forced herself to acknowledge the fact that he did not have much use for her. His health had always been excellent, his appetite indiscriminate, and whereas his father had tended him devotedly through the few childhood illnesses he had suffered, his mother had hung back, conscious of the grey hair that so offended him, conscious too that maternal concern would have had to struggle through a reserve which had now become habitual. She found it necessary to treat her son with a certain formality: overt affection on her side, she felt, would be seen as tactless, out of character, almost an error of taste. She knew, as Fibich did not, of the boy's decision to dispense with his parents as soon as he was physically and financially able to do so. If Fibich had known this, she thought, he might not have made so much money so freely available to him. In this she understood Fibich's helpless pride that his son had turned out to be so magnificent a specimen. Thus Fibich succumbed to the power of beauty as if it were a shrine before which he could only pay tribute.

The only person for whom Toto seemed to have real affection was Yvette, possibly because they both shared a vivid sense of their own importance. Indeed, Toto might have adopted for his *devise* Yvette's early formed conviction: 'I am the best'. He found her preoccupation with herself quite fascinating, and colluded willingly with her need for an audience. Out of his careless ability to please and his natural ability with women he would keep her company for hours. As a boy he loved to see her at her dressing-table, applying a delicate pink flush to her cheekbones, a silvery pink streak to her thin lips. He would watch, entranced, as she touched the pearls at her throat, eyeing her reflection critically, but also as if it were a large audience. And this was not the fascination a child might feel; it increased as he grew older. As Yvette's skin grew finer and less lustrous, Toto noted the moment at which it had to be artificially enhanced; he saw the creases and folds in the neck beneath the pearls, the rounding and thickening of the shoulders. He felt no estrangement when he witnessed this procedure, rather the contrary. Estrangement he reserved for his mother, a woman of reticent demeanour whom he regarded, quite simply, as inexpert.

This ardent appreciation of women, or rather of the sort of woman who is part glutton and part coquette, had nothing to do with the facsimile Englishman whom Toto so closely resembled, and harked back to some more distant ancestry and to a period when men were

81

allowed to witness the performance of women preparing for the day. Yvette loved it. She saw nothing incongruous in these attentions of Toto's, for she was so devoid of native sexual instincts that she found it entirely natural that a process which habitually absorbed and entertained her should afford the same amount of entertainment to someone else. 'I understand him,' she would say in the face of Christine's misgivings. 'We are very much alike in some ways.' She spoke the truth, although she did not know, nor was she ever to know, just how alike they were. It was not that Toto was in any way effeminate: the matter was more subtle than that. He seemed to have an instinct for the refinement of women which, allied to his superior looks, made him more complex an amalgam than the young men who were his physical contemporaries. As a boy he had liked to nuzzle round Yvette's neck, inhaling voluptuously the bouquet of scents that rose from her warm body. Nor was there any suspicion of vice between them. Rather they were like two actors in the same company, chatting in the dressing-room, both aware, as their profession demanded, of every corporeal action and intention. They would examine themselves quite unselfconsciously in Yvette's mirror, anxious to appear to their best advantage, for their lives depended on it. At home Toto guarded his beauty jealously from his mother, would never let her see him undressed, would wrench his head away if she tried to examine him. 'Don't fuss, Ma,' he would say, as if she were irredeemably tiresome. He sensed disapproval and would not therefore reveal himself to her.

He was otherwise devastating to women, or rather to the girls whom he dazzled and left thoughtful. From his father's fear of total physical relaxation, of accessibility to his most primitive and therefore most dangerous impulses, Toto derived his strange power, for his strength lay precisely in his ability to withhold. No matter how much he protested that he was in love with a girl – and by the time he was nineteen there had been many – he would never surrender his reserve. He might deliver himself to her desire on one occasion, an occasion she would vainly try to repeat, but usually he would regret that moment of what he considered to be weakness, would in fact be irritated and disaffected by it, antagonistic to the cause of it, and would drift away to another woman to start the manoeuvre all over again. He hated to see longing in a girl's eyes, submission, humility. He thought such emotions derogated from a woman's dignity, although he had precious little use for that dignity as such. He preferred to anger and to antagonize, thinking thereby to safeguard a woman's pride. His reputation with women was gigantic and flattering for that very reason, although all that he accomplished was a kind of spoiling. His trace was troubling, puzzling: every girl with whom he had fancied himself in love was forced to ask herself, 'Why did I lose him? Where did I go wrong?'

Such a man was Toto, and at nineteen he was adult and fully armed. Sustained by his beauty, and by those tearing spirits which had so surprised and disconcerted his parents, he attacked the girls who were drawn to him as if they were so many meals to be enjoyed, and forgotten. He became a prize that every girl thought she could win, and for that reason he set up dissension between friends who had previously been innocent confidantes. Boasting became a commonplace, where truth had been the norm, and the truth inevitably suffered. Through Toto, and through his disappearances, girls learned to rewrite their amorous history, to imply a dismissal where there had in fact been an absence, to hide disappointment in the enterprise of saving face. In this way they became adult women, holding their secrets to themselves, abandoning honesty as too costly a procedure, a tactic only to be indulged in where circumstances promised eternal security, and thus rarely. Their collective memory of Toto was of a laughing mask as he ran off into the distance, one arm through the sleeve of his coat, the other waving in his eagerness to be gone. Abandonment, flight, eclipse was his strangely alluring tactic.

He liked and admired Hartmann who had given him his first glass of champagne and wafted a cigar under his nose, urging him to appreciate the aroma. Hartmann took him out to lunch, during his first Oxford vacation. Hartmann had the gift, which Fibich never had, of finding life entertaining: his *bonhomie* rarely faltered. Therefore he saw in Toto a man who might become like himself, with a light touch and few ambitions that could not be realized. And he admired unreservedly the physical ease that would launch Toto on his career. But what career Toto was to follow was perhaps more of a problem. Fibich hoped that Toto would go into the business, although Hartmann could have told him there was little chance of that. They both retained a happy memory of a time when Toto, aged twelve, had 'helped' in the office in one of his school holidays and had been rewarded with a substantial wage. It had been near Christmas, and, in addition to the handsome bonuses that they always paid their staff, Hartmann and Fibich had succumbed to the unusual agitation for a Christmas party. Toto's work, therefore, came to consist of ordering supplies for this party; he was already sophisticated for his age, and he contacted a school-friend whose sister cooked directors' lunches in a private dining-room in the City. Great was the expenditure and equally great the appreciation. Hartmann and Fibich, proud of the boy's conviviality, had not counted the cost; that task was left to the accountant, Roger Myers. Wives and husbands were invited, and all were charmed by Toto's high spirits. Left at last amid the wreckage of the feast, Fibich, for once a happy man, made as if to embrace his son.

'Do you mind, Dad?' said Toto. 'That sort of thing is bad for my image.'

Later that evening he allowed his father to congratulate him once more, although he was already bored with the whole affair. He was good-natured enough to tolerate Fibich's excessive appreciation, but shortly afterwards he went off to another party, given by that same friend whose sister had done the catering.

'I thought he would be tired,' said Fibich, disconcerted. 'Isn't one party a day enough?'

'Apparently not for a boy like that,' said his mother. 'Anyway, I told him to be home early.'

He returned just after midnight, having been dropped off in somebody's car. Fibich and Christine, in dressing-gowns, instinctively eclipsed themselves before he could find them.

The question of Toto's career was thought to be a matter best left to Hartmann, who arranged lunch in order to broach the subject. This was not entirely to Hartmann's taste: he preferred to lunch alone. Lunch to him was a serene interval in which no serious matters were to be raised; indeed, he lunched alone for that very reason. And Toto, now at Oxford, seemed to have grown away from him; he was not sure of his ground. As ever, though, he was delighted with his first sight of the boy, so vital, so talismanic, in what suddenly seemed to be a fusty and middle-aged setting. Toto discomposed him by ordering a whisky and soda, which Hartmann cancelled. 'Orange juice,' he said severely to the barman, waiting with his tray. Toto, studying the menu, ignored him. 'I'll have the fillet of beef with mushrooms, broccoli, and fried potatoes,' he said, reaching unconcernedly for his glass. 'One fillet of beef and one sole,' said Hartmann. He watched the boy eating, his composure recovered. No serious aberrations could come from one possessed of so splendid an appetite, he thought. Youth, he mused wistfully, although he had never paid much attention to his own. It was not until they were both drinking coffee that he asked Toto if he had anything in mind for the future.

'Your father and I would like you to come into the firm,' he said. 'After all, we have no one else to leave it to.'

'I thought of the theatre,' said Toto, exhaling smoke. 'Or journalism. I haven't decided yet.'

'Both are difficult professions,' said Hartmann gently. 'How would you start?'

'I already have started. I'm producing the college play this summer. You must all come down and see it.'

This, for Toto, was promising. And he has asked us all to be with him. That was nice. And who knows? Perhaps he has a gift after all. If he has it will come out sooner or later, sooner if we are lucky. No harm in waiting a while.

'Give him time to settle down,' he said later to Fibich. 'Let him enjoy himself. He deserves it.'

This seemed to be the consensus, that Toto deserved to enjoy himself. His high spirits depended on this assumption. If he were not enjoying himself the household tended to hold its breath, prepare for the worst. Once Fibich came home to find Christine flushed and obviously concerned. It transpired that she had had a telephone call from his tutor, asking her if their doctor

86

had authorized Toto to take sleeping pills. It appeared that Toto had missed several tutorials by virtue of still being asleep at ten o'clock in the morning.

'Pills?' shouted Fibich, clutching his head. 'He's taking pills? Why is he taking them? Who gave them to him?'

And he got straight back into the car and drove to Oxford, arriving at nine-thirty in the evening. He found his son stretched out, like Chatterton, on a window-seat in his rooms.

'Calm down, Dad,' said Toto wearily. 'I'm under enough pressure as it is, with this play and everything.'

'You look pale,' said Fibich anxiously. 'Have you eaten?'

'I'll have something later,' replied Toto, again wearily.

There was a knock on the door. In response to Toto's call a girl sidled in.

'Hi, Jane,' said Toto, sitting up alertly, the colour coming back into his cheeks. 'My father,' he added. 'Jane.'

'How do you do, Mr Fibich,' said the girl politely, anxious to make a good impression. 'Are you joining us? We're meeting some people for drinks.'

'I thought perhaps dinner . . .' Fibich felt helpless, but was reassured by the girl's pleasant manners. A little lady, he thought.

'Oh, yes, we'll eat later,' the girl assured him. She was a pretty girl, and she looked healthy enough, as did his son, now risen from his fallen posture.

'Then I had better be getting back. Perhaps I could just wash my hands?'

In the bathroom he appropriated the bottle of pink pills and felt that he had done all he could. He drove, foodless, back to London. Christine had retired for the night by the time he got home. In the kitchen she had left chicken sandwiches between two plates. Fibich wolfed them down and suffered indigestion all night.

'You are making a fuss about nothing,' said Hartmann. 'What are a few pills? I take pills every night. They've never done me any harm. Leave him alone, Fibich. He will settle down in his own good time, believe me.'

But to Fibich Toto's young manhood was so unlike his own had been that it seemed to present untold difficulties and hazards. At least, he thought, with depression one knew where one was: it was a state in which nothing was possible, and therefore every action performed, every inch of territory gained, was a victory. It was life unadorned, unidealized, and therefore based on realistic premises, or rather on the lack of them. To Fibich Toto seemed encompassed about with clouds of unknowing, and what was unknown made Fibich fearful. He revered the life he now led, thinking it hardly won and even now precarious. Sometimes he thought he would have been content with less, a little shop somewhere, one of the photocopying parlours, perhaps. He had often watched young assistants shuffling and lining-up paper, and he realized, with a certain disloyalty, that he would have been content to do that all day, returning home in the evenings to a small house in the suburbs. He somehow knew that Christine would have liked this too. Instead of which he was harnessed to Hartmann's juggernaut, and to the opulence it brought with it, ill-at-ease in Hartmann's user-friendly universe.

For Christine the boy was an unacknowledged source of dissatisfaction which she experienced in the form of a pervasive lowering of her spirits, never high at the best of times. She was ashamed to find that he offended her dignity, for he so obviously found her too shadowy a presence in his life to bother with. It was her son, rather than her husband, who made her feel inadequate as a woman. He, in his turn, hated to see her sitting on her blue velvet sofa, a book neglected in her lap, her brilliant eyes clouded and gazing into space. There was discomfort between them, for it was clear, even to Toto, that if the occasion arose she might indeed be formidable, although she had as yet given no sign of this. He sensed her disapproval, yet could not bring himself to court her approval. It was against his code to solicit attention in this way, for he was used to attention being accorded to him automatically. Whereas he knew that he could treat his father lightly, yet still retain his agonized love, he was not too sure about his mother. He called her 'Ma', which irritated her.

'You are too old to call me Ma. Call me Mother.'

'All right, Ma. I mean Mother.'

After that admonition, he consciously or unconsciously called her Ma. 'I mean Mother,' he would correct himself. He avoided her whenever possible, sensing in her a sadness or perhaps a disappointment which, he thought, had nothing to do with him. He was not altogether wrong.

Christine, having successfully taken upon herself the burden of Fibich's melancholy, found her own emerging stealthily from depths which she had willed to remain obscure. Whereas Fibich, beguiled by her steadiness, had married her for the steadiness she could bring to his own troubled life, she herself longed for his rare moments of self-forgetfulness, when some motive power would briefly animate him into being a man like other men. And since the birth of her son those moments had become rare and had finally ceased altogether, as if the outcome, once reached, precluded the need for repetition. She herself was saddened by the care he took to avoid such moments. For Fibich the past was too strong. For herself it was too weak. She thought with impatient pity of her early days, her prayerful impulses, her gratitude. On some days she sat upright in her dim blue room, her eyes focused on an imaginary sun, and thought how she would like to disappear and run away to lead a truly solitary life somewhere in the light of the south, where no one would ever find her. She would leave behind her not simply her failed expectations, for she had never had any to speak of, but the effortful simulacrum of a person into which she had so arduously fashioned herself. She longed for abandonment, for a conduct that would cancel all she had ever been. She brought intense study to these imaginings, which somehow never reached a concrete form. She only knew that some fire must burn, to release her, like the phoenix, from its ashes. Fire and the sun became one in her mind, as the day darkened beyond the windows. When Toto came in, carelessly, with some girl or other in tow, she would stir as if from a long sleep. Toto, irritated by such evidence of his mother's withdrawal, would laughingly dismiss her to his girl-friend once they were out of earshot. 'Don't take any notice of Ma,' he would say. 'I sometimes think she's half gone.' Sometimes Christine overheard him, but she could not get angry. For how else could she tolerably describe the increasing distance between her son and herself?

It was Toto's attitude to the young women he brought home that most agitated her, for she sensed in it something of which she would rather have remained in ignorance. She should have been glad, she knew, that he brought them into his home so freely, but she was not, for there seemed to her to be an element of display in his behaviour of which she could not approve. After the briefest of introductions, conducted in the neutral area of the drawing-room, he would whisk the girl off to his own quarters, where, he told his mother, they were going to rehearse. The girl's rising colour betrayed her, and after their disappearance, and in the dead silence that followed, Christine found herself uncertain of the role she was to play. Was she to prepare coffee and knock carefully at the door? Or to go out, leave the flat, as instinct propelled her to do? She felt uneasy, as if Toto's lack of inhibition constrained her to a walk-on part in which an unsympathetic onlooker might have detected complicity. She knew, without being told, that Toto's behaviour was the result of what he considered to be his parents' sexual feebleness: there was rage and disgust in it. She knew this even before he did. She suspected that he would never respect or obey those parents, simply because he considered them to be burnt-out cases, having relinquished the power that sexuality confers, having perhaps never properly enjoyed it, certainly not have used it. That he could be fascinated by Yvette, to whom he laughingly and readily deferred, was, to Christine, something that had to be suffered in silence. She knew of Yvette's reluctance in the marital role, for Yvette, thinking all women like herself, or if not like her then automatically of low degree and therefore not to be taken seriously, had confided in Christine, or rather had dropped complacent hints about Hartmann's importunity and her various refusals. These, as Christine well knew, she permitted herself more frequently now that the presence of her daughter in the house imposed a certain restraint. Yet Toto seemed to appreciate her frivolousness more than his mother's depth.

Toto could have explained this, had it been nearer the surface of his mind. But it was to remain locked away for many years, until time and circumstances forced him to acknowledge it. Toto, had he been able, might have said that he abhorred depth, although in truth he was conscious of it as a matter that must at some time claim his attention. He might have said, at this stage in his life, that he adored the surface of things, and by the same token, appearance, effectiveness, easily won satisfaction, projection and impact. He appreciated self-love, the love that never fails, and in Yvette's narcissism saw the ratification of his own. At twenty, at twenty-one, Toto saw the world as a vast medley of surfaces on which he might imprint his mark.

By the beginning of his last year at Oxford he was the possessor of a proud reputation. His attendance at lectures and tutorials was negligible, and for all his real feelings for the poetry of the English language his tutors predicted that he would be lucky to get a third. It was on the strength of his performances in various theatrical productions, mostly of a semi-professional nature, that he had made his name, and of course on his reputation as what Yvette had once referred to as a *tombeur de femmes*. He had liked the phrase, had liked the image it conjured up of women falling, one after another. In truth, his part in these seductions was slight, even lazy; he had only to make the first move for the falling to take place. That first move, however, could be rough, giving a misleading impression of intent or desire. For Toto that was all that was required. The rest would follow as the night the day, and invariably did.

At twenty, at twenty-one, Toto's appearance broadcast messages of vigour and satisfaction. At over six feet he was slender but not thin. The hair was worn a little longer than Fibich thought proper these days; the look that resulted had something romantic and chivalrous about it that was found touching. He still lived at home for part of his vacations, although they knew that they could not expect to keep him much longer. Indeed, the prospect of his inevitable departure somewhat softened Christine's attitude towards her son, while Fibich hoped daily that the whole matter might be forgotten. There was still no decision about a future career, for Toto was inclined to think that there was no need to worry, that his contacts would see him through. It was true that he seemed to have made a lot of friends. He was away with them, staying in their houses so often that Christine put fresh flowers in his room each time to welcome him home. For there was something about Toto that made women, even his mother, strive for his affection, the accolade of his approval. His mother, who still had her reservations concerning his character, was forced to acknowledge that he might in time be fatally easy to love.

7

There was a nestling quality to Marianne's demeanour that seemed to predestine her for a man's indulgence and protection: she was a blank sheet on which a man might write his name. At eighteen, she was like one of the young ladies in Trollope, her favourite author, modest, decent, obedient. She was even a little pious, seeming to find peace and ease in the complicated precepts of that old religion that was not even a memory for Hartmann and Fibich. There seemed little to be done with her, for she lacked all worldly ambition and curiosity and appeared to be content to stay in the company of her mother and of Christine, ignoring the young men her father brought to the house. Quiet, self-effacing – unnaturally so for such a well-endowed young woman – she occasionally exasperated Yvette by virtue of her passivity, yet she was not lacking in confidence. This confidence came, as Yvette's had once done, from her appearance. She was an attractive girl, although she had not quite fulfilled the promise of beauty that had been hers as a child. The blue eyes and the dark hair were still the same, but the nose had broadened a little, and the shape of the mouth was full, blunt, a trifle protuberant. The expression was usually withdrawn, concentrated, disconcertingly distrait and unreachable. It was the face of a female cat, oddly powerful in its very refusal to claim power. Beneath this head, so full of information for a discerning man to read, was a slender body which Yvette kept immaculately dressed. Her insistence on presentation had taken root early in her daughter. Now both women were at one in their fastidiousness and in a formality which sat a little incongruously on Marianne, from whom one might have expected a greater show of independence, a greater vivacity, even a certain degree of opposition. Indeed, she was the very model of an old-fashioned daughter, happy to stay in her mother's drawing-room, waiting to be transferred from the parental home to the home of her eventual husband, destined to be protected, to be secure, and to marry young.

It was Yvette's exasperated contention that Marianne did nothing to help herself. As an adolescent she had been unusually silent, had had to be bullied by her mother to go to the numerous parties to which she had been invited. She had made friends easily, but they were of a confiding female sort, and her attraction for these friends was that she received, absorbed their information and never criticized or opposed it. There was in fact something impressive, unchanging, even hieratic about her silent serious listening face, behind which wisdom might or might not be seated, that inspired confidences of a more restless kind. Marianne was thus not uninformed about the activities of her contemporaries, although she saw no reason to emulate such activities. Worldliness, or an appearance of worldliness – the immaculate coiffure, the silk shirts, the long red nails – sat easily on her essential simplicity, prompting speculation as to how much she really knew.

She was thus to be found quite early on in her life

among her female friends, listening impassively to their confidences, and impressing them with an assumption of all-knowingness to which she added with unimportant but quite significant details: an examination of the flawless nails, perhaps, as if her concerns were, like theirs, to do with the general commerce of appearance, comparisons of which took up a good deal of their time. When she was away from these friends she lapsed into an inactivity which was in fact more native to her than the furious expectations that they might be presumed to share. She read hugely, Dickens and Wilkie Collins and her beloved Trollope, and at one point her parents assumed that she might take this up as some kind of career, might, like Toto, read English at the university, although her father was opposed to the idea of her leaving home. In her dreaming mind there were details of weddings and love affairs, great events for which there was no parallel in her everyday life except through the information imparted by her friends. She was, like her mother, ignorant of her own desires, ignorant even of possessing any. By virtue of this, and of other similar traits, she was the darling of her father, although to her mother she was something of an irritant. True, she was attractive and polite and manageable, as any daughter of Yvette's was destined to be, but she was fatally deficient in animation, or so her mother thought. She was often to be found, perfectly dressed, with a volume in her hand, displacing no more room than a shadow does, sitting quietly in her mother's drawing-room; looking up, her lipstick chewed off with the intensity of her attention, she was frequently unable to notice what was being said to her. 'Marianne!' her mother would sharply insist, but 'Leave her, leave her,' Hartmann would protest, passing his hand lovingly over her thick dark hair. He liked to have her sit near him, rather as if she were a cat, and gradually her intense peacefulness, or inwardness, would slow his actions and his breathing, until, with a long sigh, he would let his hand fall to the arm of his chair and be able to readjust to his domestic life, always slightly clamorous with his wife's multiple observations.

Marianne also liked to visit Christine, who loved her dearly, seeing in her the temperate child whom she would so much have preferred to her turbulent son. Christine had no fears for Marianne, whom she saw married equably to a substantial man after a suitably long engagement. For the absence of passion which was Marianne's most marked characteristic seemed, to Christine, to promise a happy life, a life appropriate for a woman of Marianne's upbringing. In this prospect Christine forgot her own disappointments: it was to her as if she were starting out again with all the advantages of which she had been deprived. Marianne's stable home, the doting affection of her father, would seem to incline her towards a similar establishment, a similar protection in the future. She saw no danger there, no ambushes along the way, and often she found herself having to reassure Yvette, whom she saw as over-anxious in her desire to see the girl settled. To Yvette, the only success for a woman was an early marriage. But to Christine the prolongation of the girlhood of which she herself had known only a poor and corrupted version seemed devoutly to be wished. As Hartmann reassured Fibich, she used nearly the same words to reassure Yvette.

'Leave her alone,' she would say. 'Let her find her feet. She moves at a different pace from you. Girls marry later now. And of course she'll marry, have no fears on that score. You must give her time to make her own choice. You simply mustn't force her or you'll ruin everything.'

97

Thus she became Marianne's ally and a source of comfort to Yvette, and felt quite proud that she had achieved a measure of influence over them both. It was the only influence she had, since she so signally failed to have any over her son, and Fibich rarely looked to her these days for guidance, using her, much as he had used the analyst, as a repository for his worried musings or accounts of his dreams.

However, Marianne could not stay at home doing nothing, although Hartmann secretly hoped that she might be allowed to. Carefully dressed in primrose yellow cashmere and grey flannel, she entered London University to read English and to become assimilated, as they thought, into her own age group. But she found her own age group attired in combat gear and engaged in protest against the teaching body. When she refused to join in or to listen to the heated propaganda that was being dispensed all around her she was regarded as something of a class enemy and left severely alone. After a few months she was so unhappy that she asked her father if she might leave. After all, she had no desire for a career: she was out of phase even in that. And when she described the grim corridors and the dingy classrooms, the endless clamorous staircases and the penitential refectories, it was as if she had been consigned to Kafka's Castle, so bewildered and distressed did she become. She made no friends there, and that, to her mother, signalled the failure of the whole enterprise. To Yvette, undergraduates were attractive high-born young men in sports cars, rather like Toto, in fact. If they were merely indiscriminate young people in jeans she saw no prospect for her daughter in their midst. It was a relief for them all when Marianne brought home her books, her unsullied ring binders, and her Parker 51 pen, and installed them once again at the desk in her room. 'I didn't like it,' she would say, wrinkling her white forehead, without exactly specifying what it was she did not like. 'I wasn't happy there.'

After a short interval of peace her mother became restless again. Remembering her own success in the business world, Yvette decided that Marianne must have a job, although she was without any qualifications or even the slightest incentive. It was Christine who came up with the idea of voluntary work with a charitable organization whose main activity consisted of raising money, in the form of balls, concerts and book fairs, for neurological units in children's hospitals. This seemed to them all far more to the point. Once again attired in cashmere and flannel, Marianne went off in the bus to the top of Park Lane, where, in a formerly elegant house, she was put to work transcribing addresses from one list to another. This kept her perfectly happy. She concealed from her mother the fact that her fellow workers were young women like herself, and the only men the board of directors who met once a month and for whom she was allowed to fill the silver water jugs in the austere room in which they held their deliberations. For these occasions she exchanged the cashmere and flannel for lighter yet at the same time more formal garments in silk and fine wool. Seeing her daughter depart the flat in a blue silk shirt, a longish black skirt, and a raw silk jacket in black and white, Yvette took heart and thought that Marianne would surely bring back a hostage in the form of a husband. For such an outfit a large sapphire and diamond ring would be the perfect, the inevitable accessory.

Marianne liked going to work. She liked queuing for the bus every morning; she liked the feeling of being one of a crowd. She liked the girls she met, usually the same ones; she liked to see them brave and decked out in their morning armour. She liked to see them drawn ineluctably to the adventures in the thick paperback books they brought out from their capacious bags. She felt at one with them, although she brought no book for the short journey herself: she had discovered the delights of watching. She was less interested in the men, their newspapers draped over metal briefcases; on the whole the bus, which briefly had the atmosphere of an informal study centre, delighted her. Above all she liked the obedience of being part of a group. Her journey home, at four-thirty in the afternoon, brought her into contact with a different set of people, a curious population of old ladies, usually in groups of four, innocent as schoolgirls in their sensible shoes and tight mackintoshes, untidy grey curls escaping from hats in the form of jelly moulds. Like schoolgirls they seemed convulsed with merriment, seeking and finding protection in their own kind, returned to their former selves, having dispensed with the bothersome business of husbands and children. Marianne had the impression that they were relieved of a burden, sex no more than a hilarious memory. She felt happy for them, was quite sorry to reach home and find that she was still young and had it all to go through before she could be similarly carefree herself.

She made a friend at work, a bold skinny girl called Belinda. Distinguished from others of her kind by an enormous appetite, Belinda's cheeks usually bulged with forbidden chocolate. 'My skin!' she would moan, examining her chin and adding another layer of powder. 'You're so lucky.' 'Did he telephone?' Marianne would ask seriously, paying her dues to friendship before putting her handbag down beside one of the two adjacent desks that they shared. There would be a sigh. Then, 'I think I'll give him a ring. In fact I think I'll take a table for the ball at the Dorchester and ask a whole lot of people. Then he'll have to come. You'll come, won't you? I'll get someone for you. You ought to mix more.'

'I don't think so,' Marianne would start to say, anxious not to hurt Belinda's feelings. But, 'I'll just give him a ring to sound him out. If he says no, I'll go ahead anyway. Just send the ticket. That way he'll have to come. To hell with him. Who does he think he is, anyway?'

She would be gone for half an hour. On return her cheeks would be flushed with triumph, the triumph of the will. Seconds later the drawer of her desk would open, and seconds after that small shreds of silver paper would be consigned to the waste-paper basket. As Belinda's mind was always and entirely on her own affairs Marianne found her a restful and congenial companion. They worked cheerfully together and were much liked by the woman who was supposed to supervise what little they did, a glossy woman of forty-five whose hands and wrists seemed weighted down by the evidence of various engagements and marriages. Engagements, if not marriages, were always in the air.

On one splendid occasion Marianne and Belinda were co-opted to help at a fund-raising book fair, where, seated behind a table, they packed up the books signed by a bemused writer of historical memoirs. Belinda, her streaked hair flapping wildly round her face, engaged everyone in animated conversation. It was one of their more successful events: the hall was crowded, the attendance gratifying. Marianne felt the stirrings of a mild spirit of recklessness as the money changed hands. Hartmann, strolling over with an air of studied uncon- cern, enquired, 'Are you girls all right? Not overdoing it?' He then went back to Yvette, who was sitting tensely behind a cup of coffee at a small table, as if attending her daughter's début.

'Stop fussing,' he said. 'She's perfectly all right. Leave her alone.'

Five minutes later Fibich followed him.

'Do you want anything, children? A cup of tea, perhaps?'

'They're sweet, your family,' said Belinda, who had greeted him effusively and sold him a book. 'Old-fashioned, really.' They drank their cups of tea, which had appeared with two biscuits in each saucer. Fibich was good at that sort of detail.

Hartmann, who was immensely proud of his daughter, whom he thought beautiful and accomplished beyond all others, nevertheless registered the fact that she was unsophisticated, even untaught, in sexual matters. She will be like her mother, he thought, and the thought did not entirely displease him, for what is inconvenient in a wife may be treasured in a daughter. He longed to keep her for himself, yet he recognized, from Yvette's restlessness, her urgings and promptings, that a partner must be found for Marianne, who seemed to have no desire to find one for herself. Nor, despite her elegant appearance and unspoilt air, did she attract anyone on her own account. When, at Yvette's insistence, she would be obliged to accept one of Belinda's table-filling invitations, she would not be happy. She would sit gravely, putting in the hours, swallowing tiny yawns, her eyes watering slightly with tiredness, while Belinda danced frenziedly, her dress coming apart, her high heels skidding over the polished floor. Watching her friend limp back to the safe haven where her spilling handbag and other effects were kept in custody, Marianne would wonder how soon she could go home. She found these occasions exhausting, failed to see why her presence was necessary. She considered her duty as a chaperone fulfilled after half an hour, but was too fond of Belinda to refuse her company. And she was aware that her shy replies had failed to retain at her side the young man whom Belinda had asked to accompany her. She became quite good at pretending to enjoy herself, although she was not good enough to deceive her partners. These partners, essentially good-natured, were nevertheless unwilling to repeat the exercise.

She became twenty-four, twenty-five, and still there was no sign of marriage, or even, at the worst possible reckoning, of an affair. Belinda, twirling a ruby ring on her finger, had just become engaged for the second time and was even now thinking she might break it off, having someone else in mind. Marianne became aware that she was out of favour, not only with her mother, but with her friend as well. 'You *are* slow,' Belinda would say lightly, drunk with her own success. She did not mean to be unkind. Tactlessness came naturally to her. But the atmosphere at home was deteriorating. 'Do something,' said Yvette grimly to Hartmann, and, 'Ask Belinda to dinner,' she said, more reasonably, to Marianne, aware that she must now tread carefully if she were not to drive her daughter into ever more silent opposition.

In a spirit of the utmost resignation Hartmann invited Goodman and Myers from the office. The table was excellently appointed, the salmon coulibiac effectively praised, Goodman in particular exhausting himself in superlatives. Roger Myers, a thick pale tall man with sandy hair, said little enough but was found to be the more acceptable of the two. He was thirty-eight, old by Marianne's standards, just right according to Yvette's. Marianne schooled herself into acceptance of another invitation to another ball, simply in order to please her mother; Myers's invitation, when it came (and out of sheer politeness it had to come), was to a football match. He played on Sundays, with an obscure college side, in a distant park. Marianne, standing on the sidelines, found it quite restful simply to stand there and watch, without the need to be sociable. She also found herself interested, once she had got over her surprise, by Roger's enormous knees. When he joined her at the end of the game, showered, dressed, and reassuringly taciturn, she was quite glad to see him. They stood for a moment exchanging banalities, their breath puffing little clouds into the cold air. Then he took her home. The occasion had brought colour to her pale cheeks, which Yvette took as a good sign. When Myers, standing politely in the drawing-room with a glass of sherry, named the date of the next fixture, Yvette said quickly that she was sure that Marianne would enjoy it: she looked so much better for the fresh air. It was arranged that Myers should call for her in a fortnight's time.

Myers also played squash but rightly thought this too bold, too virile a game for Marianne to witness. He was correct in this: indeed he displayed a certain caution that partially allayed Hartmann's misgivings. Hartmann, who had known him for the eight years he had been with the firm, had hitherto thought him an excellent accountant if a dull stick. Now he began to appreciate his prudence, his deliberate slowness, his very uninflammability. If a daughter is to marry her father does not necessarily appreciate signs of ardour, haste, desperate intent in the man who is to be her husband. Seated side by side at the parental table, Marianne and Myers, or Roger, as they now had to call him, were relaxed, even torpid, in each other's company. And there were advantages, Hartmann saw, in having a son-in-law within daily reach. His future, of course, would be assured. Hartmann tried to tell himself that he was gaining a son, and failed. One night, uncharacteristically, he awoke from a dream in which some great fiesta was taking place, with fireworks bursting in a starry sky, and everyone in Spanish costume. It should be like that, he thought instinctively, and quashed the thought. He was exceptionally good at ordering subversive thoughts out of his mind. He had had a lifetime of practice.

At the age of twenty-seven Marianne became engaged to Roger Myers, and Hartmann trained himself to think of life without her. Immediately he began making enquiries in the building as to when a flat might become available. For as brief an interval as he could command he would lose his daughter to far-off Richmond. 'Absurdly out of the way,' he said to Myers, who had lived there for most of his life. 'We will find you something nearer. It will be my wedding present to you.' Myers thanked him courteously. There was, however, no question of Myers addressing him as anything other than Mr Hartmann. This pained him, but he saw the correctness, the entirely general correctness, of Myers's attitude. He had no fear for Marianne's future. That was something. In the final analysis it was everything, he supposed. Thus he reasoned with himself, interminably, particularly when alive to the pain of his daughter's disappearance from his home.

Yvette allowed herself a moment of triumphant relaxation before rushing into preparations for the wedding. Marianne's large sapphire and diamond ring (for Roger had thought to ask Yvette's advice on this matter) was greatly admired by Christine and Fibich. Fibich, in fact, was overjoyed, for Myers met all his criteria of gentlemanliness, having never been observed to act rashly, impetuously, or in a markedly juvenile manner. Christine gave a small party for the young people, as she chose to call them, feeling very out of it herself, and Toto was induced to be present. Toto's attitude was one of hilarity: he had never been exactly comfortable with Marianne, who, he knew, was not receptive to his particular brand of charm. On more than one occasion she had shrunk from his exuberance, as a cat shrinks from hissing rain. As the date of the wedding drew nearer he found himself unwillingly included in the proceedings, unwillingly but with a certain fascination: he had, after all, nothing better to do, and it was all good material. When, two nights before the wedding day, Yvette urged him to take a suddenly tearful Marianne out to dinner, he felt a not altogether unwelcome leap of curiosity. He was impatient, on edge, longing to break up the saccharine Victorian atmosphere in which Yvette and Christine moved so solemnly, conscious of the significance of their activities. He took her to the Savoy, Fibich having given him a cheque for this purpose.

The evening began quite well, although Toto found Marianne unbearably dull. After an hour conversation languished: Marianne seemed more silent than usual. Toto was exasperated by her mutism, her lack of sparkle. He was accustomed to more of a performance when he took a girl out for the evening. He considered Marianne young for her age, even backward, and became restless at the sight of her prudent expression. Marianne, fighting a headache, wondered how soon she would be allowed to go to bed. She was not happy. Her discomfort had more to do with Roger than with Toto, although she refused to give in to the implications of this idea. Her cat-like face was pale, even if the rest of her was in excellent order, and the fine ring looked well on her narrow hand. The impression given by the hand, and the cunningly draped silk dress, and the expensively coiffed dark hair was one of worldliness, sophistication, wealth, nurture. The fruits of a good education, thought Toto, who felt the failure of the evening as particularly insulting; he was not used to failure, even to so insignificant a failure as this. When she put her napkin down beside her untouched coffee cup, and said, 'Shall we go?' he felt the beginnings of something larger, deeper than mere irritation, felt a need to ruffle her, disarrange her. This feeling was an adult version of the pushing and hitting with which he had tried to arouse her attention when they were both children. Even then she had ignored him.

She made no attempt to thank him for the evening, being too intent on her own growing misery. As they drove back to Ashley Gardens there seemed little left for them to say to each other. After he had stopped the car he sat for a moment, waiting for her to express gratitude, flattery, as most girls were only too willing to do. Then, when no words came, he leaned over and began to say goodnight in the way he knew best. Her resistance excited him. He pinioned her arms, laughing at her, but at the same time annoyed. Anger made him act more roughly than he would have done had he considered her relative unimportance more calmly. Determined to make her relax – as if relaxation were a token of submission – he fought her head back, irritated and disconcerted by her refusal. Finally she opened the door and escaped, the skin round her mouth rubbed raw.

Fibich, coming out onto the landing with empty milk bottles, saw her streak up the stairs, in tears. Instinctively, he stepped back behind his front door, his mouth dry. He stood in the hall, his heart beating, then went into the darkened drawing-room. He stood quite still for a moment, his hand to his suddenly aching head. When he heard his son come in he waited until the boy had gone to his room. Then he followed him and flung open Toto's bedroom door.

'Burglar!' he shouted.

'What's the matter?' enquired Toto, flushed and bad-tempered.

Fibich searched for a total, a final term of abuse.

'I only kissed her,' said Toto.

'Asset-stripper!' shouted Fibich.

'What is it? What's wrong?' Christine appeared in the doorway, frightened, in a dressing-gown.

'Go to bed,' shouted Fibich, rounding on her.

'My God, my God,' she cried. 'What have you done?'

'Oh, for God's sake,' shouted Toto in his turn. 'Leave me alone.'

There was a sudden silence. They were all aware that nothing like this exchange must ever take place again, even at the risk of eternal formality. They became aware that it was late, very late. After a moment, Fibich repeated, more quietly, 'Go to bed', and took Christine by the arm to usher her out of the room. Gradually all the lights in the flat went out. The following day Toto sent a note to Yvette. He was obliged to be in Oxford, he explained: he could not come to the wedding; he sent them all his love.

The bride did not look well. Her white veil hid the reddened patches round her mouth, but she was pale, listless. Her parents put this down to an attack of sickness which had kept her in bed the previous day. In any event, Yvette was too exhausted to worry any more and was now anxious for all to be over. Hartmann, seeing his daughter through a midst of tears, was unaware that she looked any less beautiful than she always did to him. Christine and Fibich were very quiet, and of course Toto's absence was regretted. At the reception both Yvette and Fibich had a migraine, although Hartmann recovered his spirits somewhat. But when Marianne disappeared to change he felt the same inner trembling that he had felt when she had said her first word. As they left, on the first stage of their wedding journey to Sorrento, he managed to keep a smile on his face until they were out of the room. Then he sank down on to a small creaking gilt chair, pulled a white silk handkerchief from his pocket, and unashamedly wiped his eyes. Yvette hissed at him, exasperated by his sentimentality. Fibich wept in sympathy. 'Ah, Fibich,' groaned Hartmann. 'Wait till it's your turn.' Yvette, thankful that it was over, nursed a lingering irritation that somehow her daughter had once again failed to live up to the occasion. Christine signalled a waiter to bring them all a cup of tea.

They stayed on in the deserted ballroom, uncomfortable on gilt chairs, too tired to move, reminiscent, and saddened, as one is by reminiscence. How time flies, they said, wonderingly. At last they got to their feet, went in search of coats, emerged thankfully into the fresh air, where office workers were waiting quite brazenly for buses, as if this were a day like any other. Wordlessly they got into their cars. For Christine and Fibich there was the consciousness of a gulf, a little rift in their perfect amity, something to be concealed, buried, if possible forgotten. Yet the moment of reminiscence had united them as never before. They marvelled among themselves at their unbroken friendship. Never separated, they reminded each other. They shook hands, kissed each other ardently at Fibich's front door, and took themselves off to bed, no more words to be exchanged that night. All slept heavily, in the two homes deserted by their children.

When Marianne, shortly after her return from Italy, announced that she was pregnant, both Hartmann and Fibich felt very old. When, two months later, she miscarried, they realized, for the first time for many years, that all might not be well in their new lives, that a disorder had occurred which for once they were unable to put right.

8

After her daughter left home, Yvette experienced a certain restlessness. Since she was not in the habit of analysing her feelings she did not attribute this restlessness to grief but tended to blame Hartmann, in an unfocused way, for being out all day and leaving her alone. He, acknowledging a far less manageable grief, and anxious not to let it develop into Fibich-seeming proportions, agreed hastily and exited as usual. He was having to supply himself with many more small treats than usual in order to keep up his habitual good humour; he was determined to play his part with honour. The office was not much quieter without Myers, who was in any event a silent man who worked stolidly and seemed never to move at any great pace: a soft-footed sleep-walker's tread took him away at the end of the day and brought him back again without incident the following morning. His absence from the office was uneventful; he had left everything in order. Hartmann found himself lingering in Fibich's room, anxious for general reassurance, which Fibich readily supplied. Fibich understood this need only too well; he suffered permanently from it himself. It was, in fact, a relief to him to supply rather than to demand. And he liked Hartmann in this new guise of vulnerability, although he knew it to be only temporary. It suited them both not quite to know what would happen next.

Yvette, overtired, decided that she needed a rest. Having had this decision ratified by Hartmann and Christine, she then announced that she was going to redecorate the flat. Nothing pleased her; all suggestions – for a holiday, a weekend in the country – were brushed aside. While workmen installed ladders and groundsheets in her kitchen she exhibited a tearful hollow-eyed appearance, much as she had done during her pregnancy. It was indeed a difficult time for her, but that had more to do with her age than with Marianne's marriage. She was growing old unevenly, as most people do; as she was not in the habit of comparing herself with anyone else, she had no notion that her dilemma could in any way be universal. Examining herself fearfully in her mirror, she was reassured to see that her inner turmoil had left no trace, or at least no trace that she could detect. The fine etched lines on the fair skin were invisible to her, as was the mildly humped appearance of the shoulders. The waist, however, was expanding; there was no getting away from that. Well, she would get down to a proper diet as soon as she had some time to herself, without the obligations and the tasks that she so dutifully took upon herself. She began to spend more time at the hairdresser's, spreading out her hands for the manicurist's attentions. The hands, in a woman, go first, but Yvette attributed their worn shiny look to her recent exertions rather than to the passage of time. Her expertise in the kitchen was curtailed by the presence of Ken and Dave, two nice young men who were spreading peach-coloured paint over her formerly white walls.

'Peach?' said Christine doubtfully. 'In the kitchen?'

'Why not?' retorted Yvette, alert for any whisper of criticism. 'I want a change. I'm going to get rid of everything. I want red saucepans and everything else plain white. After all, if I don't like it I can always change it back again.'

'White plates get to look so boring,' said Christine, unwisely.

'Who said so?' replied Yvette. 'Anyway, I can always get others. And I want a blue blind at the window.'

For she was beginning to think in Mediterranean terms, feeling, with her thinning blood, the cruel burden of the north and remembering her mother's little flat in Nice. She suggested to Hartmann that he might buy a retirement home for them there, where she could see palm trees from her window and go shopping in a cotton dress. Hartmann did not think this was a bad idea, providing he could transport Fibich and Christine there as well. Might they not all end up spending hot lazy dreaming days in the sun, growing old amidst the reviving cynicism of the French, rather than here, where they feared the cold? The flat in Nice was a possibility, but not one that Hartmann intended to implement straightaway. It was Christine who suggested the evening classes, a suggestion that was initially brushed aside until Yvette began to consult the women's magazines and to read about the new expansion of women's consciousness. The old expansion had always been good enough for her, spending, and perfecting her appearance, and she was inclined to trust that more. Christine, perceiving a real if undiagnosed distress, kept in daily contact.

'Hello,' Yvette trilled into the telephone, managing to stretch the word out into three syllables.

'Christine here,' the dry voice answered. 'What are you doing? Are you busy?'

'I'm always busy,' came the reply. 'I'm exhausted. I've just washed all the paint.'

'But it's only just been done.'

'Yes, but I noticed a thumb mark. And anyway I like it done my way.'

'Have the men gone, then?'

'They've gone, and I gave them a lot of the plates. That will give me a chance to replace them. Plain white, I thought. In fact I was going out today to see what I could find. Why don't you come with me?'

'But if you've just washed the paint . . .'

'Oh, the paint. Well, that's done now. Do come, Christine. I thought I'd just price a few things. Peter Jones, the General Trading Company, Harvey Nichols and Harrods. We could have lunch out. And anyway I need something to wear. It's time I looked after myself a bit.'

Christine, who had witnessed the frantic provisioning of clothes and accessories that had gone on just before the wedding, said nothing. She reserved for Yvette some of the protectiveness she had initially lavished on Fibich. She saw that Yvette, though incurably frivolous, was, in all the important ways, innocent, uncorrupted by the reflections that seemed to burden her own life. Each day was new for Yvette, and whatever she felt remained unexamined. Sometimes Christine saw in her face a look of bewilderment, the eyes turning to the window, waiting, waiting. And her marriage, the birth of her daughter, and that daughter's wedding, all accomplished promptly and without complications, seemed to have left her unappeased, as if the next thing must quickly come along to occupy her, or the abyss might open. What abyss? The abyss that waits for all of us, when all our actions seem futile, when the ability to fill the day seems stalled, and the waiting takes on an edge of dread. Fortunately Yvette did not identify the onset of these adult fears. The prospect of her day fulfilled, she sang happily in her small pretty voice as she shook lace-trimmed handkerchiefs from a drawer, soaked them in cologne, and put them in her bag. I won't cook tonight, she thought. I'll pick up something at Harrods. This seemed to her a dashing, even an emancipated decision. She paused only to impart this news to Hartmann, and went down the stairs to join Christine.

The streets had been washed clear by a recent shower and a pale spring sun had brought on the crocuses. Pigeons strutted expansively on the pavements. Outside Victoria Station emerging travellers blinked in the unaccustomed light. 'We can catch the bus to Knights-bridge and walk down Sloane Street,' Yvette informed her silent companion. 'I hope you're not in a hurry. I want a good look round the shops.' She then turned her attention to the passing scene, having satisfied herself that her conditions had been stated. She often found herself putting Christine into some sort of order, mis-understanding, or rather not understanding at all, the other woman's need for quiet. Christine, for her part, found it restful to glide along in the slip-stream of Yvette's activity. She was also genuinely curious to find out how Yvette maintained her self-esteem, that un-faltering attribute, which seemed to have been conferred on her from birth. Christine had heard the story of Yvette's mythic beginnings, had felt pity where Yvette had only felt pride. The triumphant sense of survival that Yvette shared with Hartmann ('Look! We have come through!') had bred in her no sense of disaster averted. Good fortune she put down to merit rather than to luck, and if anything in her well-ordered life resulted in a minute disappointment she would loudly and uninhibitedly bewail her fate instead of bowing her head momentarily to the inevitable. By the same token, she would rally quickly, be comforted by the prospect of a treat, an outing, a holiday, a party, the promise of something nice to come. In that way they had all unconsciously been trained to offer Yvette inducements to further good humour. These were small concessions, for she was easily appeased: that was her charm. What they all pitied, without ever acknowledging the fact to each other, was that intermittent look of blankness, as if, unknowing, Yvette had discovered herself to be adrift in her life, as if that life were suddenly incomprehensible to her, as if she were still that child in the train, not understanding the desperation of her mother's injunctions, simply wanting to be and to remain a child, without the superimposition of adult hopes and fears. She had moved competently through her life, had overcome, had not consciously remembered, or perhaps had genuinely forgotten, the penumbra of sensations that had settled around her in that train to Bordeaux. This event seemed to them all, to Christine in particular, a much graver affair than it had ever seemed to Yvette, who continued to recount it as if it were a pretty story whenever she judged the occasion demanded it. Toto, in particular, had loved the story when, as a little boy, he had stood by her chair, playing with the rings on her fingers. But, 'Look after my daughter,' Martine Cazenove had said to Christine, before taking off finally to Nice and the flat bought for her by Hartmann, on the day of Marianne's wedding. Christine had agreed. What else could she do? The strong must always look after the weak, even if their strength is unwelcome, even if it has been wished on them by circumstances not of their choosing.

There was also in Yvette a will to overcome that was

translated, without the mediation of her mind, into excellent bodily health. The rapid and effortless ingestion of meals, the efficient sleep, the satisfactory regulation of her digestion, filled her with an innocent pride, as if she could not tolerate any other systems of management. Seated before an empty plate, she would lay down her spoon with a certain approval, as if her food were automatically destined to benefit her. Fibich's beleaguered stomach was a source of amazement to her. When they all dined together she would berate him for being nervous, as if she had caught him in an act of lèse-majesté towards his food, so munificent a substance. Oddly enough, he tended to eat better in her company, reassured by her appetite for life, although her food was too rich for him. Christine, who empathized with his delicate and instinctive revulsions, and who cooked him tiny careful meals, did not fare so well. 'More indigestion,' he would sigh comfortably, as they set off for Hartmann's dinner table. The ensuing night would be punctuated by the sound of tablets dissolving fizzily in glasses of water, and careful, even loving, eructations. In the morning he would wave away breakfast, but, 'It was worth it,' he would assure Yvette later, on the telephone.

Yvette was not aware of having entered her life by the back door, so to speak, although all the others were. 'Look! We have come through!' was a permanent thought in Hartmann's mind. Christine and Fibich were not so sure. Yvette's conscience, like that of her husband, was unclouded: that was why, in the final analysis, they suited each other so well, despite incompatibilities which were, in fact, growing less marked as age took a hand in the matter. They shared an innate festiveness which, in their daughter, was mysteriously absent. That their entering into possession was also a latecoming was a thought that often occurred to Hartmann, whose reaction was one of fervent gladness; to Yvette the thought never occurred at all. Any girl (for she secretly thought of herself as a girl, although as a girl she had prided herself on being a woman, in both cases wrongly) could do what she had done, if only she knew herself, as Yvette did, simply to be the best. Her good fortune, her prosperity, she dealt with expansively: that also was part of her charm. Presents were bestowed incessantly: to object to her extravagance was to induce a look of wonder, as if the recipient were in the throes of some cramping disability which she could not understand. Intolerant, therefore, but good-natured, she sailed through life much as a child does, and was in this much more of a child than her own daughter.

For she had never experienced the secret treachery of her own flesh, as Marianne had done in Toto's embrace, had never had time for the meekness that had settled on Marianne when left behind by more adventurous friends, and, more important, had never known, never would know, longing, as Marianne was to know it in the years to come, when a young man's hasty but expert appropriation had awakened in her the knowledge of what she was throwing away in marrying her so reassuring, so unexciting husband. Had Yvette known of this she would have dismissed it out of hand. 'Toto didn't mean anything,' she would have said. 'He's just a boy! How could you take him seriously? He was only trying to be kind. The business of your life is to marry. That is what I brought you up for, and that is what you will do.' She would not have understood that a trace could be left, nor could Marianne ever have confided in her. Yvette, she saw, was inexperienced by any standards, even by her own. And she could tell no one else. Who, then, could explain her to herself? In her decision to keep silent on this matter, a matter to which she was to return many times in her life, Marianne achieved a certain dignity, and a maturity which could not have been foreseen for her by the father who still thought of her – a married woman! – as a child.

On this particular day, one of not too many like it, for Christine was aware of the disparity in their expectations, the sun chased from Yvette's face the last lingering shadow of doubt, a doubt that was always experienced as dissatisfaction. Christine, schooled to keep Yvette happy, felt almost happy herself in the performance of this essentially simple task. She saw herself moving nervelessly through her life while Yvette, proudly, and at her leisure, expressed satisfaction or its absence, the latter to be loudly deplored. Today the auguries appeared to be favourable. On the bus, which, to Christine, was a mine of information simply waiting for her perusal, Yvette sat smilingly, without the smallest glance to left or right. Thus she was accustomed to solicit the attention without which she never felt entirely comfortable. 'Who is she?' she imagined her fellow passengers wondering. 'Who is that marvellously groomed woman with the fair hair?' And if the attention were not forthcoming she was able to imagine it and to suppose that open curiosity in her appearance was being suppressed or covered up out of sheer envy. She looked complacently down at her fine black cloth skirt, her shining high-heeled patent leather boots: she touched, with proprietorial carelessness, the silk scarf tucked into the collar of her black mink jacket. Opposite her Christine, in plaid skirt and blazer, looked, she thought, like a country mouse, but that was quite all right, that was what she was used to, that was just Christine. She tried to ignore the pain from the troublesome vein in her left leg, accentuated by the high heel of the boot, and as if to overcome this by sheer force of personality, as she did with all those defects that the middle period of her life was bringing her, imprinted an amused smile on her lips and condescended to look out of the window. Yet when the woman sitting beside her stumbled as she got up and nearly fell, it was Yvette who steadied her, the smile of condescension exchanged for one of genuine empathy. 'Mind how you go,' said Yvette to the woman, a poor hesitant creature, possibly the same age as herself. As she in her turn got off the bus she said to Christine, 'Dreadful the way some people let themselves go, isn't it? There's no excuse. All it needs is a little effort.' The implications of letting go, both in falling unsteadily and jettisoning her façade, put her once more in a good humour, for she was not in danger from either of these contingencies, nor did she ever intend to be.

First, they must have coffee, she announced. It was then Christine's task to find a suitable venue. This was accomplished without difficulty, since the commerce of Sloane Street is designed for women who are about their business in the middle of the morning or the middle of the afternoon. Seated at a small table, in a hot atmosphere redolent of chocolate, Yvette's face took on the solemn expression with which she greeted all nourishment. Her coffee was accompanied by a chocolate éclair. 'I know I shouldn't,' she said, in the way of women who are always intending to go on a diet. The reply was bound to be, 'No, you shouldn't', or possibly 'Why not?' Christine wisely opted for the latter, as more likely to cut matters short. She herself had had to swallow a nervous yawn at the sight of the cakes proffered on a tray rather too close to her face: she had caught some of Fibich's fastidiousness. She felt tired already at the prospect of comparing one table setting with another, as if this were genuinely beyond her powers. She knew that Yvette was a naturally energetic woman and that she would not go home until her explorations were exhaustively accomplished. And there was lunch to get through, and no doubt tea as well, for Yvette took gladly to the challenge of a day out and meant to take advantage of all its possibilities. All that Christine could look forward to was a little rallying saunter between shops. Left to herself on a day like this she would have sat in the park. She sighed briefly, and told herself not to be selfish. Opposite her Yvette sat expectantly, her lips pursed, waiting for the bill.

The agreeable lassitude brought on by the first fine day of the year inclined Christine to dreaminess. Yvette, however, was unaffected, as she was unaffected by all variations in temperature and appearance other than her own. The sun spread its rays beneficently over the London streets, where Christine would have lingered had she not been spurred on by the quickening steps of Yvette, who had sighted her goal. There followed a prolonged foray into various shops, where, amid the clash of china, the buzzing of tills, and the commotion of women, and under an unvarying synthetic light, Yvette appeared wholly absorbed in pricing, on a lengthening list, various items of increasing splendour, much as if she were the bride her daughter had so recently become. By lunchtime Christine was dazed, Yvette invigorated. They sat among women of their own kind – unoccupied, almost, to Christine's mind, obsolescent – while waitresses sped about, eventually placing before them the kind of food that women out shopping are supposed to favour: highly orchestrated but flavourless salads, manufactured cakes and desserts. 'I'm going to have a piece of that,' said Yvette, pointing to a cheesecake apparently baked by the metre. 'I know I shouldn't.' She had ingested the meal with her usual thoroughness, though Christine, drawn by the sun now pouring through the windows, had refused to take it seriously. She, to whom acquisition did not come naturally, felt a terrible strength in Yvette, as, fuelled by her cake, she prepared for the final reckoning, in Harrods.

'I miss Marianne,' Christine said involuntarily, once they were leaving the restaurant.

'Well, of course, I miss her too,' replied Yvette. She was a little annoyed, as if Christine had usurped her own unsettled feelings, although any residual sadness was fast disappearing. 'I thought I'd pick out a dinner service for her. I don't think I like the one she had from Maman. And she is so sweet about these things: I don't think she would ever say she didn't like it. She's such a funny child, so quiet, not like us at all. It was high time she got married.'

For marriage, she knew, would supply what she privately thought that Marianne lacked, the sort of natural complacency in which she had always been so proficient herself. She did not really miss her daughter, of whom she had begun to despair; the cat-like presence, the silent reading had in fact begun to worry her. She liked a bustle about her, thought women should be provocative, demanding, narcissistic, as if anything less spelled failure, unpopularity, spinsterishness. She had no time for the new woman, with her bold sexist demands, thinking that such women forfeited too much and made fools of themselves into the bargain. She herself preferred the idea of winning concessions from men, and saw no shame in doing so, even if the behaviour involved meant a certain amount of exploitation. She would have defended this position vigorously had any objections been offered. I play my part, she would have countered: I cook, I clean, I minister to my husband's comforts. I am not responsible for his needs: after all, those are not really my affair. She was not above parading accounts of her domestic activities, and even boldly advanced the theory that she was worth ten thousand a year, having read this in one of the few newspaper articles to which she bothered to address herself. Like most people who read very little, she remembered every word of it, and referred to it frequently. Her husband was rather used to impressive accounts of her exhaustion, as if she were wearing herself out on his behalf. He was wise enough to refrain from telling her what an easy life she led, but at the same time he knew that no other woman could have given herself so devotedly to his domestic peace. Hearing how this was attained was a small price to pay for a perfectly run household, and he supposed that all husbands had to endure much the same, or similar, recitals after a hard day's work. He knew that in a sense they both pretended to work much harder than they really did, and was amused to see how they could fall into Punch and Judy confrontations in which neither of them truly believed. Playing at being married was how he thought of it.

The look of profound absorption on Yvette's face as she devised a dinner party or renewed the furnishings of their bedroom touched him in some way, as if he still had in his charge the girl who had pretended to work in his office. There was no doubt in his mind that her present work, the work she claimed was worth ten thousand a year, was her true work, her life's work, trivial though it might have seemed to a busier woman. And he liked the eternal peace of a well-run household, onto which he could project his thoughts in those moments of what seemed like homesickness, when, in the middle of an idle day, he would permit himself to think back to earlier times. These memories, stirred by the disappearance of Marianne and the sadness he felt at the sight of her empty room, came now and then unbidden to his mind, a fact which appeared to him curious, more characteristic of Fibich than of himself. I am turning sentimental in my old age, he thought with surprise. No longer young, after all: two-thirds of the way there. And he tried to guard his wife against similar thoughts of her own ageing, knowing how much more vulnerable she was than himself. Therefore he indulged her, shrugged off her complaints, felt at last for her a tenderness which had perhaps escaped him in earlier years.

Harrods yielded several desirable table settings, and two goose-down quilts, a scarlet kettle, and some Italian bedlinen for Marianne's new home. Rendered speechless by a day of unbridled consumerism, Christine sank down in yet another restaurant and drank several cups of tea.

'I know what we could do,' said Yvette, helping herself to toast ('I shouldn't really'). 'We could take a taxi to that nice little shop near the office, where that woman usually has a few things put by for me. It seems silly to go home now. And anyway I haven't got anything for tonight's meal. We'll just go down to the Food Hall, and then take a taxi across the park. We'll still be home in plenty of time. Do you want that last slice? And we might find something for you, Christine. Elizabeth has such excellent taste.'

Outside, in the beautiful air, the sun had faded to a milky mist, draining colour from the day. A whitening of the atmosphere brought a renewed coldness, a reminder that the year was still in its infancy. Groups of people at bus stops reminded them both of the wedding day, when they had emerged, after what seemed like a lifetime of sensations, into streets populated by ordinary people going about their ordinary affairs. They smiled involuntarily at each other, struck by the same reflection.

'Yes, I do miss her,' said Yvette. 'Always about this time of day.'

'She'll be home soon,' Christine reassured her. 'Look, there's a taxi.' For the look of blankness had come back into Yvette's eyes, indicating depths better left undisturbed. Or shallows. In any event, uncharted territory, too delicate to meddle with. Another distraction was the remedy. So that Yvette's life, restless and unexplored, remained the one best suited to her beginnings and to her subsequent evolution.

'Why, Mrs Hartmann,' said Elizabeth resignedly. 'All right, Julie, you can go home.' She turned to Yvette, her beautiful smile put back firmly in place. 'What can I do for you?'

'I haven't been in for some time, Elizabeth. I'm sure there's lots to see.'

And she slipped off her coat, her skirt and her boots and stood expectantly in the cubicle, apparently revived by the prospect of trying on clothes. By the end of half an hour she had discarded five expensive garments of varying appeal.

'No,' she said doubtfully. 'They're too fussy. Have you nothing Italian?'

A taupe-coloured coat and skirt, in a beautiful silky material, was produced. Elizabeth, not too inconspicuously, looked at her watch.

'Yes,' said Yvette thoughtfully. 'That is more my style. I'll think about it and let you know. Could you put it on one side for me?'

She bent down to pull on her boots. Christine saw, in

the mirror, the roll of flesh above the black satin half slip, the thickening yellowing back between the black satin straps. It was the view Hartmann got these evenings when he went into the bedroom, the view that Yvette never saw. She is getting old, thought Christine. And I am getting even older. But the fact did not seem to matter so much to her as it must do to Yvette.

'I look tired,' Yvette said with some surprise, scanning her face under the cruel lighting. Not tired, thought Christine: it is more serious than that. She had seen the legendary breasts, now less prominent than before: she had caught sight of the hunched shoulders as Yvette massaged her troublesome leg.

'Yes,' she said gently. 'We must be getting home.'

Pausing only to reapply her make-up, to take a tweed jacket from a hanger, and to say, 'Wrap that up for Mrs Fibich,' Yvette sailed to the door, where Elizabeth stood with her finger on the light switches. A dark blue spring night pressed against the plate glass windows. They were a little dazed, a little humbled by the rush of traffic. The taxi, when it came, was as welcome as a rescue ship in a stormy sea. Both were glad to sink back into the comfortable cigarette-smelling gloom. Both would be glad to get home. Yvette sighed longingly.

'Oh, Christine,' she said. 'Hasn't it been a lovely day.'

9

'Harrods,' murmured Christine in a broken voice. '*All over* Harrods. Every department. And she wasn't even all that tired at the end of it. At least, not as tired as I was. And I wasn't doing anything except watch her. Or accompany her. I was her lady-in-waiting.'

Fibich smiled. He was fond of his wife in this mood: flippant, independent, viable. He liked to share with her his absorption in the Hartmanns, both of whom he perceived as stronger, superior, not for any genuine reasons but because they had a fearlessness, even an obtuseness, that made them more successful at life's game. Indeed, the very fact that Hartmann thought of life as a game, and, moreover, a game that could be won, intrigued and at the same time incapacitated Fibich. By the same token, his wife, although a genuinely good woman, whose qualities he had known and relied upon since he was a boy without a home, was somehow less effective a presence than Yvette, whose massive complacency did a great deal to reassure him. When Yvette scolded him for not eating something oppressively complicated he felt an odd gratitude to her for acting in so commanding a fashion. Whereas Christine, hovering anxiously by his side while he took his first taste of a carefully bland concoction, put him in mind of a nurse, or a governess, appointed to supervise him, but not necessarily to give him pleasure. He knew that he could have married no one else. He knew that he loved her. Yet he also knew, in an unrealized way, that his true life lay elsewhere, that it remained undiscovered, that his task was to reclaim it, to repossess it, and that for as long as it remained hidden from him he would be a sleepwalker, doomed to pass through a life designed for him by others, with no place he recognized as home. Increasingly, what he felt was a kind of homesickness, although he could not have explained this.

In the meantime this would have to do, this hazy blue flat, always in half shadow, always encountered by him with a start of surprise. And this anxious, sometimes dolorous wife. And the extravagant son who had somehow been foisted on them and who was the main reason, he thought, for his wife's silence and withdrawal. They had not really discussed the son, whom they suspected of ignominy: each wanted to preserve, for a little longer, the peace of his absence, which would soon come to an end. Only one more term at Oxford, and then the question of his future would have to take a more definite, a more practical form. With a heavy heart Fibich realized that he could offer no guidance, or none that Toto would respect. And, to be honest, he felt in such need of a compass himself, so ardently desirous of an explanation, that practical suggestions died on his lips. There was also a curious reluctance to have the boy back in the flat, as if his sexual adventures were an insult to his parents, who should not be expected to collude with them, to witness them, to know about them. Their odd reticence, he saw, could do them no good in this respect. In the blind state in which he and Christine lived, there was a genuine fear of taking on the world's complications that could pass for innocence, but was in fact nothing but cowardice, lack of the right stuff. Both had been so deprived of childhood that in a sense they were both still waiting in the wings, unaware that, happy or unhappy, this stage must be passed, that all beginnings are to a certain extent situated in limbo, and are only an introduction to the definitive actions to which they are a prologue. What, in his view, incapacitated both Christine and himself and constituted their inalienable but unwelcome bond, was that they had been deprived of their childhood through the involuntary absence of adults, that his own parents and Christine's mother had vanished without a trace, spirited away by a turn of events that wholly excluded their offspring, without being known, and that they had been left in the charge of strangers who, though tolerably well disposed, were uninvolved, uninterested. They had grown up, therefore, without true instruction, without the saws and homilies, the customs and idiosyncrasies, that, for children, constitute a philosophy.

At least, that was true of his own case, which, once more, was beginning to worry him, to absorb him, to obtrude into the more reassuring aspects of everyday living. His dreams, since the incident with Toto, were also becoming more bizarre, more frightening. Recently, for example, he had had a dream about his dentist. (He was aware, from his discussions with the analyst, that his mouth was a focus of anxiety for him.) In his dream he had found the normally rather vain and meticulous Mr Gilmour seated with his feet up on his desk, reading the *Daily Mirror* and eating a coarse and overfilled sandwich. With shreds of ham and lettuce dribbling on to his obviously second-hand suit, Mr Gilmour, whose face now had a dusky and inflamed look, invited Fibich to take his place in the dentist's chair. He then opened the door of the surgery and invited a few of his friends in to watch the ensuing operation. Fibich himself was the helpless and gagged recipient of unwarranted attention, in a setting which had mysteriously become vast and shadowy, panoramic. On waking he recognized this setting as Courbet's *Atelier*, in which the painter, dead centre, is surrounded by a disparate crowd of poets, writers, gamekeepers, and crinolined society women, at the same time posturing and self-absorbed. Fibich, in Courbet's place, was not performing before an admiring crowd, as the painter was presumably doing, but was a victim on whom some dental indignity was about to be perpetrated. There was no help to be sought from the onlookers, most of whom had peevish abstracted expressions that boded no good. He had awoken from his dream in a state of panic and had gone into the bathroom to check if his teeth were still present or whether they had somehow been removed, without his knowledge, in the course of the night.

For these many reasons – the obstreperousness of his son, the sadness of his wife, and his own bad dreams – Fibich was glad of this respite, this account of a normal seeming day, this appropriate reaction of physical tiredness, caused by nothing more problematic than a walk round the shops in the reassuring company of Yvette. Christine, who was exaggerating the amusing nature of the enterprise in order to lift the heaviness from Fibich's face, was in fact watching him narrowly. Although her motives were entirely altruistic she despised herself. So, as a hapless girl, she had tried to divert her father and to draw to herself some of his mysteriously absent attention. In those days her efforts had met with no success. Mr Hardy had not been much of a father. Indeed he seemed to take a certain pride in his lack of interest in his only child, as if begetting her had been an act of munificence to which, out of sheer modesty, he wished no further reference to be made. His perception of the world had not extended much beyond his own needs, which were simple but unlimited. Christine's desire to captivate him was, as he saw it, misplaced. On many occasions he had sent her back, disconcerted, to her room, and settled down for a sleep. She had known her efforts to be inappropriate, unbecoming, yet she was still compelled to perform, to try to make life agreeable for those too nerveless to make life agreeable for themselves. Or for her.

She knew that something momentous had happened in her married life, and she knew that it had happened to Fibich and not to herself. What she thought of quite coldly as Toto's cruelty to Marianne would not be so easily objectified by Fibich. She envied Yvette Hartmann, whose child had flown the nest in entirely honourable circumstances. Toto could not decently be got rid of, yet she wished that he would go. She saw him clinging on to them, an incubus that would drain the remaining energy from them in later years. Sometimes, when she felt a little more optimistic – in the early morning, or when the sun unexpectedly shone – she would reason with herself, 'After all, he only kissed her.' Whether or not something more had taken place (and that she was never to find out) she also knew that Toto had inflicted some damage on Marianne, and that the damage was in the nature of an appropriation, or rather a misappropriation, the motive power behind which was sheer levity, speculation, curiosity, a sort of childish impulse to knock down another boy's sandcastle or to steal his ball. The girl, Christine knew, meant nothing to him. By the same token, she also knew that the slightly prudish Marianne, who moved much too slowly for her mother's liking, would inspire in a man like Toto exactly the blend of dislike, mockery and amusement to make his advances to her inevitable. And even if they were to let the matter rest – for Marianne, she knew, would effectively be silent on the matter, and Toto almost certainly would either genuinely forget it or decently, masculinely, bury it, that being his code in such matters – Christine knew that in some monstrous and mysterious way she had given birth to a man who hated women. And as she was the first woman he had ever known, she must in some way be responsible for this. The thought chilled her and made her a colder woman than she should have been.

She knew that, unlike herself, Fibich felt for the boy a palpitating, almost a maternal love. It struck her as a further anomaly that their roles should be reversed in this way, that it should be left to her to be objective and authoritarian, while he, the father, reserved the right to be anxious and helpless. She knew that the injury to Fibich would take some time to surface, bound up as it was with his sense of loss, already so overwhelming, that would be preparing its travail in his always overloaded dreams. This grotesque state of affairs, which saw her entertaining her husband in order that he should not brood ineffectually about his son, managed to reduce for her the small but genuine pleasure she had taken in having spent her day in the always reassuring company of Yvette, to whom no thought deeper than her own well-being ever seemed to occur. The knowledge that she had also, to a limited yet ascertainable extent, been responsible for keeping Yvette happy lay on her retrospectively like a weight. She dreamed, increasingly, of flight.

The following day, she thought, while allowing

Fibich for once to make the coffee, she must write to Toto, asking him about his plans for the future, for she saw there was to be no future for any of them until definite plans had been made for Toto. Once he was taken care of, theoretically by somebody or something else, she could persuade Fibich to travel more: with his native anxieties still rampant, Fibich was timorous about leaving home. They had been happy once and could be again, she reasoned. She was aware that she was not a good mother, or rather not good enough for the overwhelming creature that Toto had turned out to be, and that an onlooker might accuse her of trying too hard and too soon to loosen the knot that had once tied her to her son. This knowledge afflicted her with a deep sorrow, in comparison with which her other sorrows were mere indulgences.

There should, she thought, be a middle way, one which would allow her some interior freedom while still making room for maternal or wifely solicitude. For solicitude, she realized, was still to be her portion. Whether there was another mode she did not know, for her closest model, Yvette, seemed to her too airy a mother, a mother who too often knew best, leaving too unexamined the nature of her child's fate. Yet that airiness became her, and Marianne might even now have been provided for, largely through her mother's intervention, in the best possible manner. Myers, the accessorized husband, was steady if dull: no further shocks would be inflicted on that unprepared girl. Whereas, for Toto, she could foresee endless liaisons, mostly of an unsatisfactory nature, with fervent beginnings and unfinished endings, and all taking place in the flat from which, emotionally, she had begun to detach herself. The best thing would be for him to get a job (but even that now seemed unlikely: the *Comus* he had

133

produced at Oxford had inspired in him thoughts of a life in the theatre) and for him to find a flat somewhere, with Fibich's help, where they could keep an eye on him but not be brought into daily contact with his abrasive personality. She saw discussions about Toto's future stretching on into infinity, lasting for the rest of the life that she and Fibich might have left to them. At the same time she saw the sun or the fire of her imaginings. Somehow the two must be brought together, and it would be left to her, with an immense effort, to make this come about. Her genuine physical tiredness faded into insignificance in comparison with the great weight of obligation she felt settle on her shoulders.

The next day she sat down determinedly at her writing-desk. 'My dearest boy', she wrote, for he had been that once and in a corner of her mind, the corner in which everything worked out for the unhoped-for best, he still was. 'My dearest boy, you will soon have finished at Oxford, and Daddy and I were wondering if you had had further thoughts about your future. The theatre is such an overcrowded profession, as you must already know, and such an unsettled one. We wondered if it might not be a good idea for you to apply to the BBC? There is an excellent drama section there, for which you would be ideally suited. We should, of course, help you for as long as you needed time to find your feet, but you must be wanting to strike out on your own, particularly as by now you have got used to being away from home. Have you a friend at Oxford with the same ideas as yourself? Daddy and I would be delighted if the two of you were to decide to share a flat, and that could easily be arranged. We want to see you settled. Of course, that is what all parents want, and I know how irritating it must sound to you. But now is the time to make some decisions, or at least to think about making them. Life is so much easier when you have something interesting to do all day and a nice place to come home to in the evenings, a place where you could entertain your friends. Of course you can do that here, but Daddy and I like to live quietly, as you know, and we should hate to cramp your style. Will you promise to think about this and to let us know fairly soon what it is you want to do?

'You have been such a surprise to us, with talents we never dreamed of, and we long for you to have a happy life. Parents, alas, cannot always arrange this for their children. That is why we urge you to do something that will ensure you a proper place in the scheme of things, and not let those precious gifts be squandered.

'We are both well and think about you so much. Don't work too hard. I know that Finals will be a strain but at the same time I know that they are worth taking seriously. Write and tell us, dear, what you are thinking and feeling, and we shall do our best to help you on your way.'

Wondering how to finish this letter without being too insistent, her attention was attracted by a shadow moving rhythmically across the window: the edge of a ladder propped against the outer sill informed her of the monthly visit of Mr Crickmay, the window cleaner. Presently a round red face appeared in her field of vision. A hand waved: she waved back and made drinking motions with an imaginary cup, holding an imaginary saucer in her raised left hand. Mr Crickmay mimed delight, as he always did, and she got up thankfully to go to the kitchen and arrange cups and plates on a tray.

Mr Crickmay stood, a heraldic figure, with ladder in one hand and bucket in the other. He always declined to sit down, and would cautiously consign the ladder to a corner while he drank his cup of tea. She welcomed his visits: he was an elderly man with a weak chest and she thought perhaps that he should not be out in all weathers, his hands permanently in water. But he was self-employed and admirably independent. Since the death of his wife he had buckled to, taken cookery lessons at night school, and was now an apparently contented man, busy all day, as she had just enjoined Toto to be, although well past the age of retirement. He was a good window cleaner, and an uncomplaining one; no weather ever put him out. In addition, he had developed into something of a gourmet cook, and she liked to find out from him how he was looking after himself. Today, however, he seemed to move more heavily than usual, to make an uncharacteristically clumsy movement with the ladder, which would have fallen had he not caught it.

'I have sad news for you, Madam,' he said, refusing a biscuit, but taking a long draught of his tea. 'My little dog passed away.'

'Oh, Mr Crickmay,' said Christine. 'I am so sorry.'

'Yes, poor Gyp is no more. Old age, you see. He just seemed to know his time had come. I bought him some nice steak, and braised it, so it wouldn't hurt his mouth, but he turned away from it. I tried to put some in his mouth, but he just let it drop. Then I took him up to the Common, to give him a bit of air, but he wouldn't move. In the end we had to go to the vet. Miss Bannister, a very nice lady. She gave him an injection. I held him until he passed over.'

In his small very blue eyes two tears formed with difficulty. He brought out a large red and white handkerchief and unselfconsciously wiped them away.

'I am so sorry, Mr Crickmay,' said Christine, genuinely distressed. 'I know he was company for you.'

136

'Well, that's it, Madam. The company. I used to have him in the van with me all day. And when we got home I'd get his lead and he'd be waiting for me at the door to take him up on the Common. Well, naturally, I miss him.'

'Will you get another dog, do you think?' asked Christine, passing him another cup of tea.

'Oh no, I couldn't have another after Gyp. What I thought I'd do is to take up a hobby. My friend suggested fishing.'

'Your friend from Brighton?' For he went off at weekends to stay with a family: he had been in the Navy with the husband, and had kept in close touch since the end of the war.

'Yes. He said he'd take me fishing to see how I liked it. Of course,' he said sadly, 'my time's my own now.'

'I hope we're not going to lose you, Mr Crickmay.'

'Oh, no, Madam. Work keeps me going. And I've got my little flat. No, it'll be weekends. That way I won't grieve too much.'

'I made those chicken wings in lemon sauce that you told me about,' said Christine. 'My husband thought they were delicious.'

He brightened. 'And they come up nice on a bed of rice,' he said. 'Did you serve them with rice?'

'I did,' Christine affirmed. 'They were a great success.'

'Sometimes I grate a little lemon into the rice,' he went on. 'Quite exotic. Well, Madam, I mustn't waste your time. I've got Mrs Humphries still to do.'

'Don't despair, Mr Crickmay,' said Christine, a hand on his arm.

He grinned bravely. 'Never! There's so much going on, isn't there? And so many people worse off. I always keep my fingers crossed for another bit of luck like Gyp.

I keep them crossed for you too, Madam. If you don't mind my saying so.'

She was absurdly touched. He stood there, a bulky elderly man in blue dungarees and an old green cardigan. Valiant, a war hero; standing waist-deep in icy waters, pulling his mate to safety. Honest and simple, as people no longer seemed to be. And thus fatally removed from her own complicated projections.

But he moved unsteadily to the door and she feared for him on the ladder.

'Not too tired, Mr Crickmay?'

'No, no, Madam. Mrs Humphries is my last.'

'What will you eat tonight?' she asked.

'I thought lamb cutlets *forestière*,' he said. 'With rice, instead of potatoes. Got to watch my weight.' He patted his expansive stomach.

'What a good idea. I might do those myself.'

They discussed ways of bringing these to perfection, until finally he stood outside the door.

'Never give up, Mr Crickmay.'

'Never, Madam. That's what I say to myself every morning. You never know what's round the corner. Nice seeing you, as always, Madam. And that was a lovely cup of tea.'

They shook hands, as they always did, and then Christine was alone again.

The brilliance of the windows faded as the late darkening sky of spring turned the room steadily into dusk. Christine moved nervously back into the drawing-room, striking her hands together as she compared Mr Crickmay's honest unmediated sadness with her own. We don't get out enough, she thought. We should see more people. In the early days of their married life they had been very convivial, spending many evenings together, at the opera, the ballet, concerts on Sunday afternoons, little late supper parties. When the children had come along these activities had fallen into abeyance and had never been renewed. She supposed that given a little energy she might start them up again, but she thought not. These days they seemed to be confined to their homes, half hoping that the children might come back, half glad of the respite of their absence, modest now, retiring, a little timorous despite themselves, glad of the excuse to watch television and not go out into the dark night, glad of the comforts of their bedrooms and the solace of early sleep. This will not do, thought Christine: we are not old yet. We are too comfortable, that is the trouble: we have settled down, given up. Thinking of the many inducements to giving up that she might find in her own life, she felt a moment of repugnance for this slothfulness, as if an endless old age were being prepared, and she herself, unresisting, were being rendered old in order to accommodate her husband. I shall give a dinner party, she thought. I shall give a party for Marianne and her husband. That friend of hers, Belinda, can come. And that poor young man from Fibich's office. For she felt discomfort, and always had, at the thought of Goodman, with his radiant pleading eyes, so incongruously framed in dense black lashes, the eyes of a houri, overshadowing an otherwise nondescript face permanently set in lines of propitiation. What damage had been done to Goodman Christine had no way of knowing, yet there was no mistaking its trace. Perhaps that was the quality that embarrassed Fibich. There was no doubting Goodman's efficiency and loyalty: he was an excellent company secretary. It was simply that one could never praise him sufficiently to relieve his anxiety. That anxiety was present in his ardour to please, an ardour always in excess of his actual duties, which he

139

performed with ease. An atmosphere of effort surrounded him: he imparted a sense of strain. He seemed early to have vowed himself to nothing less than supreme excellence, in the teeth of who knew what private misgivings. He lived with his mother, to whom he was devoted. Christine doubted that he would ever marry. And the circumstances of life with mother had affected his social skills: he praised and thanked continuously. Nevertheless, she thought, he will be asked. And that friend of Marianne's, who keeps getting engaged and unengaged all the time – for Belinda, surprisingly, was still on the loose – might perhaps be persuaded to take him in hand.

Despite the early darkness she thought she would go out and post her letter before Fibich got home. Once outside the enclosed warmth of the flat the chilly evening surprised her. The coldness of the hour settled on her skin like a coating of mercury. But when she was out of the flat she was reluctant to go back in again, and she wandered down to the Cathedral, whose hybrid red and white striped mass reared up ahead of her as she crossed the broad pavement that preceded it. From the café on her right, presumably sited there for the relief of pilgrims, came an obscene smell of stale cooking; inside the large glass windows she could see hunched humbled figures drinking from plastic cups. Indignation welled up in her: why were they allowed nothing better? Her indignation continued once she was inside the building, which was strangely warm, although designed in conformity with the age of iron: bulky, lofty, ugly, commodious, authoritative. She passed the silver-faced effigy of St John Southworth, whose body beneath its covering was only dust, and lit a candle, as she always did, out of superstition rather than piety. She darted awkwardly in front of the few worshippers, rather as if she were a latecomer at the theatre, unwilling to spoil the performance for others; that awkwardness distinguished her from the faithful – the young man in the anorak, the pretty girl who looked as if she might have nothing to do with the place, the capacious woman who might have dropped in between two committee meetings – and made her feel her isolation. She envied these people, yet at the same time did not fancy paying her dues to the obscure saints in the calendar who might be thought to favour particular causes. And unlike the faithful she could not even pray for special intentions, more specific pleas, but must suppress her needs, silence the interior clamour, live outside the myth of protection. She found no difficulty in repudiating the notion of a loving father: she suspected that, for her, the deity might be an enlarged and majestic version of Mr Hardy, and the idea brought an instinctive shudder. Better on the whole to bear one's own burdens, soldier on without help. Not a trace was left, she realized, of her initial trustingness, her hopes. She thought of the evil smelling café with another burst of indignation. Jesus would have cast out those caterers, she thought, yet exploiters proliferate endlessly. And people are grateful, that is the worst of it. They are made to feel grateful, and the process reduces them.

She turned to go, drifted down an aisle, wrestled with the reluctant swing door. The warmth inside and the cold outside struck her as symbolic; now she could not wait to get home. A young woman, encumbered by a push-chair, was on the other side of the door, and thanked Christine for holding it open for her. Christine looked at the child in the chair, and instinctively turned away. The huge head, the features as if flattened by a clumsy thumb . . . She hoped that God would be there for the mother. She wished that she had added more endearments to the letter to her son. She went back into the church, bought a postcard, forced herself to go into the café, and, ignoring the cup of coffee she had bought, wrote on the card, 'Dearest boy, when are you coming home? We send you all our love.'

10

Quite suddenly, it seemed overnight, the false spring was eclipsed by returning cold: early frosts and a chill mist descended at the end of the afternoon. People searched in vain for the sun, now mysteriously occluded or reduced to a whitish blur in the white sky. In this bleached light the purples and yellows of the early crocuses looked garish, unconvincing, almost tactless. Pink blossom, frostbitten, darkened on the trees.

In the dismay that was his immediate reaction to this apparent reversal of the seasons Fibich felt doubly threatened. His inability to banish his now habitual feeling of alarm decided him in secret to go back to the analyst whom he had tried vainly to reach by telephone. An answering machine informed him that Mrs Gebhardt was away and would not return for three weeks. It was too long: he did not think he could wait. He tried, on successive days, to telephone again, to see whether Mrs Gebhardt might not have returned unexpectedly, but he was always answered by the implacable machine. Finally, he gave up in disgust, and threw himself back in his chair as if he had caught himself out in an indignified stratagem, something furtive and disgraceful, an old bad habit or addiction which had never particularly benefited him in the first place. He liked Mrs Gebhardt but was uneasily conscious of the force of her will; she seemed to have more to gain from his hangdog appearances than he did. He was not, he would have reasoned, there to provide her with professional satisfactions of an inordinate nature, as if, each time, she had briefly wrestled with him and brought him down. He was there, he would have said, to reach enlightenment. Mrs Gebhardt dismissed this as a fantasy. *She* was there, she said, to conduct him into the heart of darkness; only there, she told him, would he find what he was looking for. But something in him had always rebelled at the idea of pursuing this objective under her benign yet rigorous supervision. The discovering should be spontaneous, he thought, dreamlike, a deliverance almost mythical in its sudden completeness, an apocalypse, or an epiphany. Without this mythic sanction the discovery, if there was a discovery to be made, would be hard, bitter. And he wanted it to be instantaneous, a blinding light, so that he could get it over, put it behind him, instead of feeling it dogging his footsteps, clouding his waking hours, accompanying him every minute of the day. He dreamed of a light-filled future, in which the past would receive an absolution, leaving him free to live out the rest of his life in peace and harmony.

In the meantime he consulted Hartmann. Hartmann was euphoric, dismissive.

'Leave it alone,' he said. 'You have a wife, a son, a decent home, enough money. What more do you want at your age? A second childhood? That will come in good time, believe me. Anyway, what can this man do for you?'

'My analyst is a woman,' explained Fibich.

Hartmann cocked his head. 'A woman, eh? Attractive?'

144

'No, no.' It was Fibich's turn to be dismissive. 'Middle-aged, grey hair. Surprisingly untidy.'

Hartmann looked disappointed. 'And what does this woman do for you?'

'She listens,' said Fibich, feeling faint at the prospect of describing to Hartmann those wordless afternoons when he failed to find anything for her to listen to. 'She wants me to tell her about my childhood.'

'Tell her to mind her own business,' said Hartmann. 'You went through it once, why go through it again?'

'But that isn't the problem. The problem is that I can't remember it. Oh, I remember coming to London all right. Compayne Gardens, Aunt: I remember all that. But everything that went before is a total blank. Literally a blank. Sometimes I think that I ought to go back there, try to find the street, the house. That way I might know that I had a beginning.'

Hartmann looked grave. 'Back to Berlin? Are you mad?'

'I feel', said Fibich with difficulty, 'like a survivor. As if I arrived where I am by accident. After a shipwreck, or some sort of disaster that blacked out my memory. As if I will never catch up until I find out what went before.'

Hartmann sighed. 'You are not a survivor. You are a latecomer, like me. Like Yvette, for that matter. You had a bad start. Why go back to the beginning? One thing is certain: you can't start again.'

'Do you never look back?' asked Fibich.

'Not if I can help it,' said Hartmann. 'I remember Munich, oddly enough. That is, I remember it in flashes. It looks beautiful to me, a beautiful city. But I have never been back, and I will never go back.'

Fibich smiled. 'What is your secret?' he asked.

'The present is my secret. Living in the present. My

daughter. And, please God, the children she will have. And our success. Does that mean nothing to you? Isn't that a battle we won, however late we came?'

But Fibich was unsmiling again, remembering Marianne, whom his son might have damaged, and seeing Hartmann's still undimmed pleasure in her.

'I sometimes think it has all been a dream,' he said presently. 'That it has all happened to somebody else. And I have no understanding of the person – not myself – to whom it has all happened.'

'Ah, but that may be the way of things,' said Hartmann. 'We change so much from what we once were. To me time is a wonder. I love it. Time has brought me this good life, the food I eat, the family I enjoy. And if I got here by an unorthodox route I rejoice all the more that I got here at all. That I *am* here. Believe me, that is all there is.'

Fibich saw, from Hartmann's expression, that it would be pointless to go on. Pointless and unkind. For he also saw that Hartmann did in fact retain something of the past, his past. Somewhere in Hartmann's past had been the unthinking confidence of the loved child, the robustness, the carefreeness. Those qualities, which had survived, had been there at the very beginning. And with the true gift of the mentally secure he was unaware of them, their roots, their origin. Hartmann was a latecomer only in the sense that he was enjoying his latter age more than most people are supposed to enjoy their youth. Hartmann felt the relief of being no longer the boy at school, the soldier in rough khaki. He had triumphantly turned the tables on his miserable boyhood by becoming a mature and satisfied man in late middle age, and by enjoying the comforts of that age, not by bemoaning his lost years, but by discovering the voluptuous pleasure that each shortening day might bring. Look! We have come through! To spoil that pleasure would be indecent, unthinkable. To reconnect Hartmann with his losses would be an act of treachery, and of cowardice. Whereas for himself those losses had coloured his entire life, like ink dropped in water. For him it was all different: a hunger for absent knowledge, a longing, a yearning, not for those losses to be made good – that, he knew, could not come about – but to be assuaged by fact, by circumstantial detail, by a history, a geography. He longed to know what his life had been before he could remember it. He longed to walk a foreign street and be recognized. He imagined it, the start of wonder on an elderly person's face. Is it you, Fibich's boy? You used to play with my children. That was what he longed for. That, and the suddenly re-stored familiarity of the foreign street, that café, that theatre, that park. And surely a new sun would burst in the sky at that moment, restoring spring, summer, restoring the strength to his body and sleep to his nights. Then might he sleep as Toto slept, carelessly, no longer on guard. Then might he too feel triumph, bring back the smile to Christine's face, and live the rest of his life in peace.

And love might be released at last, not pity, not hunger, but the love on which one looks with calm smiling gratitude. And the ability to be absorbed in lives other than his own, which, he was sure, would come with the deliverance that he craved, had always craved, and was no nearer possessing now than he had been as a young man. Indeed, he seemed to be moving farther and farther away from it, and he feared that unless he took some direct action it would soon be out of reach for ever. At the same time he knew himself to be a coward, puny, feeble, one to whom action of any kind is anathema. He told himself that the testing time had come, and that if he took no action at all he would perish. In this uneasy state he lived out the last days of his old life, knowing that he must do something, yet drawing back fearfully from the very possibility of initiating a change.

So great, so overwhelming did the decision he had not yet made but would soon have to make become that it crowded out thoughts of his son, whose path in life he should be contemplating. It may even have been the aura of difficulty which surrounded thoughts of Toto that forced his mind away from the future and back to that dark or misty past which he felt to be so compelling. He found himself trying to remember or to conjure up a landscape, an interior, which were always out of reach and coming no nearer despite the intensity of his efforts. All he could see was the small fat boy in the chair, the Voltaire, but that was literally all: even the walls of the room were absent. And what he craved was an edge of wallpaper, a plant in a pot, a footstool, to furnish the room in which he must have sat, and still they eluded him, as they always had. And he saw no practical way of finding that room, of discovering its position in a house, of situating the house in a street.

Fearfully his mind explored the possibility of returning to that city which he had not seen for fifty years, and which had somehow, in his mind, been irradiated out of existence. On the surface, in the areas of reason and practicality, there was nothing to prevent him from buying a ticket, getting on a plane, and wandering, like any other tourist, around that city, just to see if anything were restored to him. His heart beat faster at the very thought of such an expedition: the rising hairs on the back of his neck told him that he was entering dangerous territory. And if nothing were restored to him? Could he retrieve anything from a city every atom of whose history and geography had been violently changed, and of which his only relic was the memory of a chair? He had been bundled off so quickly, in circumstances of such terror, that there had been no time to collect photographs or souvenirs, and the details of his address had been obliterated by the awfulness of his leavetaking: his mother, embracing him for the last time, had turned away and fainted into her husband's arms. As the train began to move off into the dark night, all that he could see was the turning and sinking motion of his mother, her face white, her eyes closed, falling lifeless into his father's arms. Vainly he had searched, through the open windows of the night express, for signs of her return to life, to her normal position; he wanted to see her eyes smiling at him once again, and his father waving reassuringly. But they had been attached to each other as a mourning group, with no thought for him, or so it seemed, and all that he had to comfort him was a packet of boiled sweets in his coat pocket, in case he felt sick on the boat, and the address of a school where a place had been found for him. A silent elderly woman had been asked to take care of him on the journey. At Dover he had been met by the representative of a refugee organization which specialized in the transfer of children, out of danger, into England. He had been escorted to the school and there had met Hartmann.

The task of confronting this nightmare again, in comparison with which his present nightmares were of no account, sickened and wearied him, until he empathized all too physically with his fainting mother. But beyond that image, or before it, there must be something more stable, less tragic, and that was what he desired so ardently to see restored. He was a grown man now, he reasoned with himself, not a frightened child, yet in everything pertaining to his past he was pre-rational. He possessed inexhaustible reserves of terror, or rather of horror, which could be, and were, activated in defiance of his conscious will. He felt uneasy to this day on station platforms: before any journey he had to wrestle with himself, even if the end in sight were pleasure or diversion. This was one of the reasons why Hartmann was so precious to him. With Hartmann nothing could go wrong. Hartmann was his guarantee of a safe passage. That enquiring yet ineffable smile, that excellence of presentation, seemed to assume that attention would be paid, service be forthcoming; it rearranged the boundaries of exchange, so that momentarily Fibich would feel like the substantial business man that he in reality was and was taken to be, able to command, to dismiss, to choose. And if any arrangement were not to his liking he could decline it, demand better. All this was an illusion, of course, but an illusion which had served him well in certain critical moments. 'This is not to my taste,' he would say to himself, as if he were practising a foreign language. 'Something better must be arranged. Something more to my liking.' Yet, while exercising himself in this manner, he continued to accumulate fetishes, to obey obscure superstitions, the meanings of which were known only to himself. His ravening appetite returning, he gorged himself on sugar. But he could not bear to have boiled sweets in the house.

At home he was preoccupied. Christine saw, with pity and despair, a re-enactment of that absent ardent haunted adolescence which had first commanded her love and her attention. When she tried to talk to him about Toto he would answer as if a huge distance separated them. 'Yes, yes, of course,' he would say. 'The BBC. Excellent.' What he meant was, Please see to it. You must have noticed that I am temporarily incapacitated. Please be the stronger of the two of us, and take me with you. His hands trembled as he cut up his food, yet he ate voraciously, as if storing up strength for the ordeal ahead. Yet nothing was ordained, laid down as ineluctable. He could still not go, stay quietly in his warm drawing-room until this madness passed. For he thought it was a form of madness and he wished to be sane again. And sanity could only be restored if the madness were put to flight.

He dreamed a strange dream at that time, strange because it was ironic and seemed cynically irrelevant. He dreamed that he was looking down on his dead or unconscious body from some vantage point in the middle of a small crowd that had gathered to witness the event. 'His faith kept him going,' said the man immediately adjacent to him. 'Either that or he was a very good actor.' This was so consummately inappropriate that he laughed when he remembered it the following day, although it continued to trouble him disproportionately. Seeing him pass from deep thought to this intermittent laughter Christine asked him what was wrong.

'Has anything happened at the office?' she asked.

'No, no. As long as Hartmann is there nothing will ever happen that you don't already know about.'

This reply gave Christine pause. She had never known him to express or even to feel the slightest envy of Hartmann's easy-going and dictatorial ways.

'Surely you don't resent him?' she asked. 'I thought you worked so well together.'

'Resent him?' said Fibich, appalled. 'He is my dearest friend. Why should I resent him? Because he is different from me? Because he finds life easier? But, don't you see, I love him for those very reasons. He saved my life, not once, but many times. If it weren't for him I shouldn't be here. *We* shouldn't be here. We shouldn't have met if it hadn't been for Hartmann's aunt. How could I resent him? I love him.'

Yet her question had been a fatal one. Fibich was forced to examine his tender conscience, his labouring memory, to find out whether he felt that Hartmann had in fact taken over the direction of his life, had always done so. He found no evidence of this, but the exercise bothered him deeply, driving the matter of his possible return to Berlin temporarily from his mind. Deeply troubled by this, and by the image of his dead self that he had seen in the dream, he began to retreat from his wife, whom he perceived as the agent of this new pain. Some higher consciousness told him that this recent difficulty could be overcome, that he did in truth love Hartmann, that his wife had been uncharacteristically tactless rather than ill-intentioned. Nevertheless he began to crave solitude and to avoid Christine's company. Until I get over this, he promised himself. Christine looked at him sorrowfully but forebore to intervene. Until he gets over this, she thought.

One Sunday, when an iron cold and stillness had settled over London, when the false early spring was less than a distant memory, Fibich took his hat, told Christine he would be back in an hour or two, and went out for a solitary walk. He was profoundly uneasy. He walked round a deserted Victoria, the cold white mist blurring the tiny milky disk of the sun. The exercise of reviewing his life was proving monstrous in so far as it revealed the places in which it had gone irredeemably wrong. He felt alienation from his son, from his wife whom he would like to think of as his mother, without sexual overtones. He walked unseeingly round the wide pavement of Westminster Cathedral, although his lack of faith was so extreme that he could not, unlike his wife, go inside the building. He walked into Buckingham Palace Road, where listless snack bars were open for business, where Indian-owned supermarkets displayed the cruel greens and oranges of winter fruit. A tourist bus disgorged a party of bleak but stoical Scandinavians outside the Queen's Gallery. In anguish he turned towards Belgravia, walked up Elizabeth Street, turned into Chester Square. All was deserted, as deserted as he felt himself to be. The thought of retracing his steps was intolerable to him, yet he was shivering and longed for hot coffee. In an effort to prolong his absence he turned into a workmen's café, inexplicable in this area, although it was near the bus station, inexplicably open, two men in donkey jackets sitting silently at the only occupied table, steam covering the windows, condensing into trickles. His hands round a mug of tea, Fibich felt sorrowfully that he was returned to his days of poverty. He stumbled to his feet, instinctively raised his hat to the company, and plunged through the door into the street. Cold mist was thickening into grey fog. The milky sun had turned blood red, the red of an apocalypse. Darkness seemed to envelop him in the short distance between Elizabeth Street and Ashley Gardens. When he entered the flat the dull heat went to his head, making him dizzy. His vision seemed to blur into the pink and blue haze of Christine's drawing-room. In this room, which seemed to him, on first entering it, deserted, he finally discerned the upright figure of his wife.

'Fibich,' said Christine gently. 'Won't you sit down and get warm? I have made you a honey cake. Your favourite.'

'Thank you, thank you,' he said. 'But I had a cup of tea out.'

If she was disappointed she was practised enough not to show it.

'Yvette telephoned,' she said. 'She would like us to go up for dinner tonight.'

In fact it was she who had telephoned Yvette, as she always did when Fibich was troubled. It was Yvette's contention that they both worried too much. 'Life is too short,' she would say, although to her life was immeasurably and enjoyably long.

'Just a light meal,' said Christine. 'Some leek and potato soup and a spinach and mushroom roulade. And a pear in wine. Nothing to upset you.'

'Thank you, thank you,' he said, again distractedly. 'I should like that.'

Then he subsided into silence. Christine, watching him over the edge of the Sunday paper, said nothing.

With Toto absent they spent too many weekends in this manner. Their evenings were easier: Fibich would return from the office, the usual enquiries about the day would be made, dinner would be eaten, and after dinner they would either watch television or read. Their silence on these occasions was companionable, although there was resignation in it for both of them. Each, too late, wanted some other quality in the partner. For Christine this dull alliance stimulated thoughts of flight, to that place in the sun which she was sure she would find if only she were free to seek it, if she were not retained, in this semi-curatorial capacity, by a husband who had yet to effect his emancipation from the curious thraldom in which she had first found him. For Fibich, the companion of his life, without whom life itself would be intolerable, was nevertheless a burden. He knew he had not made her happy. He blamed himself entirely for this incapacity of his, his need to proceed with caution, his desire to sink back into himself, his fearfulness. These qualities, he knew, were not the qualities for which a woman looked in a husband. And yet, on those quiet Sunday afternoons, in the dim hazy light of Christine's drawing-room, he could not resist the temptation to sink back into his reverie, the eternal reverie that was the very climate of his mind and from which he could no more detach himself than he could from the colour of his eyes or the texture of his skin. And Christine, on these occasions, had to learn to be silent, to proffer a wordless cup of tea, even to move noiselessly about the room, as if she were merely a personage in one of Fibich's dreams.

With Toto there the problem was different but equally complex. The problem was not only how to accommodate him but to hide from him the fact that the lives of his parents were enacted against a background that was essentially tragic. Toto turned them into conspirators in their effort to behave like ordinary people, but even here their collusion was painful, for they knew that in Toto's eyes they had failed to be the parents he wanted. They were either too old or too joyless or too easily shocked to please him: whatever their faults, they knew that he found them reprehensible. Fibich's hysterical fears for his son's well-being, and Christine's abstraction and restraint, were, they knew, not good for a young man who had rapidly become more emancipated than either of them. They felt that they could only be themselves when he was not there, and the thought was distressing to them both, for they remembered the joy of his birth, so easy, so pleasurable, and their pride in his robustness, his great beauty. He had overwhelmed them with gratitude merely by being viable, when they themselves had proved hesitant, latent. Nevertheless, he had grown up restless, disruptive, and thus their very opposite. Sometimes they felt that his brutality would explode the fallacy that their marriage had become. They saw in him no evidence of tolerance, and were too proud to ask of him understanding.

The Hartmanns were their best resource in these moments of doubt, indeed their only resource. The Hartmanns absorbed anxiety by not noticing it: they accepted that Christine and Fibich were 'nervy', as Yvette put it, without being unrealistic enough to try to change them. Yvette, in particular, liked the opportunity to scold and advise them, and they in their turn found it easy to sink passively beneath the weight of her benign reproaches. Indeed, they were grateful to her for assuming, as she always did, that they were making a fuss over nothing. Being entirely incurious, she was not conscious of undercurrents; on the other hand, she always had the grace to be kind. Christine and Fibich found her wholesome. Her self-generating activities, her bustle, even her egotism were reassuring to them; her very opacity seemed to promise them safety. Hartmann, becoming more of a dilettante with the passing years, found her exquisitely amusing and had come to value her profoundly. Who else, apart from Fibich, would pay such serious attention to the home that he had created out of nothing, out of thin air? Who else could have made it so real to him? And who else would so love his friends, making a home for them as well as for himself?

This evening found him sitting in front of an outsize television, watching the conclusion of an American hospital drama. He held up a hand to impose silence.

'One moment, my dears. The operation is about to be a success.'

They sat politely, as the young and handsome American surgeon reassured the parents of the girl whose life had recently hung in the balance. The episode ended with soaring celestial music. Hartmann wiped his eyes and blew his nose loudly.

'I don't know why I'm crying,' he said. 'There is an operation every week, and they are always successful. America! Such optimism! So. How are we?'

Fibich smiled. 'Thank you. Ask Christine. I'm afraid I haven't been very good company for her today.'

'She didn't marry you for your sense of fun,' said Hartmann, getting up and giving Christine a kiss. 'Any more than I married Yvette for her mind.' He knew that Yvette would take this as a compliment. Her faith in her appearance was still intact, and indeed time had if anything improved her, making her both more substantial and more elegant. Defiantly blonde and more than a little overweight, she nevertheless presented an appealing picture of a woman who repaid the infinite consideration she invested in herself.

'There's nothing wrong with my mind,' she said. 'At least I exercise it instead of watching that rubbish.' She indicated a copy of *Madame Bovary* on a side table. 'You should come to my class with me, Christine. It's really very satisfying. We're doing Flaubert,' she said proudly. 'And I think a woman owes it to herself to get out of the house and have an interest.'

'Speaking of interests,' said Hartmann. 'I am extremely interested in getting my grey suit back from the cleaners. Did you, by any chance, find an opportunity to pick it up?'

Yvette gave him a look in which superiority mingled with forbearance.

'All in good time,' she said. 'After all, I can't be expected to do everything.'

Hartmann shrugged and ventured an imperceptible wink in Fibich's direction. Thus had he behaved when

Yvette was queen of the office in the Farringdon Road. Fibich nodded gratefully, his immediate problem put to flight. *Fingerspitzengefühl*: Hartmann still had it, he reflected.

They passed a pleasantly inconsequential evening, like so many they had passed before. Praises rang loudly enough to satisfy Yvette that her immaculate cooking had once again passed the test. Fibich even drank coffee: as he took his cup Christine smiled and mimed permission. Night enfolded them, in the warm room. How could I leave them, thought Fibich. What would become of them if I were not to return, if something were to happen to me? Hartmann takes no interest in the business these days, and if I am not there, where will the money come from? Money for Toto, for Christine, for Yvette, even for Marianne and Roger? No, no, it is not to be thought of.

The decision brought relief, and increased gratitude. When the moment for leavetaking arrived he kissed Yvette, pinched Hartmann's cheek, as he occasionally did in moments of exceptional effervescence, and taking his wife's hand in his, led her home to bed.

———————   11   ———————

Hartmann sighed. A discomfort which he could neither locate nor analyse had kept him inactive for the first hours of the working day and seemed set fair to paralyse him for some hours to come. 'Go, go,' Fibich had said to him. 'You are no good here. Go out. Buy something. Eat lunch. I'll telephone you later, and we'll talk then.' So Hartmann had walked out of the office into chill spring sunshine, and wondered what to do with himself, knowing only that he could not have tolerated the mild routines of Spanish Place, could not, above all, have tolerated the presence of his son-in-law, Roger Myers.

His uncharacteristic and thus to him awful downheartedness had deprived him of initiative. This had not happened to him in living memory and depressed him even further. He treated himself carefully, as if he might be seriously ill. For a long time he sat in a patisserie in Marylebone High Street, at a small table with a false marble top, his coat hung on the coat-stand by the door, his hat on a chair beside him. Carefully, tenderly, he drank his coffee, as if it might contain life-giving properties. He tried to observe the patrons of the establishment – dentists, he supposed, rich widows from St John's Wood – but the fact of being temporarily without resource made him feel timorous, as if he were guilty of some major defection. The disruption of the day's activities was to him a momentous act, to be dealt with cautiously, whereas in truth nothing had occurred that would change his own life, which, tomorrow, after this interval ('sick leave', he thought) would go on its way undisturbed. He was well, Yvette was well, and Fibich had been diverted from his plan to go to Berlin. What was more, he, Hartmann, was now a grandfather, surely an occasion for rejoicing. Mouse-like Henry Myers, sleeping in his carry-cot, had already been presented at his grandparents' flat on three occasions, and on all of them he had slept obediently, too obediently, throughout the afternoon. Hartmann, who would have welcomed a show of vivacity, of charm, on the part of the infant, had, when no one was looking, extended a cautious finger to the sleeping baby's cheek and had been rewarded by nothing more than a slow and experimental flexing of the tiny star-shaped hands. Hartmann had longed to hold the child, to dance him up and down, to put a drop of champagne on his tongue, to accustom him to the conviviality of the tea-table, the smell of a fine cigar. Whereas he had been all tenderness when Marianne was a baby, age and impatience now made him long for the responses of an active child: he wished to enjoy him before it was too late, for sometimes, these days, he felt a trifle old. But Yvette had drawn him away from the carry-cot, which Roger had soon taken into Marianne's old bedroom. Hartmann had hated him, hated the important way he had ushered Marianne in front of him, hated the idea of Roger watching Marianne feeding the baby, hated his production manager's air of competence. Hartmann and Yvette had instinctively raised an eyebrow at each other when

160

contemplating this low scenario. And later, when the child was left to sleep in the bedroom, and Hartmann had stolen back for another look, he had noticed a smell of sicked-up milk on the air, and, bending over the carry-cot and peering into its depths, he had detected, on Henry's unprotected head, the unmistakable fuzz of Roger's sandy hair.

He was a pale inert baby, with none of the beauty that Marianne had shown from her earliest weeks. He lay in his mother's arms with the tip of his tongue protruding from his mouth: his eyes were a lashless navy blue, and his cheeks a chilly white. In vain they tried to see in him traces of his mother, but it was clear from his birth that he was his father's child. He would, in due course, grow up to be tall, colourless, and thick-limbed, like Roger, and whereas Roger had, briefly, been considered to be suitable, or perhaps appropriate, as a husband, they were not at all sure that they were prepared to accept him as a father. He was not one of them: that was becoming very clear. For although his quietness, his reticence, his obedience, his all too blameless decency, had previously recommended themselves, those qual- ities had now taken on a more positive emphasis. Roger, now, was uxorious to the point of suffocation. His possession of Marianne translated itself into labor- ious care for her, for her habits, her clothes, her movements. An altogether defensible pride in her motherhood made him hover over her when she was changing or feeding her child in a way that made Hartmann feel positively ill. He could remember none of this tactlessness when Marianne was a baby: Yvette would never have dreamed of involving him as a witness to procedures which they both felt should be accomplished in private, with modesty, and without trace. There had never been around Marianne that

161

aroma of soiled garments: the child had always been as fresh as a flower, while Yvette herself had been anxious to put the whole business of pregnancy and lactation as far behind her as possible, and had consequently regained both her figure and her autonomy in record time. Her deportment throughout those first few weeks of Marianne's babyhood had been excellent. But now Marianne, under the intrusive guardianship of her husband, seemed content to sit back, overweight and wordless, aggressively full of milk, or so it seemed to Hartmann. He felt, for the first time in his life, uncomfortable in her presence.

He had never particularly liked Roger but was wise enough to know that nobody would have met with his approval. It was quite simply that no one would have been good enough. He knew that. And knowing that he had thought that the soft-voiced, soft-footed Roger would be as good as any other man: he would take care of Marianne, would never be unfaithful, would be patient and scrupulous and kind; he would look after Yvette if anything happened to Hartmann, discharge the firm's responsibilities, remain loyal to Fibich . . . He was even good-looking in a well-built, broad-shouldered way.

So what was wrong with him? He was too quiet, for one thing, too slow, too immoveable. Hartmann, after half an hour in his company, would find himself seething with restlessness. He longed to madden Roger with an uncensored response or even a graceful unconsidered movement: he longed to displace those heavy careful limbs which had about them a terrible solidity; he longed to bring a flare of anger to the nostrils, a flush of red to the cheek. Hartmann loved impetuosity in a man, an ability to amuse, a capacity for entertainment, both given and received, a festiveness, and although initially he would have felt sorrow, even jealousy, to see Marianne in the thrall of such a man, he would have got over these shameful but inevitable (and fortunately fleeting) emotions, if only he could have looked forward to enjoying his son-in-law's company. But it seemed as though this were not on the cards. In the office they got on as well as they had always got on: well, but distantly. In the course of his duties Myers had more to do with Fibich than with Hartmann. But at home, or rather in Hartmann's home, there was something proprietorial about him that irritated Hartmann. It was not that he begrudged Roger the joys of fatherhood: it was just that the man's participation, his exemplary co-operation, as if preparing for a houseful of children, unnerved Hartmann. More; it gave him a thrill of revulsion. Yvette too was out of her depth. Faced with the peasant-like immobility of their daughter and son-in-law, Yvette and Hartmann felt like survivors from another era: nervous, fastidious, modest, and secret.

They felt thrown back on themselves. Whereas, with the birth of Marianne's baby, they had thought to see their lives extended into an unknown future, they had in fact seen that door closed in their faces, for there was something about the breeding capacity, and willingness, of Marianne and Roger that was quite alien to them. Old now, or almost, they saw that when the time came Marianne would look after them in an extremity, but that some deep conspiracy would draw her back to Roger. It did not even seem that this conspiracy was sexual: it seemed to be purely reproductive, as if reproduction were the only honourable way of conquering sex. Hartmann saw this and it made him uneasy. Yvette saw nothing but her daughter's fading looks, her fading appeal. These days Marianne tended to appear in trousers, even dungarees, and her swollen figure, which had not retained its earlier narrow elegance, gave her a mildly embarrassing appearance, too fecund, too exaggerated. Yvette put her discontent down to Marianne's poor looks: she scolded her, or would have done, had Roger not been there. His presence inhibited her slightly, for she thought he did not like her. This was the first time in Yvette's life that she had been aware of someone else's dislike; she was generally thought too frivolous to be taken seriously.

There was something about Roger's censorious interventions that made her see herself in another light: as trivial, as lightweight, as negligible. She became aware of the make-up on her face, the artless vanity of the bright colours that she wore, her gilded hair, as if they were suddenly shameful, the follies of an ageing woman. This was strange, for normally she felt quite young. But when she had said to her daughter, 'Why, Marianne! You have let your hair get quite out of shape. And you could do with a rinse of some sort: I can see a grey hair. I'll make an appointment for you tomorrow, dear. I'll have a word with Jean-Louis myself', Roger replied, 'She doesn't need to resort to dyeing her hair, you know. I prefer women to look natural.' Yvette had felt quite foolish, and had cast her eyes down. Soon Hartmann's hand had taken hers, the hand he knew so well, with its rosy nails, and the gold bracelets still on the wrists. The hand was trembling slightly, and he stroked it, feeling with melancholy the loose skin on the back, seeing in his mind's eye the veins that now stood out, and the occasional brown spot. She was a silly woman, he knew that; but her silliness was a private, not a public, affair. He did not like to see her reprimanded. And Marianne had not risen to her mother's defence. Indeed, there was no real position to defend; it was a matter of opinion. But they were both hurt.

Yvette had returned his clasp, had smiled determinedly, and had stood up to clear the tea-table. 'Darling, you shouldn't eat so much cake,' she could not quite resist saying. 'You have put on quite a bit of weight you know.' 'I like her as she is,' said Roger, and as Yvette turned to carry the tray into the kitchen Hartmann had seen on her face a look of frightened smiling incomprehension which he guessed she had worn as a very small child in that train travelling down to Bordeaux.

Later, in their bedroom, Yvette had wept. As he had feared, her instinctive response to trouble had been to turn younger. 'I want to see Maman,' she had said. 'She is an old lady now, and so far away. I want to go to Nice.' He had comforted her, knowing that that was not what she wanted. What she wanted was what had been lost, her own youth, and her still beautiful daughter, and the comfort and security that Hartmann had given her, and which she now felt slipping away. She was no longer young, although she had retained a naïveté, a capacity for self-deception, that had long given her an air of youth. And sometimes she was quite stiff in the mornings: he feared arthritis for her later. He said nothing. What was wrong with her was *Torschlusspanik*: the panic of the shutting of the door. For not only was the future closed to them, for reasons which were all too natural, but it seemed as if they had lost their daughter, lost her to this curatorial stranger who had made her fat and plain and kept her in Richmond so that she could not visit her parents unless he drove her over in the car. And the poor little baby, smelling of sick. The smell had offended Yvette, but now she wept when she thought of it and said that she wanted her mother.

So he had taken her to Nice for a weekend. It was October, and the warm air greeted them as they descended the steps of the plane. 'Ah,' they breathed gratefully, as if coming home. Ostensibly they had come to visit Yvette's mother, but both knew that Hartmann would be looking for a little property. He wanted flats for Yvette and himself and for Fibich and Christine: dare he also buy one for Marianne and Roger? He would see. He had felt his optimism returning as he had contemplated the blue blue sea, and the ceaseless rushing traffic, but Yvette had hurried him out of his contemplation, was anxious to reach her mother, as if her mother were in some kind of danger, had only relaxed when in sight of the modest apartment block a few miles out of Nice, on the sea front, where Martine Cazenove now lived all the year round since her husband's stroke. The flat was hers: Hartmann had given it to her. Martine and Cazenove were an old couple now, but both looked fit. Martine had that hardy appearance of French women past the age of pleasure, still flushed, thin-lipped, the head held high, dour, unsmiling, a natural recluse now that her husband was so diminished. But every morning at nine o'clock she was at the market, with her wheeled shopping basket. After her return she would settle Cazenove on the balcony, and join him there with her knitting and the magazine she had bought. They said little; they were not discontented. Cazenove, now slow in his words and movements, nevertheless bore testament to her lifelong care. With a crimson sheen on his cheeks, he would sit, in his panama hat, his stick between his legs, gazing for hours at the passing cars. They would spend whole days on their balcony, largely wordless, turning in at night to sleep in the old walnut bed that dominated their small bedroom. It was not a bad life, lived manageably within the confines of a small routine. They said little to each other, but their thoughts were occupied, and the weather was kind.

Yvette had telephoned them from the hotel, professing herself anxious to see them. From this Mrs Cazenove deduced that her daughter was unhappy for reasons which had nothing to do with the situation in Nice. She had made coffee and wheeled Cazenove in from the balcony. He had greeted Hartmann with an appearance of rapture. She had noticed how much more vivid his facial expressions were now that he was old: joy seemed to brim from his largely wordless mouth. And she had gone downstairs and bought a glazed mirabelle tart; they murmured how good it was, eating it with their teaspoons. When they had drunk their coffee, Cazenove was returned to the balcony, this time with a rug over his knees, and a promise that they would bring him in when Martine was preparing dinner. 'Oh, we won't stay,' said Yvette. 'But we'll come back tomorrow.' A complicated series of grimaces animated Cazenove's face. 'Dear girl,' he finally brought out.

Seated at the round dining-table, Hartmann and Yvette watched Martine, as she smoothed the plush cloth with steady hands, moved the vase of carnations, bought that morning in the market, so that she could see them both, and waited for her to tell them what to do. Sun washed through the balcony windows, with their looped-back tulle curtains: a plane droned overhead. It was all quite ugly, and they felt entirely comfortable there. Hartmann, requesting Martine's permission and receiving it, lit a small cigar and sat back, for this was not his conversation and he knew it. In a little while he discovered the reason. 'Maman,' said Yvette, her hands, like her mother's, folded on the blue plush cloth. 'Tell me about my father.'

The older woman sighed. 'He was handsome,' she said.

'Is that all?' Yvette protested.

'All you need to know.'

'But I know nothing about him! I don't even know his name!'

'His name was Daniel. Daniel Besnard. He died young,' said Martine slowly. 'You don't remember him.'

'No, I don't,' said Yvette. 'That's why I asked. What did he die of?'

'He was shot,' said Martine.

Shock hung in the air. Hartmann felt the hairs on the back of his neck rise.

'He liked Germans,' Martine went on inexorably. 'And he didn't like Jews. Many Frenchmen didn't. When the Germans came, Daniel made himself very useful to them. That was when I left him. I was living in one room, starving, while he was entertaining them at the gallery. His family were art dealers. They didn't get on well, and they didn't like me. And he didn't like work. So he lived by selling the odd picture. To the Germans, of course. Selling information, too.'

'Did you love him?' Yvette faltered.

Martine smiled grimly. 'Oh, yes, I loved him. I hated him too. That can happen, you know. He died just in time. It was a private act of revenge, nothing official. His German friends couldn't save him. Or wouldn't have bothered to. He was not important to them, and they despised him. I was allowed to get away. And we were lucky, we caught the last train out. After that, things closed down. We spent the rest of the war in Bordeaux.'

She remembered leaving the rue Washington, the child's hand in hers, a suitcase banging against her leg. She had gone to the gallery, taken up the floorboard, only to find the stock of money greatly diminished, had

168

taken what little was left, and fled, with the child, to the station.

'How old was I?' asked Yvette.

'You were two,' said her mother. 'And I was thirty.' She glanced across at Hartmann. He smiled at her, though he was shaken. But it was what he had always suspected.

She sighed again. 'He was no good, you see. Some people are like that: it is their nature. It was not that he didn't know the difference. He didn't care. I don't suppose you understand. I didn't understand myself.'

'Then I . . .', said Yvette slowly, 'am I like that?'

They both moved towards her. 'Why no, *ma fille*,' said Martine. 'You were brought up by Papa.' She nodded towards the immobile figure on the balcony. 'Your father was only a silly boy. Not even a man.'

Hartmann kissed his wife and held her hand. She should not have told her, he thought. He was sick and angry. But Hartmann was not as old as his mother-in-law, did not yet know the relentlessness of old age, anxious to unburden itself of its secrets, its growing indifference to the sensibilities of others, its sudden carelessness of other lives. Hartmann dreaded the effect on his wife of Martine's revelations.

'Handsome, you say?' said Yvette. 'An art dealer? That must be where I get my taste from.'

After that he thought she must be all right. But he hurried her away as soon as he decently could, said he was tired, must get back to the hotel to telephone London. Martine indicated her own telephone, then let her hand fall, defeated. She understood. She hoped that he would get over it, knew that she must leave him alone to do so. For Yvette she was not worried: she understood her daughter, measured her self-concern. Was it not her own creation? For herself she did not care. Her task now was to ensure as peaceful an old age as possible. She hoped that Hartmann, nearer to her own age than to Yvette's, would understand. If not, not. There was no more that she could do, or would care to do. She had made good the original damage to the best of her ability. Yvette was Hartmann's responsibility now.

'And Marianne?' she asked, as they stood at the door. 'Well and happy?'

'Well and happy,' they answered, knowing that there would be no help from this quarter, and took their leave.

'Will you wear your blue tonight?' Hartmann asked tenderly in the taxi. 'It is my favourite.'

'Mine too,' said Yvette, but she sighed a little. 'I think Maman looked older,' she said.

'But quite well,' said Hartmann. 'Telephone her tomorrow. Tell her we will be busy. We deserve a day to ourselves.'

And so they had spent the following day quite companionably, sitting on the terrace of the hotel, reading newspapers, talking little. The plan to settle in Nice was dropped: at least, Hartmann did nothing in the way of looking at flats. Later, he thought. Then, he thought, perhaps not. There are other places. There is no hurry. But he changed their tickets for a late flight on the same evening, and they both felt relief when the plane touched down at Heathrow.

'Back already?' said Fibich, startled, when, alerted by footsteps, he went up to the flat. 'Anything wrong?'

'No, no,' said Hartmann, embracing him. 'We missed Marianne, that's all.'

For they missed her, not as she was now, plump, silent, submissive and plain, but as she had been, a young girl like any other, but so much better, prettier,

quieter, and more lady-like. Better than her friend
Belinda, for example, whose hedonism Yvette had
hoped Marianne might emulate: superior. And how had
the change come about? Surely the insipid Roger had
not changed her? For there was no harm in him, only a
rather too rigid puritanism that had led to this almost
biblical eschewal of adornment, this irksome insistence
on the solemnity of marriage and procreation.

'Women have had babies before, you know,' Hartmann had said to his daughter, viewing with mounting
dismay her surrender to her condition. When pregnant
she had sat with her stomach out, Roger beside her.
And as there was little conversation on those afternoons
when they drove themselves over to Richmond, they
began to wonder if they were expected to keep their
distance. The idea was unthinkable! With the excitement of the birth they had felt entitled to take Marianne
over again, but Hartmann, calling at the hospital one
evening (Yvette had been there all the afternoon) had
found his daughter with her nightdress negligently
disarrayed, her enlarged breasts in evidence. She did not
bother to cover herself, and he was profoundly shocked.
He had kept away after that for a little while, until
Marianne was home again and he could trust her to be
properly dressed. And he preferred the children, as he
called them, to visit Ashley Gardens, where he felt his
own authority to be stronger, rather than to go to them
in their own home, the home that had been Roger's, and
which still bore the faintly depressing imprint of Roger's self-effacing but nevertheless rigorous personality.
Green, it was, pale green, with a large desk rather too
prominent in the half of the long room that was the
drawing-room, and a table and chairs in the half that
was the dining-room. There was space at that table,
Hartmann gloomily reflected, for quite a large family.

Dusty displays of dried flowers fanned out in the empty grates. It was never quite warm enough in that house.

'I must find them somewhere to live,' thought Hartmann, as he had often thought before. He knew that Roger liked the house, which had been left to him by his mother: he knew too that he planned to fill it with children.

In comparison with the irritating solemnity of Roger and now of Marianne, Hartmann found himself to be weightless, soaring like a bird, and, like a bird, not serious. 'And yet we tried harder,' he thought. He included Fibich and Yvette in his thought, and even Christine, although she was in a different category, having known not hardship but only loneliness. He had a feeling that Myers would take over the business when he and Fibich were gone, and he meant to change his will, leaving it in trust for poor little Henry. Toto would have shares in it: Fibich could see to that. For it was unlikely that Toto would settle down in Fibich's lifetime, although Hartmann still had hopes for him. He liked the boy's beauty, his way with women: he shook his head, laughed, and admired him. He saw in Toto the grace that had been so singularly denied to Roger. Marianne should have had a man like that, he thought, someone to tease her out of her shyness, make her laugh. But that could not be: there were too few men like Toto. And her mother had wanted to see her married. And he had let it happen, giving in to faint fears of having protected the girl too much. Wanting grandchildren.

Fibich managed better with the children, he thought, although he was far too frightened of his own son. Fibich liked Roger, and had always loved Marianne. Fibich did not mind when Henry dribbled over him, laughed at his perpetual dampness. Hartmann could see the larva-like Henry, his uncertain head propped on Fibich's shoulder, a string of saliva hanging endlessly from his mouth. There was no one like Fibich with a shy and woeful baby, whereas Hartmann would have liked to see the boy more active, more colourful, more strongly committed to subversive acts which he would, in the fullness of time, perform. At least Fibich was no longer a problem, thought Hartmann. That reckless plan of going back to Berlin had been shelved, and Fibich seemed at ease, relieved by his decision. There was still the matter of Toto's future, of course. But in comparison with Marianne, Toto somehow seemed less of a problem, less heavy on the heart. He would ruin them all, given half a chance: Hartmann could see that. But at least he would engage their attention, keep them absorbed, horrified, necessary. Hartmann felt quite grateful to Toto for being so impossible.

Hartmann sighed again. The well-preserved widow who had dropped in for a light lunch on her way from St John's Wood to the Royal Academy, where she was to meet her daughter, glanced at him discreetly.

'Would you mind if I sat here?' she asked. 'It always fills up so quickly.'

'My pleasure,' he said, removing his hat from the chair. Getting on, he thought, the same age as Yvette, or thereabouts, but looking older, discontented, bored, nicely turned out. He noticed the pearls, the large diamond on the wedding finger. No husband, he adduced: used to making these little overtures. There was, after all, an empty seat at the table by the door. But what did it all matter? Those days were gone. Once he would have paid attention, delighting in the game. Now his thoughts were all with his wife, his fatherless, and apparently childless wife. Yvette had rallied, of course. She always did, and he thought she always

173

would. Her days were not as empty as this one was proving to be for him. But he feared the look of abandonment on her face, the look which she had in fact never seen herself. He feared the day when she would become a widow. Fibich, of course, would look after her, for as long as Fibich was still there. He knew that. It was just that, suddenly, he could not bear the thought of her on her own. He wanted to be at home, safe, away from this awful day. He wanted it to be night, and to take the pill that always put him so beautifully to sleep. And it was only half-past twelve, he saw, resigning himself to an endless afternoon. He did not have the heart for his usual ceremonious lunch. He would eat here, peck at an omelette, eat one of those little meals designed for women. He groaned inwardly at the thought of his dereliction, his temporary fall from grace. But his manners did not desert him. Inclining his head courteously in the widow's direction, he smiled and offered her the menu.

'What would you recommend?' he asked.

12

Toto, leaving Oxford with a poor degree and a large following, had given much thought to his future. The details were vague in his mind but the outline was bold: he simply knew that he would be prodigious. In an exemplary way – exemplary in the sense of accurate foreknowledge – he knew that he was born to be a prodigy, for the word had suggested itself to him when he was still a young boy, fretting at the confines of his bourgeois home. '*Je suis en enfant prodigue,*' he had said to himself; he was in his Baudelaire phase at the time and longed to have a stepfather whom he could hate, instead of Fibich who forgave him everything. The path he was to take was unclear to him, but he was convinced that it led to stardom. He idly contemplated notions of couture or modelling; however, acting was his *métier*, he felt, not the old fustian stuff of drama school and years spent in provincial repertory, but instant fame on the small screen, springing into a million homes, knocking the inhabitants flat with the sheer lustre of his personality. In the meantime, until the day of his discovery, he had little to do, for it was simply a question of waiting until somebody noticed him. That someone, he saw, would be a woman, one of the new hard-pressed breed, working frantically for a television company, but taken off guard and becalmed into wistfulness by his unusual good looks, his splendid body: he would present his profile to her, then turn full-face and look her brazenly in the eye, and the next thing he knew she would have secured him a part in her next production. Anything would do: he would accept a serial to begin with. But what he had in mind was one of those masterly fictional exposés of the condition of England, in which corrupt schoolboys prefigure the handsome damaged adults who habitually compete for eminence in the inflated world of espionage. In this he was prescient. He could look both young and unfledged and adult and knowing: sometimes the two sets of impressions merged, and then he was mystifying to those of his entourage who thought they had him taped.

He was something of an enigma to his friends, especially to his women friends, who suspected or liked to think in terms of a tortured sensibility beneath the expressions that passed across his face like ripples on a pond. In fact Toto never submitted himself to torture of any kind. He had the true actor's make-up: he was both ruthless and narcissistic. Having thought for years in terms of the effect he had on others, he simply decided to make this effect his career. The conviction that this would inevitably come about was so strong in him that he disdained the idea of any form of work. He was content to wait until fate delivered him into the hands of those who would finally set the seal on his life.

In the meantime he had to consider the appurtenances of living. He had to invent a suitable setting for himself. A flat in London was the first necessity. His friends at Oxford, Archie and Isabel, suggested joining forces with him for a couple of years. Toto, who could not cook and who hated being alone, agreed, although he dimly perceived that Isabel, who was in love with him, might eventually prove tiresome. But she had taken some excellent photographs of him in the college gardens which would come in useful and he owed her something in return. In any case Archie and Isabel were brother and sister and could be trusted to keep an eye on each other. In that way he would be responsible for neither of them, a position which suited him perfectly. They were a well-connected couple, the son and daughter of a Scottish peer, but they had no money, which also suited Toto. He intended the flat to be in his name, so that he could turf the others out as soon as he saw signs of coming into his kingdom. In the meantime they might make themselves useful. Both were doing postgraduate work, which would keep them on a fairly tight budget. He would take care of the money side of things. That suited him too. He was prepared to be generous for an indefinite period. He was, in his limited way, fond of them both. But he knew, with his curiously far-seeing instinct, that they had little part to play in his future.

First the flat had to be found. Archie and Isabel thought in terms of Notting Hill Gate, where their grandmother lived and which they knew well: Toto favoured something more central. For the time being he was living with his parents, a condition which they all found less uncomfortable than they had expected. Indeed Toto, lulled by his mother's food and his father's indulgence, and fuelled by his endless belief in himself, had begun to make himself agreeable, and to her astonishment Christine found him to be good company. The trick, she decided, was to suspend all judgment, to abandon any hope of mutuality, with this curious son of hers: the trick was simply to treat him as a phenomenon. She therefore turned over her kitchen to the planning committee poring over house agents' leaflets, and her drawing-room to the telephone conversations that ensued; she became used to three hands reaching out for the apple cake which she silently put before Toto and his friends, to accompany the relays of coffee that they seemed to need, and she began to cherish the company of the three young people who had taken up residence in her hitherto undisturbed home while actively planning to move on collectively, like a flight of birds, when the season changed, for they were not too desperate, she thought, to be alone together without the nurturing that she provided. They rarely went out to look at any property, the whole thing having the air of a theoretical exercise. It was a source of wonder to her that she could please them so easily.

'Marvellous cake, Mrs Fibich,' said Isabel, her cross pretty face humanized by a crumb at the corner of her mouth. 'We haven't had this before, have we? Is it difficult?'

'Why, no, Isabel. I'll show you how to make it. It's very simple. You simply drop fresh cherries or plums into your cake mixture. Remember to stone them first. It's a little trouble, but it makes all the difference.'

She must remember to buy another dozen eggs, she reminded herself.

'It's not an English cake, though, is it? At least I've never had it before.'

'It was my Aunt Jessop's recipe. She had it from her German mother. There is cold chicken in the fridge, Toto. And potato salad. And perhaps Isabel would like to mix a nice green salad. There is plenty there for all of you. I shall be with Yvette, if you want me, dear. And I shall be back to give you your tea.'

She sailed out of the flat, feeling cautiously happy. At last, it seemed, she was being an adequate mother to her son. It had required no ruse, no duplicity in order to achieve this, just submission to his will, simple subjection, of a not entirely different order from that experienced by poor Isabel. But in her case expecting no return, having learnt by experience, throughout Toto's childhood, the outlines of his imperious self-sufficiency. He would never need her, she now recognized, any more than he would ever value the love and fidelity of any woman, but if she could please him, spoil him, feed him, and of course praise him, he would tolerate all these offerings, and in return confer upon her his bemused and graceful acceptance. And to think she had tried to conquer him, to chastize him, to awaken in him a more rigorous sense of life's expectations! That was not the way of it at all with Toto. One loved him and looked for nothing in return. Many women would love him proportionately more because of receiving so little; they would be the importunate ones, the ones who would bring a grimace of well-bred distaste to his lips. Christine saw that she must never again fall into this plaintive category. To remain in her son's graces she must avoid behaving like the sort of woman he most held in disfavour.

She was fond, too, of Isabel, despite her knitted brows and her rather high petulant voice. A darkly pretty girl, Christine could see in her something of the torment which her difficult position was causing her to undergo. Was she to be sister or concubine? Christine mentally shook her head with pity that the young should have to suffer so, for to her they were all children. Yet Isabel, despite the modish clothes that outlined her fine figure, wore her hair drawn back into a modest bow, and her physical restlessness – the twining of her legs and feet, the sudden expansive yawns – were undercut by a wistfulness of expression, as if she were wondering what she could be doing in this so comfortable flat, and whether she would ever get out of it. And if she did, what then? There was no way, Christine could see, of making it easier for her, of ensuring her maturity without pain. She would be brought to a dreadful humility if she continued to love Toto, and continued to make it so clear. He liked her for her very crossness, which intrigued him, and which he thought protected them both. And for her glossy black looks, the raven's wing hair and eyebrows, which gave him a detached aesthetic pleasure. He had decided some time ago that she was worthy of him. Christine, knowing her son, could see that this was only a temporary arrangement. And Isabel, although she did not yet understand why this should be so, felt it in the air between them. It was Isabel who kept them to the task of finding a flat. Archie, her brother, had long ago abandoned the whole idea and simply brought his law books to these consultations. With his fingers in his ears to shut out his sister's scolding voice, he got quite a lot of work done. Not having to go out for meals helped. He said very little, but always smiled at Christine and held the door open for her when she left the kitchen. Christine liked Archie too.

All in all, she thought, Toto had made nice friends, although she knew that he would eventually dispense with them. In the meantime she enjoyed this respite from conflict. She even looked forward to their daily taking up residence in her kitchen, although it did occur to her to wonder how long they intended to be there. 'My young people,' she described them proudly to Yvette, who was vaguely annoyed at this erosion of her sovereignty. 'My young people are downstairs,' Christine would say. 'Can I take you out to lunch? There doesn't seem to be any room for me.' Thus she became, briefly, the leader of those little expeditions to stores and restaurants to which she had previously submitted without much enthusiasm. Yvette found her more animated these days. And Fibich, returning home to a depleted supper of cold chicken and the remnants of an apple cake, was delighted with her. After greeting his father, Toto would sail out for the evening, although he rarely said where he was going. 'Leave him alone,' Christine would say severely. 'It's only natural that he should want to be with his friends.' Thus she repossessed Toto from his father's anxiety, and in so doing decreed a measure of calm for them both.

When the dazzle of this new activity momentarily subsided it would occur to her to wonder, yet again, where this exorbitant son had come from. She could see in him no trace of either Fibich or herself, which she supposed was a measure of congratulation all round. Yet once, when she had come upon him in the drawing-room, asleep in a chair, with his legs flung out, she had had a disturbing memory of her graceless father in his most characteristic position. Surely not, she wondered. Mr Hardy had been so very horrible, and anyway he had been short and stout. And Toto was so tall and graceful. Yet there had been something in the totality of his repose that took her back to those ominously silent afternoons in St James's Mansions. So disagreeable was this impression that she mentioned it to Fibich. 'Surely not,' he protested in his turn. He had never known Mr Hardy, but he disavowed him just the same. 'He must surely take after my father.' 'You don't remember him,' she said. 'I don't remember anything *about* him,' he corrected her. 'But I remember him as looking tall and distinguished.' The memory for once did not upset him. He saw in his son a kind of worldliness that must have come from somewhere, and it pleased him to think that the paternal genes had been passed on. A modest man, he could not see that he himself was tall and disting- uished looking. And indeed his habitual mildness of expression militated against an imposing physical pres- ence. Yet as they grew older both he and Christine began to improve in looks. Awkward when they were young, they had remained slender, and although Chris- tine's hair was now white Yvette had persuaded her to have it cut short, and with the addition of a subtle rouge on her cheeks, also Yvette's suggestion, she looked not unlike an eighteenth-century pastel, with a suggestion of veiled wit about her that made her look, paradox- ically, quite ageless. The eyes were still splendid. And Fibich too had an absent-minded and harmless air about him, which, allied to the correctness of his bearing, produced a favourable impression. Toto appreciated their fastidiousness, which he had entirely inherited. These days he did not mind them at all.

After six months in the kitchen (the happiest six months of her life, she often thought), Christine found them one day drooping in discouragement. Her table was covered with Archie's books and papers, and the elaborate and discarded lists which Isabel made each day and forgot to take home with her. She noticed that her now completely beloved son was growing sleek and lazy on apple cake. 'Toto,' she was moved to say, for she prized his looks almost as much as he did himself. 'It is time you made a decision. No, don't put more sugar in your coffee. *You are putting on weight.*' These words electrified them, as if a doom had been pronounced. Isabel blushed deeply. Archie, aware of their changed expressions, removed his fingers from his ears. 'It's all right, Mrs Fibich,' he said. 'We've decided on Fulham Road.' 'Have we?' said Isabel, startled.

'It's there in front of you,' he said, pointing to one of

her pieces of paper. 'Ground floor, three bedrooms, west-facing garden. Handy access to excellent public transport.'

Toto laughed. 'Just like that,' he marvelled. 'And he wasn't even listening.'

Christine felt a pang, but simultaneously became aware that she was rather tired.

'I suggest we go and have a look at it,' said Toto. 'Coming, Ma?'

Sun flashed briefly on the raindrop-spattered windscreen of the car as they inched their way down the Kings Road.

'You see?' said Archie, expansive. 'All this and the Royal Court too.'

Isabel was silent, knowing that Toto's father was putting up the money. She wondered, for she was quite hard-headed in her more enlightened moments, how long she would be allowed to stay. She reasoned that as long as she stuck it out, Toto would be unable to move another woman in. Suddenly she was anxious for them to be installed. Her own thesis had been hanging fire too long: she was receiving enquiries from her tutor. Christine's kitchen had been so much more attractive than the British Library. But now, they all realized, the time had come. Toto was thoughtful.

'Have I really put on weight?' he asked, at random.

Christine consoled him. 'You will soon take it off. Just be careful what you eat.'

'You have fed us too well, Mrs Fibich,' said Archie, who was naturally gracious. 'We are terribly grateful.'

It sounded final, and Christine felt another pang. Well, it must be done, she told herself, and determined to like the flat, whatever its drawbacks. If it were terrible, as she suspected it might be, he could always come home again. And if it were not, then perhaps she and Fibich might, one day, be welcome there. For at the prospect of this parting of the ways her timidity had reasserted itself, like an unwelcome visitor from the past.

The flat was not terrible: it was large, and light, and had the extremely empty air of a recent conversion. Dusty French windows, with an ironwork grille in front of them, opened, finally, on to a rain-drenched garden in which sun flashed tormentedly on to unkempt grass. Grey clouds bowled in from the west, darkening the high-ceilinged rooms. But it was quite a solid conversion, Christine noticed, and the kitchen and bathroom were newly installed, which would save considerably on the outlay. It had been painted magnolia, which took on a shadowy aspect under the rapidly changing sky.

'I'll have this room dark green,' said Toto.

'You like it then?' she asked.

'Yep,' he said, and sat down on a packing-case full of electrical wiring that had been left in what she supposed to be the drawing-room.

'What about the others?' asked Christine.

'Oh, they'll be fine,' said Toto, pulling the *New Yorker* from his pocket and turning to the listings.

'Of course, Daddy will want to see it,' murmured Christine, but she knew that it was decided. She wandered through the empty rooms, felt the radiators. 'Do you like it, Isabel?' she asked. 'Archie?'

'Seems fine,' said Archie cheerfully.

Isabel, Christine could see, was frantically enthusiastic, her cheeks burning, holding her breath in case it should prove too expensive.

'We'll pay rent, of course,' she assured Christine.

'It seems to be settled then,' smiled Christine. 'I'll bring my husband to see it this evening. You had better leave the key with me, dear.'

'So he's leaving home?' said Hartmann, surprised that Fibich was taking it so calmly. But Fibich was so proud of having behaved like a grown-up parent, so pleased that his wife was similarly proud, that he merely sighed and smiled.

'Yes,' he said. 'Well, he is a man now.'

And they had been so happy, Christine and he, visiting the flat, where they seemed to be entirely welcome. This tolerance on the part of the young people had charmed him. Toto had painted his room himself, and the dark green walls were, they had to admit, quite handsome. The green and white striped curtains supplied by Christine had gone down very well. 'Thanks, Ma,' said Toto. 'Brilliant.' He had already lost interest. Soon Christine was conspiring to decorate Isabel's room: the outwardly subversive girl turned out to have surprisingly conventional taste, as Christine feared she might. Archie was indifferent to his surroundings and kept his magnolia walls. Christine ordered plain cream linen curtains for them both: she was suddenly exhausted. They gave a party when the flat was declared officially finished.

'This will cost you something,' said Hartmann, above the noise of the sound system that Toto had set up. 'What's he going to do now?'

'He says he has contacts in the film business,' said Fibich, he hoped with conviction. He was enjoying himself so much, and Toto's many friends seemed so nice to him, that he did not much mind what his son did at the moment.

'Such pretty girls,' he murmured, gesturing with an asparagus-filled tube of brown bread.

'And so many of them,' said Hartmann.

In the two years that ensued it was mainly Isabel who

185

kept in touch. Christine grew to expect her plaintive voice on the telephone, to be followed by her attendance at dinner. Once Fibich came home to find her asleep on the sofa. This led, in a certain measure, to a return of his original worries.

'How are they living?' he asked Christine. 'Why is she so tired?'

'She is very young,' said Christine sadly. 'We must remember that.'

Toto, they learned, had acquired an agent and was waiting for offers.

'He may wait a long time,' protested Fibich. 'It will do him no harm to put in a few months at the office while he waits.'

And when he drove Isabel back to the Fulham Road that evening he presented his son with an alternative. As this had never happened before Toto was surprised into accepting. He hated solitude and was privately bored. In any event he needed information about the world, and none seemed to be coming his way. As an amateur he rather favoured thinking his way into a part for which he was naturally wrongly cast. He consented with some amusement to Fibich's proposal.

He turned up at the office in a faultless grey suit, a Burberry over his arm, and in one hand an expensive brief-case with cruel corners, effects he had observed in others of the kind he was supposed to be imitating.

'Let me get back to you on this,' he would say on the telephone. And, 'Can you pencil it in for the 12th? I'll have a word with my partners.'

Secretaries and typists were charmed: Goodman looked at him admiringly. Only Myers was unimpressed, but then Myers had never seemed enthusiastic about him. Toto was in fact capable of quite considerable work, but once he had mastered the idiom his usual

186

subversive indifference took over. As a worker he was one of the naturally disruptive kind. He would arrive very early, surprising them all by being there ahead of them, and then be out for most of the rest of the day. 'I have to see my agent,' he would explain airily.

'His agent seems to be a woman,' Hartmann observed to Fibich. 'I saw them lunching together in my restaurant.'

He regarded this as a bit of an imposition – it was, after all, *his* restaurant – but had the grace to laugh at himself for this. I am getting old, he thought wonderingly, and felt none of his usual satisfaction. It was an awkward moment. He had waved his hand in a discreet greeting to Toto, who had nodded back. The agent was very pretty, though he did not mention this to Fibich, and one strand of her fair hair had slipped from its swept-back moorings and lay attractively across her brow and cheek. She was talking so hard, and concentrating so entirely on Toto, that she did not notice Hartmann. She had a beseeching expression. Hartmann had always supposed the transaction to be conducted on rather different lines. Well, never mind, he thought. What was clear to him was that the woman did not stand a chance. It occurred to him, quite surprisingly, that Toto might never marry.

The thought had also occurred to Christine. There was something hard, high and distant about Toto which seemed to intensify as time went on. His adult personality, built as it was on a form of accurate self-regard, also emerged in due season, and by the time he was twenty-six he was his own man. It appeared to Christine that he was gradually removing himself from the sphere of child-like affections, hasty friendships, innocent love affairs, liaisons based on simple taste and need, all those dangerous areas of human vulnerability in which a false move or a disappointment can lead at worst to suffer-ing, at best to boredom. Toto had no time for any of this. Time that was not spent perfecting himself was so strictly rationed that it was almost non-existent. He had, for example, to keep himself fit. This involved hours of swimming, a long run before breakfast, another at night, no cigarettes, no alcohol, and a strictly supervised diet. The result was an almost inhuman burnish to his already impressive looks. As he withdrew from others he practised an extreme form of courtesy which did duty for emotion and saved him a certain mental investment. This courtesy was maddening to the girl-friends he continued to attach to himself and who were amazed, after a night of love, to be addressed as formally as if they had just been introduced.

It was reassuring to his mother to be telephoned from time to time, and then more regularly, by this prodigy who had become almost a stranger but in whom she could detect the faint tracings of the melancholy that had so overwhelmed his father at the same age. This lofty and beautiful stranger also came to dinner with his parents, ate carefully, thanked his mother, and delighted his father by asking about the family background. Toto's interest in this background related entirely to himself, but was none the less genuine. He had a curious empathy, which made him try out for roles which had not yet been assigned to him. Thus for a whole week following one of his visits, he loped down the Fulham Road with a shopping bag, his hair carefully combed the wrong way, pretending to be Fibich. He was so success-ful that the chemist said to him, 'We usually get your young brother in for these.' Isabel found him in-creasingly frightening.

Christine did not think he would marry because, in Tolstoy's words, he lacked the necessary weakness.

188

But, by the same token, he was nostalgic for some kind of safety, the safety that is provided by two people rather than by one. For this reason she saw that she and Fibich must remain in readiness, discreet, uncritical, and always welcoming; that they must stand back, ask no questions that could not be answered with the minimum of travail, and always be prepared for a return of the prodigal to the fold. For Toto was both prodigy and prodigal, as perhaps he had always been, and their initial failure to understand him could, in the light of this truth, be more easily explained and understood. They feared for him, largely on account of his inner solitariness, his gifts: what would happen to him when they were no longer there? Would he live alone, spending his evenings with other couples, couples perhaps less well-intentioned, less self-effacing than themselves, more ready to back this dark horse in a variety of sexual speculations, seeing in him an object of baffling fascination? She wished for him a calm wise older woman, a woman experienced enough to leave him alone, delicate in her attentions, all-forgiving. She feared to die while he was still, as she saw it, unprotected.

When Archie finished his thesis and Isabel abandoned hers, having devoted her best energies to the task of getting Toto to love her and failing, there came a parting of the ways that was not entirely harmonious. Archie blamed Toto for his indifference: he blamed his sister for her endless delusion. He had watched their liaison with increasing distaste, had seen Isabel reduced to pure longing, and, worse, to pure waiting, when Toto, mysteriously absent for several days, would return and appear to wonder what Isabel was doing in his bed.

'We're going home,' said Archie, seeing his sister in tears for the hundredth time. 'I've had enough of this.

Go and pack. There's no need to explain.'

There was apparently so little need to explain that Toto seemed to them to have anticipated this development all along.

'Goodbye, then, old thing,' he said to Isabel, and patted her on the head.

His goodbyes were pitiful: he was never to master the art of dismissing a woman gracefully. After that Archie did not feel that he could shake hands with him. They clattered down the stairs with their bags and cases as if in a sudden hurry to be gone. When the door had finally closed on them Toto sat listening to the silence and wondering whether or not he was happy. He sat in his room while the pattern of the sunlight shifted round the walls, and when the light began to fade he got up, went out into the little entrance hall, and carefully closed the doors to Archie's and Isabel's rooms, leaving only the door to his own room open. Then, curiously anxious to make no sound, he picked up his keys and tip-toed out of the flat.

By this stage, at twenty-six, he was working one day a week at the office, still in his young executive's outfit, and pursuing his own affairs for the rest of the time. Occasionally, he would drop in on his mother for lunch. These visits, though largely uncommunicative, brought joy to Christine's heart. Fibich, returning from the office, would say, 'Any news today? Did Toto come?' and though Christine would too often reply, 'No, nothing today,' they both had the warm and comforting feeling that something had been restored. They floated in a calm which they had thought would never be theirs, and, strange to say, Toto began to match them in mood. He was discovering that intense quiet and solitude brought him his best effects, and he, who had been so exuberant as a child, began to take on a more silent presence as a result of his self-communing. He often sat in his room, willing himself to immobility, the only object of his attention the pattern of the sunlit window on his green wall. These descents into concentration he found laborious though rewarding. He could not have said what he discovered in their depths; he simply knew that they led him on, from chasm to chasm, to a sort of revelation that he could not define. He would emerge with a sigh, yet a profound feeling of peace, of something stored for future use. When the light went, the sound of 'The Archers' on a neighbour's radio brought him back to the present. This was a sign to resume normal living.

In this curious state, which a mystic might have recognized, work became an irrelevance. Yet it was about this time, and possibly as a result of sheer indifference, of a general cessation of the will, that he landed his first part, on the strength of only two television commercials, in which his presence had been obscured by busy lighting effects, and through the dedicated efforts of that very agent whom Hartmann had mistaken for quite another sort of woman. He was to play a waiter, in a story of love and treachery in high places, just such a production as he had always imagined, or rather foreseen. His role was small, indeed minimal, but he was on camera throughout a long and crucial passage. The black and white of his costume showed up his fine looks to advantage, and he was clever enough and assured enough to be pure background, not to add his modicum to the thrust of the scene. Nevertheless, his presence was so unmistakable that one newspaper, the following morning, was to report, 'The ambiguity of the scene showing Prescott trading with his superior was underlined by the enigmatic figure of the waiter, whose rigorously neutral presence threw the deceptions of the main characters into high relief.'

'But they haven't given him any lines,' protested Yvette.

'Quiet,' ordered Hartmann, his handkerchief at the ready.

The four of them were seated on chairs pulled round the Hartmanns' television. Fibich and Christine, alternately blushing and paling, sought each other's hands. They examined their son's image with something like curiosity: did he still belong to them? Or was he already on his way to a thousand hearts? Was he really to act, or merely be a seductive presence, a fantasy for housewives? They could not judge. They leaned closer to the screen, hardly daring to believe that he had grown so serious. Whatever strange property was there already seemed to belong to others, not to them at all. The very slowness of his development, this unexpected reversal of all the signs by which they had thought to know him, this very belatedness, amazed them. It was as if their own characters, their own mysterious and even dolorous inheritance, were receiving some strange and dignified form of recognition. They did not know this new adult son who had emerged from his unruly boyhood like a legendary princeling attaining his majority. What they did recognize was a quality of inwardness bordering on enchantment, a quality not remote from melancholy but with a strength about it that they had never known. He was theirs, and yet not theirs. He was their apotheosis.

They switched off the television and ran to the telephone. Christine spoke first, trying, and almost succeeding, in keeping her voice steady. Then Yvette spoke, then Hartmann. Fibich was content to wait until last. After the praises which were Toto's due, Fibich said, 'When will we see you, my dear? We miss you. And now that you are famous we are afraid that you might forget us.'

'Oh, I'll see you soon,' said Toto. Even his voice was calm.

'I'll make coffee,' said Yvette, as they trooped back to the drawing-room.

'No, tea,' Hartmann called after her, blowing his nose. 'Tea is better for the nerves. The strain was terrible. Are we to go through this every time he appears? My heart was beating so hard I thought I would have an attack.'

He laid a reverent hand on his left breast, as if to solicit further news, then sighed, and put his handkerchief back into his pocket.

'Marvellous,' he said. 'Marvellous. Well, Fibich? Latecomer? Feel better?'

'I wonder if Marianne was watching,' Yvette said some time in the course of the evening. 'I must ring her in the morning.'

Toto's next part was in a romantic serial for children which went out at five o'clock. In this he acted very well, for he had come to take children seriously. This was to remain Christine's favourite, a moment of innocence in a career that already held promise. Then he got a part in a film on Channel Four. The part was small, but at one point he was required to take off his shirt. It was an event that was to open up the future to him, although Christine never liked it. She foresaw a conflict for her son, in which his extreme physical attractiveness would war with his new-found seriousness. She dreaded for him the vulgarities that the publicity would bring. For a moment she longed to have him back as he was, even as he had been, inordinate, unmanageable. Then she was led to reflect on the marvellous power that had brought him to this moment. She hoped he was strong enough to withstand the temptations, the corruptions of his new career.

Toto was not surprised by being famous. He had always known that he would be, and therefore took it all as a matter of course. The only difference was that now he had less time to practise those strange descents into the abyss of himself. Now that the telephone rang all the time, and that there were suddenly so many more women in his life, it was all he could do to make excuses and retreat to his green room: nobody would believe that he was really alone. But he was, and he continued to be. On his green walls the outline of the sunny window glided steadily with the hours. In the entrance hall the doors to Archie's and Isabel's rooms remained closed.

13

At the end of another spring Fibich made up his mind. His decision, when it came, was dream-like in its simplicity. He walked into a travel agent's office and announced that he wanted to go to Berlin. He was to remember that very walk, and the sight of the golden forsythia frothing in the London gardens. It had been a cold year, and by the beginning of April the daffodils were only just out in the park: their frail heads trembled in a keen wind. But there was a lightness in the sky that promised a change of season: it was as if a wheel had turned, cancelling the hesitations of the past and promising a quicker pace, a new effectiveness. He said, mildly, to Christine, 'I have to go to Berlin next week. Just for a few days.' So mildly did he say it, with so little anxiety, that she was not suspicious. 'What a pity that it has to be Berlin,' she answered him. 'If it were somewhere warmer I might have come with you.' He had smiled at her. 'I will take you away later,' he promised her. 'We will go to the sun.'

She had never known the extent, the depth, and the location of his fears, only that he was troubled, hesitant, by nature. Having so little desire to review or revive her own childhood she could not quite understand why he should want to recapture his. In this, oddly, he was coming round to her point of view. He regarded those who rhapsodized about their childhoods with amusement and some impatience; Hartmann was the same. In the office both Myers and Goodman were apt to be stimulated to unusual loquacity on the subject of past days, days from the beginnings of their lives, and their anecdotes struck Hartmann and Fibich as uninteresting, insignificant. Both felt cut off from such attachments, and also from the need to sentimentalize them, knowing instinctively how endangered they were in this respect. Nostalgia is only for the securely based. When Goodman relayed news of his mother, or Myers recounted what merry games had taken place in what Hartmann privately considered to be his appalling house in Richmond – and which accounted for his reluctance to move from it – he and Fibich would look at each other with perfect understanding. Of the two of them Hartmann was the more impatient. 'Why do they go on about it?' he would ask. 'It is not polite. After all, no one can join in.' Fibich was more indulgent. 'It is not their fault that you were grown-up at twelve,' he would say. They both regarded childhood reminiscence on the part of other people as at best an embarrassment, almost in the same category as public discussion of one's amorous preoccupations, an imprudence, an imposition, an error of taste, as if the whole purpose of growing older had been mislaid. Such reminiscences excluded them, reminded them of their uncertainty of status. Only Yvette was to be indulged in this way, and even in Yvette's case there was a certain uneasiness to be evoked. Both Hartmann and Fibich now knew the nature of the subterfuge that surrounded her famous story of the train to Bordeaux. Certain things they could only share between the two of them. When Fibich told Hartmann

196

that he had bought a ticket to Berlin, had booked a room at the Kempinski, would be leaving in three days' time, they entered a conspiracy, unmentioned but understood by both of them, to say nothing of the purpose of Fibich's visit to their wives. They recognized it as too grave, too historic a matter even to be explained.

In the three days that separated Fibich's announcement of his departure from his actual leave-taking, his mood underwent several inevitable alterations. The serenity with which the decision had been made – a serenity which he associated with the golden showers of the forsythia – gave way, as he knew it would, to dread, the dread to longing, and the longing to a homesickness which was more for the home he was leaving than for the one he intended, if possible, to recover. The day before his departure he was unable to keep still, would start up from his desk to knock on Hartmann's door, then let his hand fall without knocking, so intimately did he realize that what he felt could not be shared with anyone, not even with Hartmann. In bed, on his last night, he lay rigid, sleepless, until his rigidity was interrupted by convulsive involuntary movements. Christine awoke. 'Is anything wrong?' she asked. 'Can't you sleep? I'll make you a hot drink.' 'No,' he said. 'Let me do it.' He was glad of an excuse to get up. He returned with a tray of tea and a plate of biscuits. She watched him over the rim of her cup, at last aware of something momentous. 'My dear,' she said. 'Must you go?' Fibich summoned a smile of enormous cheerfulness. 'Of course,' he reassured her. 'It's only for a few days.' But she noticed that his hand reached out for the biscuits until he had finished them, storing up sugar again for the terrible adventure ahead.

They made love that night. 'I have always loved you,

Christine,' said Fibich. 'And I have loved our son. Please thank him for me.' Then, all too soon, morning came.

His plane did not leave until the afternoon. He went to the office as usual and surprised them all with his good humour. Staggering courage was required to keep the smile on his face: he felt as if he were to undergo an operation that might leave him for dead. This was the false cheer of the condemned, summoned up to leave a happy memory for those who loved him. And behind that smile the slow sad opening of the abyss, into which he thought momentarily that he might vanish. As the time drew near it seemed to him as if he might die before he got to Berlin. He felt layers of the life he had sought heroically to maintain as reasonable peeling away and leaving him as sorrowful as a medieval sinner deserted by his God, the God in whom he, Fibich, had never believed. Yet, as Hartmann drove him to the airport, he summoned up the smile once more, pointing out to him, as he might to a slight acquaintance, the flowering cherry in one of the gardens bordering the thundering road. Overhead a plane came in low to land. By the time that Hartmann left him he could only register two states, restlessness and homesickness. Yet he knew that his action, the action that had brought him to this echoing scurrying place, was ineluctable. In a corner of his mind he knew that one day he would be glad that he had taken it.

Restless and homesick, he entered upon an altered state. The homesickness, he knew, he was attempting to sort out. The restlessness – and the realization came to him only slowly – would be with him to the end. That was what his life amounted to, he could see it now: he was doomed from the start to have his condition unchanged. And perhaps death was the only resolution he would ever be permitted for his insoluble lifelong problems. Perhaps death was that good thing that some pretended it to be: death as the end of longing. He felt, on this flight, among these nice people eating their cold meat and their rum baba, as if his life were drawing to a conclusion, as if it would not now be long before he was delivered. This pilgrimage, undertaken for Toto, to answer Toto's questions, to furnish Toto with a lineage that would survive the death of his parents, was, he thought, a rehearsal for the real thing, the true home-coming. He expected nothing from it now, although he had undertaken it in a spirit of quixotry and what now struck him as absurd valour. He had intended to look for signs which he would relay to his son, but now, quite suddenly, miles up in the air, he lacked the energy to go through with it. He had no heart for what he had promised himself to do.

Hartmann had shaken his head. 'You are not a young man,' he had said. 'This is too much for you. Leave the past alone. How can you tell Toto what you do not even know yourself?' But Fibich had still been possessed by the idea that the past would be returned to him as an illumination, and that that illumination would render him whole. Without it he must suffer the homesickness that had dogged him since his earliest days, the home-sickness that had no end.

He had thought, gallantly, that he must open himself to this experiment, after which he could take whatever rest was owing to him. One more effort, he had thought, and then my slate is clean: I shall not have shirked the task that has frightened me all my life. After that, nothing: the beatitude of complete repose, a life at home with those I love. For suddenly he loved them beyond measure, the little family that had kept him whole. He saw Hartmann's face as he had last seen him

199

at the airport: grave, uncharacteristically stern, his hand smoothing his now silver hair with a gesture that suddenly seemed that of an elderly man. By the entrance to the passport control Hartmann had taken him in his arms and embraced him, then had stalked off without a word. Fibich knew that he would be there to greet him in five days' time. And Yvette would prepare dinner, for Christine would be too nervous. Perhaps Marianne would be there. But no, she was expecting another baby, and seemed to be unwell. And Toto? He did not think that Toto would be present. They did not see him often, nor did they expect to. Out of modesty they did not telephone, in case a woman's voice answered. But sometimes, on a Sunday afternoon, he would appear as if by magic, and sit with them quite peacefully, eating his mother's cake at teatime with his usual appetite. He was studying them, Fibich thought: maybe he too knew that there was not much time left. What Fibich could not bear to see was Toto's solitariness, which seemed now to be an important component of his uniqueness. He wanted to give him roots, a family, an inheritance, more than he had ever wanted such things for himself. He wanted, for his son, to be a man among men, and not simply the terrified creature he knew himself to be. And for this reason he was taking this journey, as a proof of his manhood, to earn the respect of his son, even if his son knew nothing of why this should come about. As far as Toto was concerned, Fibich was taking a business trip. Nothing of Fibich's intention had been discussed with him. If there were a happy outcome Toto would know of it. And if, as Fibich now suspected, nothing was restored to him, then there was no need to burden Toto with the uneasy depths of Fibich's autobiography. He must remember to buy them all presents, he thought. He was already looking forward to getting home.

It was dusk when he reached Berlin, and a huge dark blue sky, moonless and starless, stretched over the curiously silent city. He realized that he was unaccustomed to these quiet wide streets, these blank-faced apartment houses with their austere windows, this isolation of a landlocked place far from the winds of the sea and the subtle odours of grass and river water. In the brief interval between the airport and the taxi rank he had noticed that the weather was unusually cold, had smelled only a faint aroma of petrol, had tasted nothing on his tongue. This atmosphere, this savourless air, was not in the least familiar to him. His taxi took him efficiently to the Kurfürstendamm, where the sky was momentarily obliterated by city lights, high buildings bearing advertisement signs like heraldic devices or the badges of ancient guilds, the outline of a ruined church which reminded him of a rotten tooth, and cautious tables outside cafés at which nobody sat. At the Kempinski the welcome was efficient, smiling, deft, but lacked, he thought, effusiveness. He surprised himself by responding in the same manner, having retrieved some kind of effectiveness from the fact that he had arrived at all. In his room he pulled aside the heavy white curtain on to a provincial calm interrupted only by the low rumble of a U–Bahn train. Suddenly exhausted, he undressed quickly, washed his face and mouth; with his last available energy he dragged his limbs beneath the white eiderdown, and fell into a deep sleep.

His sleep was so deep, so uninterrupted, that when he awoke he felt peaceful and even faintly optimistic. He understood, from the silence, that it must still be very early, and yet he felt as if a great deal of time had passed and that he had been transferred, with complete precision, from one world to another. He got up and took a bath, still in his becalmed state, dressed carefully, and studied himself in the mirror. He saw a tall thin grey-haired man with a faintly olive-coloured face, narrow slightly-hunched shoulders, and an enviably slender figure: despite his appetite he had never put on weight. The expression on his face surprised him, for his lips were stretched into a mild smile in which affability and innocence were exactly mingled. I am here, he thought, and I did not die of it. I will take breakfast and wander about the streets. Something is bound to come of it. And if not, it will not matter, for I have already done what I meant to do, taken the chance, returned. And if I find nothing, if absolutely nothing occurs, then perhaps I can go home a little earlier than I had planned. Yet this thought struck him as cowardly, although no one but himself had devised this test, the test that he had already passed. He looked at his watch: half-past seven. He thought it might be all right to begin his day.

They treated him kindly in the restaurant, and his hesitant spirit, already reinforced by his success, seemed to revive. By half-past eight he was on the street, anxious to begin his experiment. A dense blanket of grey cloud seemed not low but high above the wide boulevard, where few cars passed and only the occasional businessman, prudently belted into a sub-stantial trenchcoat, seemed to be abroad. The silence amazed him, and also the grey air, so grey that it seemed to blur his vision. At wide intersections sparse knots of people stood obediently, waiting for the lights to change. The city appeared featureless, recent but already shabby looking; it had a grim worn look, dominated by apartment blocks of an unadorned nature, set down endlessly along broad streets. Only when he raised his eyes to the horizon, and to the roofs of the larger buildings, did he see signs of industrial or commercial life: banks and corporations raising their standards and their devices as they might have done in earlier days. He turned off the oppressive street and soon found himself in a vast concourse filled with hurrying workers. He recognized, without being told about it, the Zoo station. It was, he knew, the way to the East. At this he hesitated, lost heart a little, and retraced his steps. At the Kempinski he sat down again in the restaurant and drank another cup of coffee.

Without entirely losing his new-found assurance he realized that his problem was that he did not know what to do with his time, or even what was expected of him. His age was against him, and the prospect of wandering about all day defeated him; in any event he had misjudged the size of the city, which was huge, unmanageable. Those apartment houses, stretching to infinity, the wide unconquerable streets, the rumbling trains, all filled him with bewilderment. He was forced to revise his original plan, in which he merely wandered, seeking landmarks: he was already tired and it was only half-past nine. Was he, then, to be a tourist, like any other? With a melancholy smile he went to the desk and bought a guidebook. What did tourists do in foreign cities? He supposed that they went first to the museum. He hurried out of the hotel, walked to a taxi-stand, opened the door of the first taxi parked there. '*Morgen*,' said the driver, without turning round. '*Morgen*,' said Fibich. 'Dahlem, *bitte*.' '*Ja, bitte schön*.' Collapsing in the back of the cab he wondered if he were going to be able to manage more than the average tourist's German.

Ah, but Dahlem was much more like what he expected to remember, a suburb of silent villas painted yellow, with pitched roofs and green shutters. The museum, like a giant funeral chamber, rose among ragged tangles of bramble in corner beds untouched by spring, rusty relics of a petrified autumn prolonged into this early season of the new year. As he paid off the driver, and arranged to be collected in two hours' time, he straightened up and breathed deeply. Standing on the steps of the museum and looking around him he courted recognition, but nothing came. Birds sounded muted, sad: under a sky of solid cloud, wide streets of cobbled pavements were void of any human presence. On the door of one of the houses he saw a bunch of balloons tied to the knocker. A child's party, he supposed, and he tried to remember if he had ever had one. A schoolgirl, wobbling along on a bicycle, made him wonder if he had ever had a bicycle, and had ridden along just such a silent street. But nothing came, and he turned resignedly into the museum.

He recognized nothing of what he saw: why should he? He wandered through the empty rooms, amazed that he was capable of doing so, that collapse did not seem imminent. He winced at the contorted, almost corrupt, nudes of the German school, at the agonized cosmeticized sculptures that had once adorned the altars of churches. When he smiled with recognition, it was at an English face that he smiled, at Gainsborough's *Joshua Grigby*, alert and confident in his subtle pink coat, unthreatened by the rocks against which he posed or by the lowering grey sky under which he so aristocratically lounged. A fiction, Fibich knew, but what a reassuring one, and he gained a little courage from it. He wandered, the only visitor, through rooms in which the attendant stood up when he entered and waited politely for inspection to have taken place, so that he could sit down again. Fibich saw the vast stone heads of a brutal ancient culture, and in a darkened gallery blurred dancing Indian figures worn in places to a smudge, a trace. Then, when he could stand it no longer – for the range of sensation on offer seemed to him to stretch only from pain to indifference – he escaped into the street and started to walk.

Lansstrasse, Fabeckstrasse. He walked, his feet twisting on the cobbles, to a stand of apparently dead silver birches. Summer and winter seemed equally distant in this mournful quiet. The Hansel and Gretel houses disclosed no inhabitants. He tried to find a shop, a café: anything to break this unearthly silence. He felt at home, and not at home. The only way he could judge his progress was that he was no longer homesick. He thought of Christine wonderingly, as if she were a stranger he had once known. He thought of Hartmann, whom he now saw to be lively, exuberant, festive, not stricken by this *fatigue du nord* which hung over Berlin. Hartmann, of course, was from Munich, an elegant and already southerly city. He understood Goethe's longing for the sun and the slender trees of Italy. Yet Goethe was from Weimar and was surely spared the blankness that afflicted this place. He retraced his steps to the museum and with relief heard the taxi approach. He looked at his watch. Only half-past eleven.

In the afternoon, already exhausted, he took another taxi to Charlottenburg. This was not familiar to him, although he supposed that he had seen the vast yellow palace before. He joined the crowd, put on a pair of felt slippers under the stern eye of the guide, and shuffled miserably through the ugly rooms with their coarse gilding and parvenu display of blue and white porcelain. Longingly he looked out into the gardens, composed of gravel and box; geometric parterres, carved into the red dirt, were destined never to be disturbed. He felt weighed down with fatigue, could not wait for the visit

205

to be over. And this was only his first day! He took a taxi back, sat at the Café Kranzler, furtively ate two slices of strawberry shortcake. The rush of sugar to his bloodstream revived him, and he was able to walk back, on painful feet, to the hotel. There he asked for his key, hobbled now to the lift, and greeted his white room with something like pleasure. Hartmann was right, he thought. I am no longer young.

He feared the night, with no one beside him to comfort him. But once again sleep came swiftly, a calm sleep of extraordinary depth, which, when he awoke, left him self-possessed, reconciled to this odd interval, as if, hour by hour, he were undergoing some test which, incredibly, he was managing to survive. A whiteness in the sky outside his window promised a lifting of that numbing cloud that had dimmed, hazed, and eventually weakened him the previous day. Again, he wondered what to do with his time but resigned himself, as he never thought he would be able to do: first breakfast, and then whatever the anonymous tourist did, for it seemed to him that he was no different. Outside the Kempinski coffee room the promise of a fine day had inspired the waitresses to unlock the chains that bound the iron chairs to the tables on the pavements. Was he, then, to turn temporarily into a stroller, a dilettante, sipping coffee, watching the crowds? But no, he felt, that was Hartmann's role. His was and always had been the harder part. He resolved to go to the East, to try, once more, to find that illumination, that shock of recognition that would tell him that he had come home.

At the Zoo station he bought a ticket for Friedrichstrasse, momentarily frightened by the crowds. Among the anonymous Germans were noisy French tourists, Japanese students with backpacks. He reminded himself that he, a correct elderly gentleman, was not destined to be as free of association as they were: he felt lonely, not belonging to any group, unaided. If he fell ill, he thought, no one would come to his rescue. What was more, if he fell ill in East Berlin, no one would know who he was. Thus restored to refugee status, his mind sank to familiar depths of melancholy, as, standing in trance-like stillness by the doors of the shabby train, he watched the endless lines of apartment houses advancing and retreating down wide, quiet and seemingly deserted streets, crossing and recrossing like railway lines in the segmented landscape, which had the appearance of a huge deserted junction. At the Friedrichstrasse crossing point he was herded into a discordant queue, and was hard put to contain his rising panic as the line shuffled forward into the narrow glass pen where the visas were issued. Here nationality reclaimed everyone. The French laughed and smoked, the Japanese chattered and pushed, the Germans waited patiently. Fibich felt rather faint: this alienation, at least, he recognized. He recognized it as the feeling that underlay his habitual homesickness, and then he recognized the homesickness itself as the luxury that had replaced the raw and fundamental terror that had powered him from one country to another all those years ago. The homesickness, he perceived, might be what others felt, although cleverer minds dressed it up as nostalgia or replaced it with an attachment to childhood that was or seemed artificial. But for him it was not so easy to look back. And yet, if he were to learn anything from this excursion, it would be that although he was face to face with the terror and the alienation and the longing, he was nevertheless somehow still on his feet. He had not died of it.

Squeezing through the narrow door to which the

queue had been inching its way was so like a symbolic birth that he laughed, and, once more in the open air, under the mild sun, straightened up and headed for the Unter den Linden, to which, mysteriously, he knew the way. Here was a street even wider than those which had gone before, but again overlaid with that unpeaceful quietness, that absence of some vital ingredient, some metropolitan effervescence that was intensified in the Eastern zone, where few people sauntered for pleasure, where flat square buildings faced each other across the great avenue, and where no buds broke on the famous trees. In the distance, in a faint mild haze of sunshine, Fibich could see the Brandenburg Gate. That recognized, he decided that he had passed whatever test he had set himself. He found a modest glassed-in café, and went inside. The coffee that they brought him was dark and strong. Delicious! He looked around him, feeling suddenly well-disposed, like a student released from his final examinations. A young man in a corner was eating fried eggs. Subdued conversation, of an unusually orderly nature, rose from adjoining tables. No music: a provincial calm. He paid his bill, raised his hat to the company, and went out into the sunshine, back to the Friedrichstrasse station.

And, once back on the Kurfürstendamm, he felt free, free of his curious life-long obligation, free, even, of his fear. Sun glinted on the chrome of cars: the tables outside the Kempinski were full. He wondered whether it had been his own blindness to the matters of ordinary life and the way in which this blindness had been lifted that made the city now seem populated, businesslike, good-humoured. He thought not, for he had never been mad, simply troubled to his depths by that last vision of his fainting mother and his father, bent to succour her, their faces turned away from him. Had she recovered?

Had they survived? Or rather, how long had they survived? What had happened to the house (for now he knew it was a house), the house with the chair in it, the Voltaire? And how much was he to blame for any of this? Ah, that was getting nearer to the source of his anguish. His adult self, the adult he had so unexpectedly become, almost in spite of himself, knew that all children blame themselves for their parents' unhappiness, and even for what becomes of them. That was what he must have been doing all these years. What was to deliver him was the thought of his own death, which he somehow knew was not far off, and he brushed aside the past – remote now, dully coloured, almost dark – in the interest of seeing to whatever future remained to him, leaving matters in good order for those who came after him. Time the regulator, he thought, bringer of philosophical awareness. Looking back now, from this distance, even his own life seemed precious to him, blessed with a wife and son, with a friend like Hartmann, living always in amity.

He thought of Christine, as he had first known her, a shy, timid girl, awkward, self-effacing, not happy, but too modest even to register the fact. Denied much, almost as much as he had been, in the way of family relationships, trying so very hard to belong to Aunt Marie Jessop, who was not, despite her natural kindness, any sort of a mother. Christine had not changed much, he thought: behind her odd and appealing face there still lurked the timorous girl. The only time he had ever known her to shed her reserve was with those friends that Toto had brought home: with Toto himself she was still shy. He thought of Hartmann, his valiant friend, and of Yvette, another little girl who had never shed her former self. How he understood them suddenly; how dear they were! And Marianne, who had been his darling, and who even now might be in the hospital, having another baby of her own, yet, to him still a child. Ah, he thought, the truth bursting on him suddenly, nobody grows up. Everyone carries around all the selves that they have ever been, intact, waiting to be reactivated in moments of pain, of fear, of danger. Everything is retrievable, every shock, every hurt. But perhaps it becomes a duty to abandon the stock of time that one carries within oneself, to discard it in favour of the present, so that one's embrace may be turned outwards to the world in which one has made one's home.

This thought brought him to his son. His boy, his dearest boy! How could he ever have thought his own life more precious, more interesting, than this great achievement, this Toto, this marvellous stranger, who had been given to him to show him that stable edifices can be built on ruins, that honey might indeed come from the rock? So unlike him as to seem to belong to a different species, and yet not entirely rejecting him, his poor father, coming round, in fact, after his turbulent boyhood, to their own quiet ways, reconciled at last to loving them in his own fashion, keeping in touch, however infrequently, dropping in to see them, bringing no news but apt to sit quietly at his mother's side until another impulse took him away again. Fibich, sitting in the sun outside the Kranzler, watching the crowd, felt a great peace come upon him, recognizing at last that his purpose in life had been not to find his own father but to be a father himself.

Yet, he thought, was it to be as easy as that? The part of him that was and always had been an adult warned him against the euphoria, the sense of revelation that was overtaking him, but so anxious was he to sustain the feeling that he brushed aside his misgivings. He was, after all, still on dangerous ground, and his purpose was to get home safely: he could not afford to be riven by doubt. He looked up and saw the ugly ruin of the church, the obscure blackened stump of the tower, an outrageous reminder of a past he was now anxious to forget. At the next table a woman, dressed in a white satin blouse, a full black skirt, a black hat, and wearing a gold bracelet round her ankle, smiled at him, revealing long white teeth between grotesquely exaggerated vermilion lips. He raised his hat to her, and left hurriedly, uneasily aware that she may have been, probably was, a man. Only three days left, he told himself. He was already finished with Berlin.

But the revivifying sleep continued to reclaim him and to cast him up safely on to the shores of the following day. He began to treat himself more kindly, dropped his guidebook into the wastepaper basket, stayed for long hours in his quiet room, emerging only for meals, for a gentle stroll to the shop that sold English newspapers, to the Kranzler, or, for lunch, to the Paris Bar. He alternated between feeling stranded and feeling becalmed, a state of mind common, he supposed, to most travellers. For now he felt himself to be just that, a traveller. It was a dispensation he could not have foreseen. Still the obscure voice warned him, but he silenced it. He felt well, unexpectedly restored: the slower pace of life he had allowed himself must suit him. And he began to think, luxuriously, that when he got home he would talk to Hartmann again about buying homes for them all in the South, where their wives could shop for olives and melons in the market and he and Hartmann could relax in the sun. Their work was over, he saw that now. It was time to go, time to make arrangments for them all – and for Toto, and Myers, and poor Goodman, who would perish without the office to go to each morning – and to leave, say goodbye, harvest a few years before the end. Nothing to wait for now, he thought: I have done what I meant to do, tied up what loose ends there were. And if certain things remained puzzling, what of it? Not everything is capable of being resolved in this life. And since, as he was almost certain, there was no other, and that therefore he would never see his mother and father again, what of it? It was the fate of all children. He frowned. And I am no longer a child, he reminded himself. Nevertheless, he would feel safer once he was on the plane.

He left early for the airport, allowing too much time, which he spent drinking more coffee. When it became time for him to board he felt an enormous surge of joy. In the plane sunshine flooded the cabin, signalling to him his release from stress. He saw, quite clearly, the evening ahead of him, the reunion of the four of them, the telephone call to Toto. He had bought scent for Christine and Yvette, quite unnecessary, he knew, a bottle of apricot brandy for Hartmann who liked sweet drinks, and for Toto a black crocodile belt. Marianne would have, for Henry, the little piped jacket just like the one he had seen on a boy with his mother in a café. Despite the droning of the plane he felt cocooned in silence.

The journey passed with dream-like efficiency and speed. Standing up to leave, he raised his hat to the stewardess, and shuffled with all his bags and packages through the tunnel, stepped on to firm ground, and looked around him with disbelief. He was unprepared, after the orderly little airport in Berlin, for the crowds and the noise, which was tremendous. Searching for Hartmann, and suddenly unaware of his direction, he was buffeted, stopped to rearrange his packages, and was nearly swept off his feet. After Berlin it felt warm, even hot, and stuffy. Children cried: a baby, slung over its mother's shoulder, was in the deep sleep of exhaustion. He inched slowly ahead in a queue, longing to be free, to be home. The crowd grew denser, and he was aware of a commotion behind him. 'Keep still,' cried a voice. 'Don't push. A woman has fainted.' Fibich, hampered by his parcels, felt the stirrings of the old panic. As he knew he must, he turned, in time to see the figure of a woman, collapsed into the arms of her husband, who bent over her to lay her on the ground. Together they formed a mourning group, ageless, timeless, without nationality. His mouth dry, his heart beating, Fibich pushed on, stumbling now, his peace and calm destroyed, on and on, somehow, until he reached Hartmann and fell into his arms.

14

At sixty-one Fibich grew old, perceptibly. No longer interested in his work, he put all his efforts into doing it, with fewer results. Because of his inherent meticulousness no one noticed this, but it seemed to him that the major exercise of the day was getting to the office, and then, after an aching interval, which he measured minute by minute, getting home again. He felt endangered by his absence from home, and, once home, was not much reassured. He begged Christine not to bother to devise meals for him; he would concentrate on trying to eat a little fish, which he would dismember with a tremulous knife and fork. He would discard his city clothes with a sigh of relief and put on his dressing-gown. Christine, trying to make a ceremony of this habit, which she saw as alarming, bought him a velvet smoking jacket. He wore it once or twice to please her, and then relapsed into the dressing-gown. Once she saw him shuffling along from the bathroom, the cord tied loosely round his waist, and was thankful that Toto no longer lived at home to see his father in this condition. She wondered whether it was the prospect of Toto's imminent departure to Morocco, to make a film, and his absence for a projected six months, that had brought

about this change. She even discussed this with Hartmann, since Fibich would say nothing. Hartmann, for
once, was devoid of resource. 'The trip may have tired
him,' said Hartmann. 'Let him rest. He'll be all right.
We'll plan a holiday, take a house somewhere this
summer. He will come round.'

So they let him rest. He slept voraciously, and
sometimes dreamed. His dreams were not clear to him.
In one he was being very kindly introduced by a
companion to an aristocratic tailor who was to measure
him for a suit. The fitting was to take place in Brighton,
near the station. While he waited for the tailor to attend
to him, which he never did, the scene abruptly changed
to Copenhagen on a winter's morning. This was somehow significant. In the dream Fibich took photographs
of Copenhagen which he later studied with the same
companion who had introduced him to the tailor. But in
one of the photographs the companion figured quite
prominently, standing in front of a cottage in the
grounds of a large mansion or hotel. There had been a
displacement of some kind, a fobbing off, a lack of
explanation. Fibich awoke from this dream with a sense
of alarm, relieved to find himself in his own bed. The
relief gave him a little energy with which to start the
day, which he did with a factitious enthusiasm that he
was forced to substitute for the real thing. At the office,
where he still appeared to be effective, he sat for long
periods at his desk, staring at his hands. 'He's a little
tired,' explained Hartmann, who was thereby forced
into regular attendance. Goodman, ever sympathetic,
took most of the work off his shoulders.

It was Yvette's turn to appear with covered dishes.
Turning bad into good, as was her habit, she regarded
Fibich's malaise as a challenge to her psychological
powers and excellent household management. Luxur-

ious foods appeared, were discarded by Fibich as too elaborate, and were hastily eaten by Christine in order that feelings should not be hurt. 'Don't trouble yourself,' said Christine to Yvette, as a concoction of sole with mushrooms in a cream sauce was handed in. 'He has no appetite.' 'Then he needs building up,' said Yvette firmly. Her reassurance, though of a hollow nature, was balm to Christine's anxious spirit.

To Hartmann Yvette said, 'I don't think he eats enough. Does he have a proper lunch?' 'He never has,' Hartmann informed her. 'Then you'd better see that he does. Take him to that place of yours. He'll eat if you're with him. After all, he is no longer young.' Hartmann was disgruntled, disturbed. He was the elder by five years, sixty-six to Fibich's sixty-one. Nobody remarked that he was no longer young. Of course he did not feel old. That, essentially, was the difference between Fibich and himself.

For the first time Hartmann was obliged to think about age, and about the future. He was not particularly inclined to make changes. Since his mother-in-law's revelations he no longer felt that France was a country to which he might wish to retire. This, he knew, was irrational. Nevertheless, he would wait a bit and see if the feeling passed. And if not, well, there were other places: Spain, Switzerland. And yet he had to confess that he had little taste for uprooting himself. Now that he was forced to acknowledge that he too got tired, that he was no longer eager to leave home in the mornings, that he always felt a sense of deliverance as the weekend approached, he thought it might be time to sell up, settle affairs, make arrangements, and then, perhaps, wait a little to see what everyone wanted to do. He would miss his little indulgences, his routines, but he was not without resource. By nature he was a man of

216

pleasure, and he could see that there might be a voluptuous charm in simply filling the empty days as only he
knew how: a morning of delicate shopping, a stroll, a
decent lunch somewhere. Could it be that he was at last
on the verge of that real, that ineluctable old age, in
which he had never truly believed? If so, he thought, it
had come suddenly and quickly. He pondered a moment
in disbelief, looked around at Yvette's apricot walls,
looked at Yvette herself, dressed in the bright colours she
still loved, the hair an ever more ambitious gold, saw her,
unconscious of his gaze, vigorously and importantly
moving about her drawing-room, saw, in a flash, that he
must stay alive for her sake, for she would never fare
well as a widow. He felt an unaccustomed pang in the
heart as he looked at her, never still, in her royal blue
blouse and her black skirt, humming a little under her
breath, beautifully concerned for his comfort and the
perfection of his home. He sighed. Perhaps they would
quietly remain here, and somehow carry on as they
were. Perhaps Fibich would come out of his depression,
if that was what it was, and resume his duties, bring his
attention once more to bear on the present. Suddenly all
that Hartmann required was to see smiles on the faces
around him. It was, after all, what he had always
required. In his own eyes he had changed very little, had
always, even as a young man, had an adult sense of
responsibility. He had always had the insight that if he
organized the main structures of his life – work, home,
marriage – in a satisfactory manner, then he was fully
entitled to enjoy his liberty outside them. He had had an
easy attitude to fidelity when first married, but now he
realized that he had been faithful to his wife for so long
that he would find anything else intolerable. He became
aware that Yvette had made him happy. He looked at
her, sitting at her little desk, making out her shopping

list, her mouth firm with attention. She would never understand either *La Princesse de Clèves* or *Madame Bovary*, and he was glad of it. He went over to her and kissed her hair, put an arm around her thickening shoulders.

'You know,' he said gently. 'I think you have put on a little weight.'

'I may have filled out a bit,' she admitted. 'But no one could say that I haven't kept my figure.'

'No,' he agreed. 'No one could say that.'

He patted her arm, was suddenly reluctant to leave her. She was, however, as always, sublimely unconscious of his moods.

'Are you off?' she asked. 'Don't be late this evening. I might want to see Marianne.'

'What will you do today?' he asked her in his turn.

She looked at him in surprise. 'Oh, I have plenty to do, don't you worry about me. Are you all right, Hartmann? You're usually on your way by this time.'

'Yes,' he said. 'I'm all right. I'll see you later. Have a good day.'

But he hesitated by the door, looked back at her unrealistically golden head, bent once more over her list, and wondered suddenly what it would be like not to see her there. He shivered. But this was ridiculous! They were still young! This was the malaise that was afflicting Fibich: he must have caught it from him. He straightened his shoulders and left the room, took his hat and the cane he sometimes affected, decided to walk to the office to demonstrate how young and active he was. It was a clear day, mild but sunless: rain was forecast. The white sky reflected his mood, in which he detected a certain anxiety, and absence of joy. He put this down to the strain of Marianne's second pregnancy, which had worried him, but he was aware that this was not the only cause. If Fibich went . . . Again, he told himself, this was ridiculous. Because the man had had the absurd idea of going to Berlin and had understandably been shaken up by the experience, there was no need to regard him as endangered. He had always been nervous, and now he was just a little more nervous than he had been: it was as simple as that. And even if it were not simple, they had reached the stage in life in which matters had to be made simple if they themselves were to last out the course. How could Fibich have put them all at risk with his insane journey? And what had he proved? Striding up the tree-arching avenue in the park, Hartmann felt his heart expand with anger, and also with joy, as he recovered his normal equilibrium. Fibich must pull himself together. He must be told that he owed it to Christine, to his son, and to himself, Hartmann, to behave like a grown-up for once in his life. For that was the trouble with Fibich, he thought. Although recognizable as elderly, he had never grown up. Well now, he, Hartmann, would have to talk with Fibich, as man to man, not as the boys they had once been, would tell him about the sudden recognition of old age that he had had that morning, would remind him that they must make plans, settle affairs, and, most of all, preserve themselves so as to enjoy whatever future remained to them. Hartmann, gazing up proprietorially at the arching branches, the trees now in full leaf, felt his troubled thoughts leave him, and also his ill humour. This had always been his strength, he thought, his endless tolerance of idiosyncrasy in others. Nevertheless, he was determined to speak to Fibich quite firmly. He strode on, proud of his ability to cover the distance from Ashley Gardens to Spanish Place, at a steady pace, on this dull but cloudless May morning. And not even out of breath, he remarked to himself.

The morning passed without incident. Roger brought no news of Marianne's condition. She had been in the hospital for three weeks and now the baby was almost due. Hartmann felt a thrill of fear: if bad news were to come it would come from that quarter. It was only natural that his nerves were on edge, he thought. Perhaps if Fibich were to become a grandfather he might behave more sensibly, might realize that energies have to be reinvested in that new generation, not squandered on his own past. But he thought that Fibich might be denied the opportunity to see his grandchildren. He somehow knew that Toto would remain unmarried for a very long time, would indeed regard his youth, and in turn his youthfulness, as his stock in trade, and therefore remain professionally famous as a young man until at the very least in his late thirties. Hartmann realized with a shock that Toto was already twenty-nine, nearly thirty. Where had the time gone? Again with a shiver of disquiet he determined to bring Fibich to book, as if he alone were responsible for all this ageing, as if time had less purchase on Fibich than on the rest of them, as if it devolved upon Fibich to bring them all safely through to the untroubled prospect that was, by now, surely theirs by right.

At half-past twelve he knocked on Fibich's door. Fibich, his hands folded and resting on top of an almost empty desk, looked up mildly. Hartmann resented his inactivity, as if this were proof of some private decision to abandon serious matters, until he saw that it was not inactivity at all: in the background, by the safe, was John Goodman, their all too devoted company secretary, whose eagerness was out of all proportion to what Hartmann and Fibich saw, still, as the frivolous nature of the enterprise. A small fortune built on flair, nothing but flair: how could they take credit for it? They had always had an amiable attitude towards work, the two of them, both knowing that in another life they would have done something more sensible, more serious, recognizing what they actually did do as appropriate to their uncertain position in every sort of hierarchy. Hartmann had the ideas and Fibich did the worrying: it suited them both perfectly. It was something of an effort for them to accommodate the personal career ambitions of both Myers and Goodman, young men on whom, Hartmann thought, youth was wasted, but fervid in their belief that what they did in this toy empire was important. Dark-suited, their rolled umbrellas a mark of *gravitas*, Myers and Goodman treated each other in a perfectly affable manner but with a lack of intimacy that entertained Hartmann profoundly. 'Such senators!' he had once remarked to Fibich. 'Such men of the cloth!' For he thought that work should be tackled exuberantly, lightheartedly, or not at all. Fibich was more tolerant, at least of Myers. Goodman worried him more. It was Goodman's assiduity he found hard to bear, his almost feminine desire to be necessary and wanted. And those extraordinary pleading eyes, the eyes of a harem favourite, quickly cast down, at the merest hint of reproof, into a double arc of dense, almost tangled lashes. Fibich had devised many ways to outwit Goodman's sensibility, and had been forced to improvise many others, but that sensibility had never been exhausted. Trying to spare Goodman's feelings frequently brought on one of Fibich's migraine headaches. Hartmann treated him more teasingly and suffered from him accordingly less. Fibich could hardly bear to think about Goodman's life with his mother, in their little house in Putney, the news of the day faithfully served up to her over the evening meal. He saw them as himself and Aunt Marie Jessop, all those years ago. Nevertheless he continued to enquire after Mrs Goodman's health, although the radiant answers made him uneasy. Hartmann quite simply saw him as unawakened, waited for him to break out. In the meantime, since there were no signs of Goodman's ever breaking out, he would sportingly assume the existence of several girl-friends. 'Still out and about, John?' he would say. 'Still fancy free? Still tormenting the women?' Goodman would modestly lower his fabulous eyelashes, uncertain as to how to respond. At an admonitory shake of the head from Fibich, Hartmann would relent. 'Leave early today, John,' he would say. 'Give your mother a surprise. Everything seems to be taken care of. You do an excellent job.' Fibich often wished he had so light a touch. Goodman always appreciated Hartmann's sallies, but it was to Fibich that he looked for praise.

'Lunch,' said Hartmann firmly, determined to get down to the matter in hand. 'I am taking you out to lunch. All right, John, get some lunch yourself. And tell Tania to go too. We'll be back about two-thirty.'

Fibich looked at him in surprise. 'I am not hungry,' he said. 'Yes, John, finish up here later. I don't really want to eat.'

'I am taking you to lunch,' said Hartmann, handing him his hat. 'That is what is the matter with you, Fibich. You're neglecting yourself. And it's time we had a talk.'

In the street he looked about him with displeasure at the prolonged sunlessness, the absence of good weather. Brave girls were dressed in flimsy garments, their bare legs white, their shoes inadequate. Harsh light came down unmediated from the colourless sky: rain still threatened but refused to materialize. Turning into the hotel dining-room, Hartmann was mildly put out to see nearly all the tables occupied. He stood majestically by the door, waiting to be ferried over to safe-keeping. Reaching a table that was not his usual table, he flourished his white napkin, waved away the menu, and said, 'Sole. Grilled. Is that all right with you, Fibich? Fish is what you like, isn't it?'

'Thank you, thank you,' said Fibich. 'Sole, by all means.'

They sat in silence for a while, Fibich staring at his hands. Eventually Hartmann, who knew him so well, sighed.

'What happened there?' he asked. 'What did you find?'

Fibich looked up at him, still mildly.

'I found a foreign city that I did not remember,' he said. 'Rather a pleasant one. It meant nothing to me whatever.'

'And yet, since you came back you've been different. Changed. Something must have happened. What was it?'

Fibich smiled painfully. 'The only memory came last of all,' he said. 'Do you remember a commotion at Heathrow? A woman fainting?'

Hartmann nodded.

'The last sight of my mother,' said Fibich finally. 'She fainted when she said goodbye to me. I seemed to see her again. And since thinking about that moment, I find that I cannot endure . . .'

He dropped his head, made a helpless gesture with his hand, and knocked over a glass of water.

'Fibich!' said Hartmann warningly, summoning a waiter.

'I should have gone back,' whispered Fibich. 'I should not have left. I should have got off the train.'

'Is everything all right, gentlemen?' asked the head

waiter, removing the wet tablecloth.

'Quite all right,' said Hartmann, rather too loudly. 'But I'm afraid we are in rather a hurry.'

'Your lunch is served, sir.' And the table was put to rights, hastily, while another waiter dealt with the fish, taking it off the bone and decorating it with lemon wedges and tartare sauce. 'A little wine, perhaps? If Mr Fibich is not feeling well?'

'No, no,' said Hartmann, again too loudly. 'That will be all.'

'Thank you,' said Fibich, in a voice slightly higher than normal, feigning enthusiasm. But his face was pale, and as the smell of fish rose from the plate in front of him his eyes filled with tears.

Hartmann stared at him in alarm. A collapse here, in Durrant's Hotel, where he lunched every day? A break-down, the end of Fibich? He watched as Fibich tried to eat, raising and lowering his fork, disguising the un-tasted fragments beneath the sauce, the tears sliding down his face. He glanced round to see if anyone were watching. Conversation had ceased at the adjoining table.

'Come, Fibich,' he said. 'Thomas. You are safe. You are here. Try to eat. You have such a good appetite. Make an effort.' He was distractedly torn between anger and pity. But as the tears continued to fall he summoned the waiter again. 'On my account,' he said. 'We have to go.'

'Of course, sir. I understand.' They were outside in what seemed like record time, their passage shielded by waiters, their hats handed to them silently. Hartmann was aware of a momentary cessation of activity, a collective holding of breath, before they reached the blessed anonymity of the street.

Somehow he got Fibich back to the office, his coat

hanging off his shoulders, his hat on the back of his head. Hartmann could not bear to put him to rights, simply drew his arm through his own, walked him like a child, aware of what they must look like, an upright bourgeois with his dissolute brother. Two girls, passing, giggled, taking Fibich to be drunk. As they reached their building, Fibich stumbled on the step. Then they were inside, safe from alien eyes. Hartmann guided Fibich to his room, to his chair, removed his hat, stood there while Fibich wept.

Goodman, returning, and thinking to find the room empty, went in to finish his work at the safe. He stopped at the sight of Fibich, whose tears were now spent, sitting with his head lowered to his clenched hands, still in his coat. Hartmann lifted his hand in warning, putting his finger to his lips. But Goodman, who was all too naturally of a filial nature, disappeared, came back with a glass of water, knelt by Fibich's desk, and took his hand.

'Mr Fibich,' he said gently. 'Would you like me to make you some coffee?'

Fibich raised his head, looked around him, and then looked down into Goodman's extravagant eyes, while Hartmann eased his coat from his shoulders.

'John,' he said presently, in an almost normal voice. 'I think I must have turned a little faint.'

'Drink this, sir,' said Goodman, proffering the glass.

Fibich drank slowly, shuddering as the icy water reached his stomach. 'That's better,' he said, his face still ghastly. 'Did you have lunch, John?'

'Oh, yes, sir,' Goodman's voice was devoid of embarrassment. Life at home, even at the age he was, must have conditioned him to work of this nature. Hartmann's opinion of him rose.

'And do you look after yourself properly, John?'

'Oh, yes, sir,' said Goodman again. 'My mother sees to that. We eat very healthfully. Mother sees to it that I eat a lot of salads.'

'That's good,' said Fibich. 'Take care of your mother, John.' Hartmann turned away and looked out of the window. 'Is she in good health? Do you keep her company?'

Goodman did not appear to find these questions unusual. 'We've always been close,' he replied. 'My father left home when I was little, so there's just been the two of us. We do everything together.'

'And what will you do this weekend?' asked Fibich.

'I dare say we shall go over and visit my married sister,' said Goodman. 'I'm an uncle, you see. My sister has a small girl. We like to see her as often as we can.'

'That's good, John, very good.' Fibich's colour was returning, as if the contemplation of Goodman's home life were gradually filling him with reassurance.

'Perhaps a cup of coffee, Mr Fibich?'

'Why, yes, John, if you would be so kind.' At a nod from Hartmann Goodman left the room.

'Hartmann,' said Fibich. 'Something has happened.'

Hartmann stood behind him, his hands on Fibich's shoulders.

'Nothing has happened,' he said. 'You're still here. And so am I. Perhaps you did what you had to do, faced facts, did your grieving. Perhaps it is over for you now. I was lucky,' he went on, wiping the moisture from his eyes. 'I dismissed it all. And I was able to do this, somehow. I don't know how. I can't explain it, any of it. Perhaps you had to go through this to be free of it. A little crisis,' he said, blowing his nose. 'One might even say it was overdue. And all managed without the benefit of psychiatrists. Think of that!'

Fibich looked around him wonderingly. 'I feel better,' he said. But he did not look well, Hartmann thought. Nevertheless, his colour was nearly back to normal, and he drank the coffee that Goodman brought. Both watched him as he replaced the cup carefully in its saucer.

'Perhaps you should go home, sir, when you've had a rest.'

'Yes,' said Fibich. 'I should like to go home.'

'We will both go,' said Hartmann. 'And you too, John. Finish what you have to do and go home.'

'Buy your mother some flowers,' said Fibich. 'Give her a nice surprise.'

'I usually do, at the weekends,' said Goodman. 'We always enjoy our weekends.'

They both watched him as he collected the cups. Doomed, thought Hartmann. Saved, thought Fibich.

They took a taxi, leaving Fibich's car behind. They sat in the back, two elderly gentlemen, Hartmann resting his hands on his cane. They said nothing, simply marking the passage from danger back to normal life. The streets were empty: it seemed as if most people had left early for the weekend, despite the unpromising weather. Fibich appeared to have recovered from his attack, or whatever it was, thought Hartmann. He cautiously allowed himself to hope for the best. He resolved, at some point during the weekend, to speak to him about retirement. They would both retire, he thought, remembering his melancholy of the morning. It was time. And it was unthinkable, in any event, that he might carry on without Fibich. Their day was done, he now saw, although it terrified him to think that this might be so. Nothing too precipitate, of course: perhaps a year to wind things up, convert themselves into shareholders, make provision for the children. It could be done, he saw, and all in due season. There was no

227

need to get out immediately, no need to frighten anybody. Everyone would understand. And their wives would be glad of their company. He thought back to Yvette, as he had seen her that morning. All in due season, he thought. All in due season.

Fibich thought of his home, of Christine, of his son. How painfully he had missed them, he thought: how wrongly he had spent his time, trying to re-establish a life before the only life he knew. He longed to reach his home, which was the only haven he would ever reach, and yet how temporary, how unstable even that now seemed to him. In any event he had always had an ambivalent attitude towards his home, for while the idea was sacred to him, the reality of it always proved fugitive. This was nothing to do with its physical location, or the fashion in which it was arranged: he even liked Chrisine's hazy muted colours, although he regarded the rooms as belonging entirely to her, with himself as a visitor, agreeably housed, but, it seemed to him, on a temporary basis. When in the office he would sometimes think lovingly of his home, yet as soon as he was back there he was afflicted with a restlessness which had him seizing his hat again and calling to Christine that he was going to get a bottle of wine, or post a letter, or simply take a walk in an attempt to dislodge the beginnings of a headache. He would wonder if he might feel better somewhere else, would search the Sunday newspapers, go with Hartmann to visit blocks of flats in St John's Wood, in South Kensington, in Highgate or Chiswick. Hartmann enjoyed these visits as simple excursions – he was in any event curious about other people's living arrangements – but to Fibich they were a matter of greater importance. Would he feel better if he received the evening sun, if he had a balcony, a patio, a roof terrace, if there were a caretaker on the premises, if the shops were near to hand, if there were three bathrooms instead of two, if he faced the other way? He did not know. He only knew that he felt a dismay amounting to anguish at the thought that he was already experiencing the maximum amount of comfort to be derived from the concept 'home'. He worried that it loomed so large, yet filled him with despair. Whatever brief moments of satisfaction he had felt in his life were always lessened by the idea of going home. He could be sitting comfortably in his own chair, in his own drawing-room, doing something entirely pleasant – reading, listening to music – when the idea of home would strike through him with a pang, as if home were somewhere else. Thus the homesickness that had afflicted him in Berlin had nothing to do with any home that he had ever known, but rather as if his place were eternally elsewhere, and as if, displaced as he was, he was only safe when he was fast asleep.

Gliding down Park Lane in the taxi, with Hartmann silent beside him, he began again to wonder whether they should not all sell up and go to the sun. For surely he would feel safer in the sun, source of all life, all joy, drawing him out of that deathly sleep every morning, summoning him, challenging him, revivifying him? The white skies and the green leaves of London had never given him the comfort that burning heat and brilliant light would certainly supply. For ten months of the year he felt cold, and his longing for warmth, like his longing for home, seemed unconquerable. He was not like Hartmann, who had the gift of being able to enjoy everything, every change in the climate, every amusement in the working day, every prospect of a new life. Fibich wished only to be safe, and, once safe, to be free, and, once free, to be brave. He had always known this, but never so clearly, never so nakedly as he did in

229

this taxi, which even now was at the bottom of Grosvenor Gardens, and was taking him home to his wife, who must not be told that he was gravely damaged, merely a little tired, a little over-stressed and in need of a holiday. Hartmann would see to it. Hartmann would know what to do, what to say. For his part he felt quite calm, as if that shameful weeping had sedated him, leaving him devoid of resource, devoid too of his habitual nervousness, but cold, very cold.

They found Christine arranging pink and white tulips in a square glass vase. 'I'm so glad you're early,' she said. 'Toto is coming to dinner. You're eating with us, Hartmann. Does Yvette know you are home?'

'No,' he said, 'I haven't been upstairs yet.'

'You are more than welcome to stay,' she said. 'Will you have tea? Or did you have some at the office? You look cold, Fibich. Take your coat off. You'll soon get warm.'

She was too busy to pay them much attention. Fibich watched her, patting her tulips, straightening a couple of books on a side table, twitching curtains into place.

'Toto coming to dinner?' he asked. This was almost unprecedented.

'Apparently he is off on Monday. The dates are being put forward. And we shan't see him for six months.'

She put her hand to her heart, as if registering the full impact of this news.

Fibich smiled, went over to her. 'Then we must see that he has a nice evening,' he said.

It appeared that nothing would be mentioned of the affair of Fibich's day, for which Fibich was grateful. He had not yet decided what to make of it. He now viewed his conduct with distaste, the distaste of a rational man. He felt quiet and empty, had no desire to return to that moment of – what had it been? revelation? – which he had experienced in the hotel dining-room. Whatever it had been, he had a sense of finality, as if the episode were done with. The partial easing of his feelings (for he knew there might be more to come) had been violently registered as a physical upheaval over which he had no control, and, as with any other illness, he was too glad to have got it over to investigate it further. Health, he supposed, was an absence of physical despair, and for the moment he felt none. Like a restored invalid he welcomed the warmth of the room, the flowers in the vase, the tea in his cup. Like an invalid he drank greedily, ate, with a careful and painful exactitude, the slice of iced apricot flan that Christine made so well. Hartmann lingered, turning to the window, his cup in his hand.

'You are very quiet, Hartmann,' said Christine. 'What are you thinking?'

'I was thinking of a housekeeper we had,' he said. 'In Munich. Her name was Frau Dimke. I have just remembered it. And my nurse was Frau Zarzicki.'

But Fibich waved a hand at him, as if to say, 'That life is over. Leave it alone. It has no place here. Remember not to remember, or you will be like me.' And Hartmann nodded, as if he understood what Fibich did not need to put into words, so present was it in both their minds.

Hartmann smiled. Such smiles they both had, thought Christine. That was what had bound her to them in the first place, their wonderful smiles, eager in Hartmann's case, tentative, like an English sun, in Fibich's. And from the joyless world of her youth she had retained a nostalgia for joy, although she herself was untrained for such emotion, and was awkward with it. Toto had it, that smile, although in his case it came too rarely, and when it did come could be perverted to do

231

duty for feeling. Latterly, she thought, smiling herself, he had begun to look more like Fibich, tall, inwardly pondering, so that the smile, when it came, had a thoughtful reflective quality to it. In her eyes Fibich had changed little: it was Toto in whom all the major changes could be observed. Fibich, just today, when his hair was a little untidy and beginning to grow long again, might have been the man she married, tall and spare, absent-minded, with the same loping walk that she had often and secretly observed from behind the curtains of her father's flat in West End Lane. If anything it was Hartmann who had changed, grown pear-shaped, silver-haired. But his face, beneath the expensively barbered and flattened hair, was still the same, the face of an impudent boy impatient to grow into a fully-fledged roué. It was all a matter of expression, she thought. He still cocked his head to one side, pursed his lips as if to kiss someone, anyone, widened his eyes at the thought of treats to come. And Fibich, too, had kept his original expression. He had a characteristic way of smiling and shaking his head at the same time that she had always found endearing. She saw that in time Toto might come to have that little mannerism, although in Toto the family likeness had taken a long time to come to the surface. She hoped that there was nothing of herself in Toto, although many people had remarked on his brilliant eyes, so unusual with dark hair, and, in rare moments of exaltation Christine did suppose that he might possibly have inherited them from her.

'What are you smiling at, Hartmann?' she asked.

'I am smiling at you smiling,' he said. 'One can see your boy is coming home.' He sighed. 'If only Marianne were here. Then we could all be together. No news, I suppose?'

'Nothing in the last hour. You had better ring the hospital and give them this number. Then you can relax this evening.'

'Yes,' he said. 'I must go and change. What time do you want us, Christine?'

'Toto is coming at seven-thirty,' she told him.

He smiled again. 'Then we will come at eight.'

When Toto came in, on the stroke of seven-thirty, with a carrier bag, she almost cried out at the resemblance to his father. He had let himself in with his key, and was deep in thought, going through his lines, she supposed, for she had no notion of how films were made. He straightened up, with a visible effort, and smiled at her. That smile again! From the bag he produced a bottle of wine and a pot plant, which she put in the place of honour on a small table, sweeping aside her tulips in order to do so.

'My dear boy,' she said. 'My dear boy.'

He flapped his hand at her. 'It's only a plant, Ma,' he said. 'The wine is for Dad. Drink it when I'm not here. You're very quiet, Dad. Daddy? Are you all right?'

'Never better,' said Fibich.

This was new, he thought, this noticing. But because he now wished to preserve his son from those quaking feelings of loss and regret which were his almost constant companions, he said little, put away his anxiety and his solicitude, the enquiries about Toto's health, sleep, exercise that he longed to make and habitually did make. Now it was appropriate, on the eve of Toto's departure, to treat him like a man, and in order to do so he must behave like a man himself. For he knew, somehow, that Toto, who was about to leave them (and who knew if he, Fibich, would ever see him again?) must feel some of that melancholy experienced by all those who leave their known worlds behind, and leave

233

behind, too, those who love them, exchanging them for the more brutal attitudes of casual acquaintances, acquaintances who might see him as a novice who must undergo some rites of initiation if he were to be one of them. For whom could Toto trust, since he loved no-one? He would be for ever dependent, whether he knew it or not, on those who loved him. And Fibich, in the clarity of this unusual day, could see that Toto was beginning to be aware of this, and to begin his own life, in which the mourning process would not be entirely absent.

The arrival of Yvette, in a blast of 'Joy' and a black and gold striped dress that made her look like a wasp, lightened the atmosphere. 'Hartmann is still telephoning,' she said disgustedly. 'He telephones every hour. He is driving them all mad. I told him I would *know* when the baby was born. "I am a mother," I said. "I will *know*." He takes no notice, of course. As if I were not concerned myself.'

'And of course Roger would let you know,' said Christine.

'Oh, Roger,' said Yvette, with surprise in her voice. 'I'd forgotten about Roger, to tell you the truth.'

Toto laughed. 'I adore you, Yvette.'

'Well, of course, darling,' she smiled. 'You always did. And how's our clever boy, then?'

They ate roast lamb, with tiny carrots and turnips, and a pudding that consisted of squares of shortbread floating on a sea of fruit. Toto ate swiftly, his eyes on his plate. 'There is plenty more,' observed Fibich mildly, almost amused to see his appetite duplicated so exactly. The day had brought revelations, he thought. *Life* brings revelations. He remembered some inkling of this having come to him in Berlin. He had felt then on the verge of a great discovery. But perhaps that was the discovery, quite simply that life brings revelations, supplies all the material we need. And if it does not supply it in the right order, then we must simply wait for more to come to light. He felt a coldness at the thought that more might be revealed to him, was no longer so anxious to bring it about, might even be content, he thought, to wait, and even to hope that nothing more would be vouchsafed to him this side of the grave. He glanced at his wife, whose eyes were all for Toto. Yet Fibich knew that in those last days, if he were granted the grace to be aware of them, Toto would be his, entirely his. For at the end he knew, even if Toto were not there (and he could not help wishing, selfishly, that he might be) he would, with this knowledge, die a happy man.

'There is cheese, if anyone wants it,' said Christine. Nobody did. She put a dish of chocolate-covered marzipan on the table, and went out to make coffee.

'Why do you never put on weight?' wondered Yvette. 'You both have such a sweet tooth. Hartmann was saying this morning that he thought I had filled out a little.'

'I was mistaken,' said Hartmann gravely. 'You look to me as you looked when I first saw you. Voluptuous, sensual, a woman of mystery. You maddened us with desire, back there in the Farringdon Road. I had to tie Fibich down to his desk. He was like a werewolf. A lycanthrope,' he added, taking the last of the marzipan. 'We imagined men fighting duels over you. Not much of a typist, though, as I remember.'

'Oh, Hartmann,' protested Yvette. 'You are always making fun of me.'

'I?' He put his hand to his breast. 'Would I do that?'

'I think I ran that office very competently,' she said.

'My darling, I can safely say without fear of contradiction that we have never had another secretary like you.'

The evening passed as if there were to be no birth, no departure. Fibich reflected that it might well be the last of such evenings. He felt a sense of completion, not devoid of sadness. They would never move, he could see that now. They would stay as they were, for whatever changes would take place would take place in their children, not in themselves. He supposed that he and Hartmann would continue to go to the office, do a little less, perhaps, then a great deal less, until they could do no more. Then they would take their rest. He did not know which of them would be left to take care of the others. For himself now it would simply be a matter of trying his best. He looked around him, at the faces at the table. Toto had wandered off to watch television. Christine was flushed, as she always was in moments of pleasure. Yvette – and he could see that she was now quite plump – sat with her hand through Hartmann's arm. And Hartmann looked quite old. But just the same, still the same bold young man that he had been on leaving the army, ready for anything. Fibich turned and looked at his son, who sat, long legs stretched out in front of him, in front of the television.

'Remind him to take something warm for the evenings,' he said to Christine.

'But it will be hot!' said Yvette. 'Marvellously hot. We should go to the sun ourselves this year. What do you say, Christine?'

'It would be better to wait until the winter,' she answered. 'I don't want to be away until Toto comes back.'

'And have you forgotten Marianne?' said Hartmann. 'Oh, God. Should I telephone again?'

'Not yet,' Yvette told him. 'You know what would

be nice? If we took a house somewhere, and the children came too. Would you like that, Toto? Would you come?'

'Leave him alone,' said Fibich, smiling. 'He will come if he wants to. And if not, not.'

Toto leaned forward and switched off the television.

'Rubbish,' he commented. 'And he wasn't good. What was that, Daddy? A house? Oh, yes, I'll come. I'll come. If you really want me, that is.'

15

Hartmann, with solemn joy, realized that his life had
been restored to him with the advent of Flora Myers,
Marianne's second child. His relief and gratitude at what
he considered to be her gallantry in submitting to her
husband's demands for a large family (relief which was
cunningly mingled with hope that her marital duties
were now over) predisposed him towards the birth, for
surely, he thought, two is enough, even for Roger, with
his pale evangelical attitude towards the righteousness
of this particular activity. Marianne is too old, thought
Hartmann, prepared to do battle on her behalf, although
he viewed his daughter's conjugal arrangements with
unmitigated distaste, thinking, secretly, that he would
rather have kept her at home unmarried than see her
waxy and plump in her boiler suit, her hair already
showing strands of grey. What had happened, he wondered, to that sleek fastidious girl who was almost too
fine, too unprotected for this world of sharp dealing and
broken promises? How had she turned into this silent
middle-aged woman, whom, truth to tell, he loved
even more now, although her every visit inspired him
with the sort of dismay he would have felt at the sight of
a badly served meal or a neglected and disordered room.

His dismay was of an aesthetic nature, for nothing could change the agony of love he felt for her. Yet when he saw her side by side with her mother he wondered what had gone wrong, and even whether the easy circumstances of her childhood had deprived her of some essential rigour, some need to improve, which was the characteristic which secretly linked him with Fibich, with Yvette, and even with Christine.

Marianne, at thirty-seven, looked quite simply indistinguishable from a million other tired mothers, although she had a nanny (paid for by Hartmann) and a car of her own (also bought by Hartmann, who saw it as a means of enabling her to visit her parents without Roger, which was how he preferred to see her). Yet she seemed listless under the weight of all this attention, her face pale and unadorned, her hair too long on her forehead, her slackening body indifferently clothed in a plaid shirt and blue jeans, garments which Hartmann thought should only be worn by students or those of indeterminate age who mistakenly liked to flaunt the badge of youth, middle-aged schoolmasters, gallant lady tourists, those recently retired who had taken up self-improvement. He saw such garments as deceitful, inappropriate on anyone over the age of eighteen. And Marianne never seemed to wear anything else these days, as if she had given herself over completely to the desecration of her former beauty.

Now that he thought of it, Hartmann could see that the light had gone out of Marianne some time ago, around about the time of her marriage. He had no sense of why this should be so, although he was convinced that it had much to do with Roger's holy and purposeful manner of making love. Squeamishly, he closed his mind against the prospect of his daughter's intimate life, although he sighed when he thought of it, and would have wished for her a different kind of husband, even a lover, who would make her laugh and put some colour in her cheeks. But it was not to be, for she seemed determined to play another part, and no lover, however demonic, would seek her out in her present condition.

When he compared her with Yvette, he would shake his head in a mixture of wonder and amusement. Marianne, with her pale face, looked both younger and older than her mother. With every year that passed Yvette became more refulgent. Past the age of fifty-five, and now at last heading in the same direction as himself, she seemed to have undergone a second wave of femininity and now devoted more time than ever to her appearance. Hartmann supposed that this ease of passage was some kind of compensation for her untroubled instincts, which had preserved her in happy ignorance for so many years. Whatever the reason, she presented a brave appearance, golden-haired, her face bright with colour, her clothes voluptuously bold, her little feet squeezed into high-heeled shoes, the bracelets still tinkling on her wrists. She was like a schoolgirl, he reflected, knowing something of her life as a poor boarder in that Swiss school, who had at last found herself able to afford all the things that she had wanted at that earlier age, and who had bought exactly what she would have bought had she had the money when she was a girl: bottles of scent, make-up, frivolous underwear. Yet he had to admit that she looked well on it. He liked to see a woman still flaunting her powers of attraction. His taste, these days, ran not to the young, not even to the middle-aged, but to those about to enter their late fifties or even early sixties. He liked to see what a woman could make of herself then, as if he might catch her out on her whole amorous history by virtue of the signals she still displayed. A disappointed woman, he thought, would not bother, whereas a woman whose faith in herself had been preserved would go to town, embrace every remaining year, enjoy the afterglow of her past, and thus earn his indulgent and always amused approval.

He knew, of course, that the signs could be misleading, that not all decorative, or indeed decorated, women had had a gallant past, and yet as he got older that consideration no longer seemed to weigh with him. What he admired now, he thought, was a sort of pluck, the quality that made a woman want to dress herself boldly and sally forth in spite of the damage that the years were doing to her. Contemplation of this quality, which Yvette possessed in abundance, filled him with gratitude, and also with a sort of reassurance, not merely that life could go on but that it could go on undimmed. Undimmed! That was his watchword now that he was getting older – but did he really believe that? He would not, could not, countenance any unsavoury change, and would resist to the very end the laziness, the inertia, that he knew must come eventually. For this reason he had decided not to retire, and had without difficulty managed to convince Fibich (who needed little convincing) that it would be better to change their lives as little as possible. 'Time enough to think about it later on,' he had said. 'When we are old. When we are ready to go to the sun.' Fibich had agreed with him. Now that Toto was so rarely in England, Fibich would have found the days long without his scrupulous routines, and in the office both he and Hartmann were able to recapture the essence of their friendship before the advent of wives and children had cemented the two families into one indissoluble unit.

Such memories now were sweet to Hartmann, as was the position of safety that he had made for himself in this uncertain world. He would talk to Fibich of the early days in England, and indeed Fibich was now able to reminisce with him, although discussion of what had gone before was still out of bounds. And yet, Hartmann thought, later we may even come to talk of that, of those matters, of what must have happened. Not yet. He knew the time would come, near the very end, perhaps. And Fibich, he knew, was writing some kind of memoir, for his son, he said, of all he could remember, which was very little, but which was coming into a sort of low relief as he wrote. He said little of this to Hartmann, although he asked if he might give the papers to him for safe-keeping, if anything were to happen to him. Nowadays he was quite eager, even enthusiastic, when the discussion turned to those early days at school (here they were apt to look round fearfully, to see if they had made good their escape) and at the print shop and in Compayne Gardens and the Farringdon Road, until they looked at each other, amazed to find that they were still on their feet. Look! We have come through!

Hartmann, for whom the working day had always been long when not furnished with diversions, had instituted a new, though atavistic, ceremony: second breakfast. To this end he would summon Fibich to a café he had discovered, for scrambled eggs and toast at ten forty-five every morning. It was in this atmosphere, with the beneficent smells of innocent food rising around them, that the memories would be exchanged, a haze of goodwill emanating from the realization that their appetites were still excellent. Did they eat more than other men of their generation? Or did they simply come from well-nourished backgrounds? Whatever the explanation, they were easily able to accommodate four meals a day, and they liked to have at hand fruit or chocolates to sustain them through the comforting evenings. Food was still a source of pleasure, and why not? All sources of pleasure – those of the faculties and of the senses – must now be enjoyed to the full.

It was in comparison with the enjoyment he still felt, and with the brilliant appearance of his wife, that he viewed his daughter's pale and lack-lustre presence when she drove herself over to see them. It was understood that Roger would not accompany her because he saw Hartmann every day at the office, and this did duty for family intimacy. Hartmann, who could tolerate him in Spanish Place, where relations were naturally formal, found his presence in Ashley Gardens inappropriate: he could not reconcile this pale, freckled, righteous stranger with his own frivolity. He considered the other man to be benighted, rendered bloodless by his irritating single-mindedness, and by the puritanism which decreed that his wife should wear no make-up and should bear children until the time for such matters ran out. And Marianne had not even put up a fight! She is so different from us, he thought. What has made her different? Did we look after her too well, see that no harm came to her? Did it deprive her of initiative? He knew she was not happy. And he knew there was nothing to be done about it. There was no getting rid of Roger: he was too obviously impeccable. And Hartmann drew the line at inciting his daughter to revolt: that was too unseemly to contemplate. If only she had my vanity, he thought, and her mother's complacency. If only she were light-minded like me, subversive, wilful, sensationally charming. If only she had my flair, my bad character. But she was good, passively, obediently good. And he loved her all the more for it.

Some of the distaste he felt for Roger also affected his

243

attitude to Henry Myers, which he felt was probably unfair, if on the whole justified. Henry was a pale freckled boy, a miniature version of his father, with his father's thick white limbs and large pale blue eyes englobed in mauvish eyelids. Although he no longer smelled of sick his appetite was poor and his flesh was not attractive. When invited to tea at his grandmother's he would peer suspiciously inside sandwiches to see if they contained anything he disliked, and would halt his mastication of sponge cake in mid-flow to wonder if it were agreeing with him. Yvette, naturally, found this exasperating. 'Henry!' she would say. 'We do not serve bad food in this house! Sit up and swallow properly!' He would abandon what was on his plate, and drink his tea steadily, eyeing his grandmother over the rim of his cup. He often neglected to wipe his mouth with his linen napkin, and had to be reminded. He was not an endearing child, and, for his part, he seemed to have decided that his grandparents were not serious enough for him, or rather not weighty enough to be taken seriously. They loved him, of course, but failed to like him very much.

But Flora was in every way different. Flora was, quite simply, what Marianne had been as a baby, before she grew up and began her fall from grace. From his first sight of Flora, with her damp dark hair and tiny purposeful mouth, Hartmann was lost to reason. He worshipped her, cunningly contrived to ingratiate himself, to integrate his presence into her sensibility, her receptivity, removed her from her mother's arms and sat down happily with her, talking to her even when she was fast asleep. When no one was looking, when his wife and his daughter were in the kitchen or were engaged in talk, he would give Flora a gentle nudge and wake her up. She might cry a little, but after a few minutes was always pleased to see him, opening her blue eyes at him as he lovingly wiped away her tears. 'Time for her nap, Daddy,' Marianne would say. Or, 'We must be going.' 'Not yet,' he would plead. 'She's not tired.' 'Leave her alone, Hartmann,' Yvette would pronounce. 'You are breathing on her.' Even Yvette, who was by no means afflicted with Hartmann's senti-mentality, would linger over the child, and smooth her perfect cheek with the back of an index finger. When Hartmann saw the contrast between the bloom of the infant's face and the wrinkling flesh on the back of Yvette's well-kept but ageing hand, he felt over-whelmed with love for them both, felt an overflowing of such loving-kindness that he would have to go out for a walk. In any event, once Flora was removed his home seemed to him momentarily intolerable. Yvette, although she looked at him with a sceptical eye, under-stood. He was in love, she knew, and there was no point in trying to reason with him. And of all the rivals with whom he might have presented her, Flora was the only one above suspicion.

When night fell on the afternoons of Flora's visits, Hartmann would take his wife by the hand, and, putting on some appropriate music, would waltz her slowly round the drawing-room. Fibich, coming up-stairs on one such evening to ask Hartmann about some aspect of their early life, was astonished to see them both dancing, with serious expressions, and very gracefully too, he had to admit, although neither of them was as slim as they once had been. Fibich was charmed, and, forgetting his errand, sat down to watch. He saw his friend as a brilliant success, brilliant as he himself had never been, and counted himself fortunate to have known him. He thought of the time they had spent together, time that encompassed two lives, then four, then six. He did not count Roger, the incomer, although he liked him well enough, liked him rather better than Hartmann did. He sat quietly, for five minutes or so, watching them dance, and saw that they were old. He gazed round the room he knew so well, with its apricot walls and dark green carpet, and striped apricot and white curtains, and at Yvette, spectacular in royal blue, her feet in small black sandals. As she waltzed past him, her hair, he saw, was brighter and perhaps thinner than it had been: he saw the strands parted at the back, as if she had got up from a little sleep and had not effaced the impression of a pillow or a cushion. Hartmann's face was grave and serene, as he danced: he had always been a good dancer. Fibich had seen him dance at Deauville, at Monte Carlo, when they had gone on their youthful holidays together, after he and Christine were married, the four of them, before the babies came. How Hartmann had loved a party! He had had a charmed life, thought Fibich. When he gambled in the casino he always won, not much, but enough to enable him to gamble again the following evening. He and Christine had sat quietly, watching the people, watching Hartmann dancing with Yvette, always with Yvette. He had been a good man, thought Fibich. Such considerations were important to him these days.

After a while he waved his hand at Hartmann, as if to tell him not to disturb himself, and took his notebook back downstairs with him. Although he had wanted Hartmann's opinion that opinion was not really necessary: his work was finished. He found Christine sitting in her chair, her head thrown back, her eyes fixed on the window as if a sun were blazing there. He knew that she was thinking of Toto, and of the day when she would see him again. He himself felt no anxiety for the boy, although Toto's life was so unlike his own that he could no longer imagine it. He drew the curtains, and Christine stirred herself, as if the sun had been eclipsed, although the sky was black beyond the windows. She looked around her, as if she were coming back to full consciousness after a long absence, and said, 'Is it late? Are you coming to bed?' He smiled at her. 'Not yet. But don't wait for me.' She rubbed her eyes, picked up her book and her new glasses, and stood up. He took her in his arms and kissed her, as if he might not see her again. 'You look tired,' she said. 'Are you all right?'

'Never better,' he said.

He went into his study, took a large envelope from the drawer of his desk, and put his notebook inside it. Before sealing it, he thought for a moment, and then uncapped his pen again, drew a sheet of paper towards him, and began a letter.

'My dearest boy,' he wrote.

'I want you to have this little memoir, which contains your history and as much of mine as I can remember. There is a copy, typed, in the safe in the office, which Hartmann will look after for you, providing, that is, that you find it of value. So don't worry if the notebook is tiresome to carry around: you can leave it anywhere, or even throw it away, if you want to. Don't have a bad conscience about it. It was not intended to be solemn or significant. But I wanted you to know that I have been thinking of you. When have I not been thinking of you? I wanted you to know that these past few weeks, when you have been so far away, have brought you back to me most vividly. I wanted to tell you about your home, and how it came into being.

'You know the story in outline, and when you read the notebook you will know it as I remember it. I wanted in particular to tell you what a good life it has been. I have been blessed with everything a man desires, and it is my most fervent wish – unfortunately, I cannot pray – that you will be similarly blessed. Marry, have children, and you will know my joy.

'How is it out there, in America? Have you made friends? Good friends are like gold. I, who have had Hartmann as a friend all my life, know the truth of this.

'We are all well. Your mother is well. Do not worry about us. But come back to us, if your work permits.

'Your grandfather's name was Manfred. Your grandmother was Rosa. She was very beautiful. You will read all about them in the notebook.

'Take great care of yourself, and, I repeat, don't worry about us. We are still here, and will be here as long as you want us. Life has taught me that death is only a small interruption. This I now know to be an unalterable truth.

'Do you remember that poem I used to read you night after night, in an attempt to get you to sleep? Do you remember "battle's magnificently stern array"? I was never able to capture that spirit myself. Some battles, however, are fought in the mind, and sometimes won there.

'If I were a religious man I would ask God to bless you. And as I am not I will ask Him just the same. And I send you all my thoughts and hopes.

Your loving father,
Thomas Manfred Fibich.'

A B O U T   T H E   A U T H O R

Anita Brookner is the author of the best-selling *Hotel du Lac* as well as the novels *A Start in Life, Providence, Look at Me, Family and Friends, The Misalliance*, and *A Friend from England*. An international authority on eighteenth-century painting, Brookner teaches at the Courtauld Institute of Art and has also written *Watteau, The Genius of the Future, Grueze*, and *Jacques-Louis David*.